THE GREEN MURPHY SUCCESSION

Book 1—War, Power, & Bloodlines

A NOVEL

BY

GLENN W. STURM

Published by E&R Publishers
New York, NY, USA

An imprint of MillsoCo Publishing, USA
www.EandR.pub

ISBN: 9781966155294 Hardcover
ISBN: 9781966155300 Softcover
ISBN: 9781966155317 eBook
ISBN: 9781966155324 Audiobook
Library of Congress Control Number: 2025946763

DEDICATION

To the warriors who make our way of life possible

DISCLAIMER

None of the characters in this book are intended to resemble any person who served in any unit of the 357th Fighter Group or any of its subsidiary or support units, the United States Army Air Corps or its successor organization, the United States Air Force, Hagenah, the Israel Defense Force or Israel Air Force or any of their predecessors or successors. The battles described in this book are often fictitious, as are the incidents around which this story was built.

TABLE OF CONTENTS

Table of Contents

ACKNOWLEDGEMENTS

Col. Earl C. Sturm, Dad, I miss you so much. I loved having a dad who was also my mentor. I remember those phone calls to you when, as a young officer, I was way over my head, and you always answered the phone and gave sage advice. I can't imagine the decisions I would have made without you. I, along with the soldiers I led, continue to be grateful for your help.

Daniel B. Hodgson, you have been my mentor throughout most of my career. You guided me as I transitioned from a young Army officer to a very young partner and eventually to the Corporate Chairman of our firm. I would never have reached that position without your guidance and friendship.

Dr. Simon Mills, this book, along with my first four and several currently in various stages of creation, would never have come to fruition without your help, guidance, support, and creativity. You are one of the most talented individuals I have ever had the pleasure of meeting. Thank you, Simon, for your wizardry. You, sir, are a gentleman and an honorable fellow.

Randy Talbot has been my lifelong best friend. There's a well-known saying among dog owners: "May I be the person my dog thinks I am." It's about character—supporting your family through tough times, remaining loyal, obedient, and trustworthy. It's about striving to become the best version of yourself. That perfectly describes Mr. Talbot. He is exactly the person all dogs believe he is. He is the best version of a person, the one we all aspire to be, and the most loyal friend anyone could have. Thank you, Randy, for over 50 years of friendship.

PROLOGUE

During World War II, the U.S. Army Air Forces activated 114 fighter groups. Of these, a few units stood out as elite. The 35th Fighter Group had one of the most impressive combat records. In just over a year of combat, 42 pilots earned 'ace' status. Nicknamed "The Oxford Boys" after a village near their base in Leiston, UK, the 357th achieved the highest number of air-to-air combat victories of any P-51 group in the Eighth Air Force and ranked third among all groups fighting in Europe. As the first P-51 Fighter Group of the Eighth Air Force, the group flew 313 combat missions between February 11, 1944, and April 25, 1945.

On December 16th, 1942, the group was activated at Hamilton Field, California. Besides a few veterans, all pilots and personnel were new graduates from Air Force schools, after moving through multiple bases across the country, including Tonopah Army Airfield, Nevada, on March 4, 1943; Santa Rosa Army Airfield, California, on June 3, 1943; Oroville Army Airfield, California, on August 18, 1943; and Casper Army Airfield, Wyoming, from October 7 to November 9, 1943, for various phases of training in the P-39 Airacobra. On October 24th, 1943, ten months after being formed, the 357th Fighter Wing was approved for combat. During training, 14 men lost their lives in accidents.

357th Fighter Group training at Hamilton Army Airfield in their Bell P-390 Airacobra

On November 3, 1943, the 357th began its journey to Europe, and by November 30, 1943, they had moved into RAF Raydon Wood airfield in Suffolk under the Ninth Air Force. While the group was busy training with their limited number of North American P-51B Mustangs, the U.S. Air Force recognized the need for a long-range escort fighter, and the Mustang was identified as a suitable option. On February 1, 1944, the decision was made to assign the Mustang as the primary aircraft for the Eighth Air Force.

The 357th was not only reassigned to the Mighty Eighth but also relocated to Station F-373 (RAF Leiston airfield), situated between the Suffolk towns of Leiston, Saxmundham, and Theberton, where they would remain for the rest of the war. From this base, on February 11, the 357th FG carried out its first official mission—a sweep to the Rouren area—led by ace and recent Medal of Honor recipient Maj James Howard of the 354th FG. The group's main role in the air war was to escort heavy bombers, mainly B-17s and B-24s. These escort missions helped establish some new records for the Eighth Air Force.

After the group's first aerial victory on February 20th, 1944, when they downed a Me 109 flown by 1st Lieutenant Calvert L. Williams of the 362nd Fighter Squadron, flying a P-51B (G4-U, serial number 43-6448) named "Wee Willie," the floodgates opened for the 357th. These 313 missions resulted in the destruction of 595.5 German aircraft in the air and 106.5 on the ground, totaling 702 victories. The 357th produced 42 pilots who became aces—the highest number of any fighter group in the European Theater of Operations.

Senior Year

A group of high schoolers was standing together, waiting for trucks to arrive and take them out to the pea fields. These teens were not headed to a game or dance but to a long, hard day of work under the open sky. This was a time when school vacations usually involved farm work rather than relaxation.

In December of 1941. Mrs. Paul Murphy (Betty) was preparing for Monday's classes at Teton High School. The school was in Driggs, Idaho, but she lived with her son in the northern part of Victor, Idaho.

Mrs. Murphy, who held a bachelor's and a master's degree in applied mathematics from NYU, taught the most advanced math classes available at any high school in Idaho. She also taught calculus and other subjects like chemistry at Teton High School. Betty, at 43, was one of the most beautiful and accomplished women in Teton County. It wasn't always easy being both one of the most intelligent individuals, a widow, and a very beautiful woman while raising a son.

Her husband of almost twenty years was a highly successful rancher a wonderful dad and an even better husband. He courted her for two years while she was finishing her master's degree. He had met her on his graduation trip after finishing first in his class at BYU, where he graduated in 1921. They were engaged in 1922 and were married during her Christmas vacation 1922.

The couple's son was born in 1924 after a very traumatic pregnancy. The entire pregnancy was complicated, and the absence of specialists made it even harder. Another challenge the couple faced was that while her husband, Paul Murphy Sr., was a member of The Church of Jesus Christ of Latter-day Saints, Betty was Catholic.

Both Paul, Sr., and Betty were devout Christians who understood well the issues the other faced. Teton County's Mormon population made up about 70% of the total population, while the Catholic population was much smaller. Still, that didn't stop Betty from actively pursuing the growth of her faith.

Both Paul, Sr., and Betty were devout Christians and very understanding of the issues the other faced. Teton County's Mormon population made up about 70% of the overall population. The Catholic community was much smaller. Nonetheless, Betty was dedicated to growing her faith. However, there was no Catholic Church in the county.

Mission priests traveled a vast territory by train, then by horse, buggy, or early automobile to reach scattered Catholic families. When the priest visited, Mass was not held in a church. Instead, a designated Catholic family hosted the service in their home.

These services were significant social and spiritual events. They offered a chance to receive the sacraments, listen to a sermon, and connect with other Catholics. Betty always wanted to host these services. Without a local church or priest, the family home became the center of religious life. In most Catholic households, parents, especially mothers, were the primary teachers of their children's faith. They led daily prayers, such as the Rosary, taught catechism from a book, and read from the Bible.

At Betty's house, both Paul and Betty offered grace before meals. Both parents took turns saying prayers at bedtime. Paul and Betty were Unique in the county because they were practicing members of different religions who respected each other's beliefs and values. That didn't mean that Paul didn't get a lot of counseling from other members of his ward. He did.

Everything had been going well in the family for over a decade. Thanks to Betty's education, she was recruited to teach at the high school, and she thoroughly enjoyed it.

Paul was very successful as a rancher. He developed a line of Black Angus bulls that received awards and were in high demand. He quickly became the most successful rancher in Eastern Idaho. He quickly became the buyer of choice when a bank had a problem borrower. Banks would expeditiously loan Paul, Sr. all the money he needed to buy a troubled ranch. His bank required him to purchase substantial life insurance policies because of the debt he incurred to acquire additional ranches. The policies were always enough to cover all the debt, provide working capital if needed after his death, and cover the family's expenses for the rest of Betty's life.

It was on a late October day when it happened. Paul Sr. was riding alone in the early evening. He was supposed to be home no later than 7.00 p.m., but on that fateful day, he didn't arrive. He was always punctual so that he could read to Junior, but this time the minutes ticked by with no sign of him. At 9 PM, Betty called Wes, the ranch foreman, to express her concerns. By 11:00 p.m., Wes arrived at the house with Paul's bishop, bearing the news that Paul Sr. would not be coming home again.

The funeral attracted nearly 1,000 attendees. Not only was his entire ward there, but an additional 35% of the county was also present. You see, Paul was the Eastern Idaho Stake President of The Church of Jesus Christ of Latter-day Saints. Betty and Junior were in shock—no more rides with Dad, no more plans to expand the ranch, nothing.

A week after the funeral, Betty met with her lawyer, Pop's lawyer, and their estate planner. He made the following statement: "Pop's death was a significant financial win for the family." She was polite but resolved never to let that lawyer work for the family again. She couldn't wait to hear from the bishop of Pop's wards about his request for a tithing. Paul was supposed to give one-tenth of all their interests to his church annually. That wasn't going to happen.

The ranch manager, Wes Bowen was responsible for all of the ranches that Mrs. Murphy owned. Many capital improvements were needed, and thanks to Pop, Bette had the cash to make those upgrades. She was known as the most generous person in the valley. After all, her ranch was now second only to the Bar B Bar Ranch in size. She owned nearly a thousand sections and ran about 4,000 head of Angus cattle. Her ranches were also completely debt-free.

Bette decided, for Junior's sake, not to change their lives in any way. It was up to him which religion to follow and which college to attend. He would work for Wes on the ranch and develop the skills Pops had. She knew he'd face the usual teenage struggles. Having seen all the young men in the county while teaching at the only high school, she understood that what would differentiate her son wasn't that he'd become a highly educated, wealthy young man. Her job was to make sure he didn't find out about or expect to inherit wealth. As much as possible, he needed to live the life of a typical, red-blooded American teen.

Paul's High School years.

The Teton Valley was a place where nature set the rhythm, and the seasons shaped the spirit. In winter, snowbanks covered fenceposts. In spring, runoff thundered down the Teton River, watering fields that had been passed down like heirlooms. For Paul Murphy Jr., high school was less about growing up and more about preparing for manhood and loss.

He attended Teton High School in Driggs, where his mother taught. The building had drafty hallways, chalk-stained blackboards, and windows that framed the Grand Tetons like a cathedral. The county had only about 3,600 residents, and high school enrollment was just over 100 students—two-thirds girls, one-third boys. Most of the boys who weren't in class were in the fields or on the ranch. Paul did both.

Paul was handsome, tall, and broad-shouldered from baling hay and branding cattle. His thick, unruly dark hair complemented his blue eyes, and his skin was clear from fresh mountain air and hard work. He was the type of young man who drew the attention of every girl and the envy of half the boys.

Paul didn't rely on charm. He pushed himself in the classroom, motivated—perhaps even intimidated—by the presence of his mother, Betty, who—as every student and teacher was aware—taught advanced mathematics (calculus) and chemistry at the school. A two-degree graduate of NYU, Betty expected excellence and delivered it. In her classroom, Paul was never "her son," but he was expected to be the best.

Paul had heavy chores on the ranch and at home. As a talented athlete, he played, basketball, and ran track. Paul was also on his school's rodeo team, which played a key part in rural Idaho's cowboy culture. He was the starting quarterback, a fierce competitor in the paint, and a sprinter who rarely lost the 100-yard dash. He was also a standout in steer wrestling and calf roping. Paul was the definition of a well-mannered young man.

He was also a standout in debate, where his quick wit and calm logic—perhaps sharpened by theological discussions at home—made him an unexpected intellectual force. He worked the pea harvest in the summers, baled hay in late July and early August, picked potatoes in the fall, and split wood for the winter. While other boys were sowing wild oats, Paul was earning varsity letters and applying to Ivy League schools.

What no one knew—not even his closest friends—was that Paul had been accepted to three of the top universities in the country: Harvard, Dartmouth, and Penn. His mother knew. She kept the letters in her desk drawer and never mentioned them publicly. She believed, just like Paul, that humility was the most accurate measure of character.

But what shaped Paul most during those years wasn't the classroom or the field—it was the absence of his father.

Everyone knew that Paul Sr. was the county's most successful rancher, who died when Paul was just a freshman. They knew his death had come suddenly, during a riding accident in the high pastures. The man who had once read bedtime stories and said grace at dinner was gone in an instant. Paul Jr. never fully recovered, but he also never broke. Instead, he stepped into his father's boots—figuratively and literally—and took on the role of man of the house before most boys had found their voice.

Betty never remarried. Paul never complained. They built a quiet pact between them: work hard, live right, and don't let grief make you small.

In the spring of his junior year, as war clouds gathered over Europe, Paul asked his mother whether he should postpone college. He wanted to serve. She didn't argue and told him he still had another year to finish high school so that he could make his decision then. However, things didn't go as planned. On December 7th, during his senior year, the Japanese attacked Pearl Harbor. The next day, in a nationwide speech, President Roosevelt announced that a state of war existed between Japan and the United States. The war changed Paul's missionary plans and the promise he had made to his father to serve the church. He felt horrible about his decision, but it was his family's honor as well as his duty to serve the country. Hopefully, he could finish a mission after the war.

That night, Betty held him a little longer than usual. In the morning, she made him pancakes, kissed his forehead, and gave him a rosary she had hidden in her top drawer since the day his father died.

It was during his remaining months in high school that Paul first decided that he wanted to serve as a fighter pilot during the war. As he quickly found out, it wasn't an easy process to get into flight school. There were a lot of steps you had to go through, a lot of tests you had to pass.

Flight Training

The war did not hand out wings easily. Paul reported for Aviation Cadet examination in early spring, the courthouse hallway packed with boys who looked like men and men who looked like boys. Some were farmhands. Some were college sophomores. All of them believed they were different. All of them believed they would fly.

The written tests came first—hours of numbers, patterns, mechanical diagrams, logic puzzles designed to separate dreamers from pilots. Paul moved through them methodically, pencil steady. When the Army General Classification Test ended, he leaned back, confident but careful not to show it.

The physical exam was worse. Doctors measured everything—lungs, eyes, reflexes, heart rhythm. One minor defect could send a man to infantry instead of cockpit. Paul passed. Barely anyone celebrated. Too many still failed.

Then came waiting.

Six weeks of uncertainty. Six weeks of imagining the letter that might not come. When his acceptance arrived in April 1942, it was thin, official, and life-altering.

He would report June 1. He did not tell the valley. He simply finished high school and went.

College Training Detachment

The Army sent him to a college campus where cadets wore uniforms but slept in dormitories built for debate teams and fraternity boys. Days began before dawn—marching, push-ups, mathematics, navigation theory, aerodynamics. Professors taught them how wings generated lift; sergeants taught them how to obey.

Half the class washed out before Christmas.

Paul learned two things quickly:

Intelligence mattered.
Endurance mattered more.

Classification

A week of testing determined futures. Pilot, bombardier, navigator—or back to the Army.

When the results were posted, Paul searched the board without breathing—Pilot.

Beside his name was another:
Green, Benjamin—Pilot

When the classification results were posted, Benjamin Green did not look immediately. He stood back, allowing the louder cadets to crowd the board. He had learned early that drawing attention was rarely an advantage.

When the cluster thinned, he stepped forward.

Green, Benjamin — Pilot. He exhaled softly. Not relief. Confirmation.

Behind him, one of the cadets muttered,

"Green… that's a New York name." Benjamin turned, polite smile in place.

"It is."

"You Jewish?"

The question wasn't hostile. Not exactly. Just probing.

"Yes."

The cadet nodded, unsure what to say next. Benjamin folded the paper in his pocket and walked away. He did not argue. He did not boast. He did not invite more.

As he turned, he noticed Paul Murphy. They nodded to each other, strangers only weeks before, now bound by selection.

That night, alone in his dormitory bunk, Ben whispered the Shema before sleep. Not because he doubted. Because he understood that the sky would not care who he was.

Preflight

Preflight was not flying. It was running until lungs burned. It was memorizing aircraft silhouettes. It was Morse code tapped into forearms at midnight. It was pistols, rifles, formation drills, and leadership exercises meant to break arrogance. Instructors shouted. Cadets competed. Failure was public. Men disappeared weekly—Paul did not.

Primary Flight Training

The first time he sat in a PT-17 Stearman, he felt the war change shape.

The biplane was fabric and wire—fragile, honest. The instructor in the rear cockpit barked corrections over engine noise. Paul overcontrolled. Every cadet overcontrolled. The sky was not forgiving.

After twelve hours of instruction, his instructor climbed out, slapped the fuselage, and said:

"Don't kill yourself."

The aircraft felt suddenly enormous and impossibly small at the same time—Paul taxied out alone.

When the wheels lifted from the runway without another human aboard, something fundamental shifted. The world shrank beneath him. The controls steadied in his hands. For three minutes, he was not a cadet. He was a pilot.

He landed hard. Bounced once. Corrected. Rolled to a stop. The other cadets grabbed him and dunked him into a rain barrel. He came up sputtering and grinning.

Benjamin's first solo felt different. His instructor climbed out of the cockpit and leaned in.

"Green, you're steady. Don't overthink it."

Benjamin nodded. As he taxied onto the runway, he felt the familiar tightening in his chest—not fear, but responsibility.

Ariel's face appeared unbidden in his mind. Then Joseph's, though his child was still only a promise. The engine roared. The Stearman surged forward.

"Baruch atah Adonai…" he whispered, barely audible over the propeller wash.

The wheels lifted. For a brief moment, suspended between earth and sky, Benjamin did not feel triumph. He felt covenant. When he landed—smooth, controlled—there was no shouting, no dunking ritual. He stepped from the aircraft quietly, removed his helmet, and looked once at the horizon—the sky had accepted him. He would honor that.

Basic and Advanced

The trainers became heavier. Faster. Formation flying demanded trust. Instrument training demanded faith in dials over instinct. Night flying demanded nerve.

Aerial gunnery was different. Shooting at sleeves towed behind other aircraft made the war feel real. Missing meant embarrassment. Hitting meant something darker—proof you could destroy another machine. Washouts increased. Some cadets froze. Some lacked coordination. Some simply cracked under pressure—Paul and Benjamin did not. They gravitated toward each other—two high scorers, two men with quiet discipline. Competitive, but never reckless. By advanced training, they both knew their track.

It was during advanced training that Benjamin made his decision. He had been married for months—no one knew.

He had written Ariel weekly. He had sent money quietly. He had said nothing to command. But secrecy was becoming dishonor.

The next morning, he walked into administrative offices and filed the paperwork.

Married.
One dependent.
Another expected.

The clerk glanced up.

"You're a brave man, Lieutenant."

Benjamin met his eyes.

"No. Just honest."

***

Single-engine fighters.

The AT-6 Texan was faster, louder, unforgiving. It rolled harder and punished hesitation. This was where boys became fighter pilots.

Wings

Graduation came without ceremony worthy of the transformation. A small stage. A senior officer. Wings pinned to tunics. When the silver insignia touched Paul's chest, he felt the weight of expectation more than pride. He had survived—Many had not.

He and Benjamin stood side by side, newly minted lieutenants.

The war was waiting.

***

On April 3, 1942, Benjamin Green joined the Army Air Forces. He was a young, married man dedicated to his religious faith. He attended Shabbat services every week and was very concerned about how he would observe Shabbat regularly. Green had met a beautiful Jewish woman named Ariel before enlisting in the USAAF to become a fighter pilot, and he married Ariel before joining the military. He kept his marriage quiet, not because it was forbidden, but because he feared it

11

might mark him as distracted—or worse, cautious. As a cadet, he believed the less the brass knew about his private life, the better. In wartime, a man was expected to belong wholly to the mission. A wife, and now a child, made him something else. Something with more to lose. Although it was not ideal for his career, he knew he had to come clean and live with the consequences. That decision had freed a weight from his shoulders that he hadn't even been aware of.

Having come from a wealthy family, Benjamin was well versed in the practice of discretion to the point of secrecy. It was just better for people not to know certain things, as it gave you more room to maneuver under the watchful gaze of perception.

Benjamin's parents, Yosel and Esther, met in the early days of the West 47th Street Diamond District, where they both worked as merchants. Esther Finkelstein came from a long line of diamond traders, which is reflected in her surname—etymologically, it relates to the words sparkle and rock.

Esther was devout in her faith and knew she had found her life partner in Yosel within days of their first encounter on 47th Street. Esther was representing the seller, and Yosel was the buyer. Yosel got much more than he bargained for in that deal, and his life changed forever. Yosel and Esther fell deeply in love, and their strong faith ensured that their children would be raised with honesty, integrity, and passion.

When Benjamin was conceived, he was conceived in love, and that love would shine through him into the world all the days of his life. As he grew, even in the school yard, he would bring peace and balance. It was like he had lived life before and had learned many of its mysteries. "An old soul," they would call him, even his teachers.

His responsible nature would enrage the children with a penchant for bullying. Benjamin knew they were weak and insecure and would talk them through their shortcomings. He would either embarrass them to the point they would let it go and walk away, or they would break down and admit their shortcomings. Benjamin knew the military was for him from a very early age. It called to him and offered him authority and strength to couch his inherent nature. He also saw that he wanted to fly. He wanted to learn and lead.

Leadership and purpose coursed through his veins. His parents wondered how they could have been so fortunate, because even their robust parenting, faith, and love could not have produced all his glorious traits. He was one in a million, and they knew it.

Benjamin effortlessly passed all the tests. His score on the Aviation Cadet Test was the highest ever recorded in the eastern region. Just like Paul, it was off to aviation training immediately after graduating from high school.

Ben made many friends easily, and one was Paul Murphy, whom he met at the initial classification center and who would later become a lifelong friend. He saw many of his own virtues in Paul Murphy as their relationship strengthened in those formative weeks. Both men were selected for pilot training, but after completing pre-flight and primary school, they were sent to the same basic schools and classified for pursuits.

They both qualified to fly fighters. They had no issues flying the AT. After completing advanced flight training, Lieutenants Green and Murphy received their wings. They were the only two members of their preflight school to finish all their training together as fighter pilots. For this reason, in part, they were both then sent to transition training for the P-51, the fighter they would fly in combat. During training, Paul and Ben were inseparable; they were peers. They were both leaders, well-educated, and highly competent aviators.

Before they went on their post-graduation leave, Ben had a question for Paul.

"Have you given any thoughts about your potential call sign?"

"No, Ben, I haven't, I thought it was given to you by your initial squadron mates."

"I don't like that approach, so I have decided—aided by Ariel's suggestion—that I want my call sign to be Mensch. Are you ok with that?"

"Sure, Mench"

"Have you given any thought to yours?"

"Yeah, I believe that Rodeo would be a good one for me since that's what I enjoyed the most in high school."

Mensch and Rodeo completed their transition training in June 1943 and were assigned to Hamilton Army Airfield in Novato, California, where they joined the 357th Fighter Group. After training, the new Army Air Force aviators were granted a 21 to 30-day leave en route to their new assignment. Lt. Green was excited because he finally had some leave and could reunite with his wife, Ariel.

He was also able to attend Shabbat services. Due to a shortage of rabbis in the USAAF, participating in Shabbat services during flight training was very difficult; however, Benjamin continued studying the Torah. When he returned from leave, he knew it was time to inform the Army that he was married. He couldn't keep it a secret forever, and opening those doors was now a necessary step.

Paul, on the other hand, had been frolicking around in San Francisco. Each day, it was another woman. He was developing a well-deserved reputation for having the highest quantity of complete relationships of anyone in the Group.

It was another day—Paul believed it was going to be another day of hunting and bagging young ladies who were impressed with his flight jacket and being a fighter pilot. He had all his lines down pat, and the young ladies fell for them in record time each day.

Not suspecting today would differ from any other "on the hunt" and completely obvious to the possibility that his life was about to be offered an entirely new trajectory, he sprang through the squeaky wooden door of a small french coffee shop, the sun was streaming through a window and shining angelically on a young woman. The light created what seemed, for a split second, like a halo over her head. She was the most beautiful woman he had ever seen. A stunning blonde debutante named Katie, and all 5'9" of her was pure lust-inducing perfection.

At first, she was ice-cold toward him. She sliced right through the almost 20-year-old's lines and banter. To her, he seemed like just another jerk—an over-the-top flyboy. At first, she clipped his wings at every turn. To her, it seemed like the same thing it was to Paul. A game where superficial young men hunted for equally superficial young women in a mating ritual. She saw it for what it was and enjoyed clipping the wings of the superficial pilots. Eventually, Paul realized he was outmatched and softly surrendered.

"So, ah, have you?"

Katie looked into space rolling her eyes.

"Do you mind if I ask where you're from—are you in college?"

Fully expecting a crass pickup line, Katie was completely taken aback by the polite and straightforward question from the infamous hunter.

"One, two, three," she thought to herself before composing her reply. "Well, since you asked so kindly, I'll answer both questions. I'm from New York, and I'm attending Stanford University in the Honors Science program."

"Wow, that's impressive. If you don't mind me asking, what specifically are you studying?"

"I'm majoring in Organic Chemistry in case I decide to attend medical school after finishing my undergraduate degree. If I choose not to pursue a career in medicine, I might attend graduate business school." Lieutenant Paul Murphy couldn't believe what he was hearing. Here he was, standing with the most beautiful, and clearly the most intelligent woman—besides his calculus-obsessed mother—that he had ever met.

"Well," he exclaimed after a long silence while trying to conceal his amazement. "I am both deeply impressed and deeply jealous. I had to delay college because of the war, but I plan to major in applied math once the war is over. I'll be pursuing my Ph.D. and applying it to the business skills I've been gaining. I'm thinking about entering the securities industry."

"So, Paul, have you decided where you would like to attend university?"

"No, I am not sure. I haven't told anyone where I have been accepted. I didn't want to sound like a showoff. My mother warned me not to tell folks about my acceptances. That said, I believe you can keep my secret. I was accepted to the University of Pennsylvania,

Harvard University, and Dartmouth College. My mom went to NYU, where she received her BS and Master's degrees in Applied Math."

"Wow, impressive."

"I agree, it was very unusual for a woman to achieve those honors back then."

Paul had often wondered why more women were not like his mother. But this one was obviously brilliant, highly educated, and stunningly beautiful. He felt like he had hit the jackpot. His fast-won conquests were becoming tiresome and lacked the thrill of the hunt. Katie presented something different entirely. She inspired in him a longing for her respect which meant he respected her. Katie was another level of lady.

Paul had quickly become enamored to the point of jaw-dropping, puppy-like bewilderment. He had found his dream woman. Mensa-like intelligence, and unimaginable beauty.

They engaged in deep conversation like they were frozen in time and isolated from the rest if the world. Like they were floating inside a bubble through clouds, miles above the Earth. Eventually, there was a few seconds of silence where they had satisfied all their thoughts and questions for a moment when Katie suggested they get some dinner. That was the last time anyone saw either of them during Paul's leave.

They both enjoyed a deeply dazed whirl of profound new love where time didn't matter, and the world went on around them all by itself. While on leave, Lieutenant Green and his wife Ariel met Miss McFarland once. The rest of their leave, no one saw either of the new couple.

"Murf, where have you and Miss McFarland been? Ariel and I have left you 50 messages."

"Ms. McFarland and I have been conducting a secretive military reconnaissance. After a while, we carried out in-depth formal military maneuvers called a reconnaissance in force. That was fun. By the way... Miss McFarland and I got hitched."

Ben shot a sharp, shocked expression and blurted without thinking,

"Isn't that against regulations?"

"Isn't that the pot calling the kettle black?" Murph replied with a slight smirk."

Ben sat down with an agreeing smirk.

A week or so after they returned from leave, the two lieutenants were assigned to the 363rd Fighter Squadron. On March 4, 1943, soon after they arrived at Hamilton Army Airfield, the Group was transferred to Tonopah Army Airfield, Nevada. On June 3, 1943, the 357th moved to Santa Rosa Army Airfield, California, and then to Oroville Army Airfield, California, on August 18, 1943.

While the 363rd was in California, both Ariel and Katie found a way to spend a few days with their new husbands. Katie and Ariel became fast friends and decided to live together while Ben and Paul were deployed. This would ease the burden of loneliness and they thoroughly enjoyed each other's company.

***

The two young aviators completed their training at Casper Army Airfield, Wyoming, during October 7 to November 9, 1943. During these six months, they completed their 2v2, squadron versus squadron, and escort training.

On October 24, 1943, the 357th was cleared for combat and initially assigned the P-38. The pilots had only just begun studying its "Dash One" manuals and logging time in the cockpit when orders changed. The Eighth Air Force decided to standardize on the longer-range P-51 Mustang. The group had barely grown comfortable in the P-38 before orders came down—switch aircraft. Again.

By mid-November 1943, the 357th was deploying to RAF Raydon in England, where they would assemble their new Mustangs and prepare for combat. Their first mission would come on February 11, 1944.

PART I: THE FIRST MISSION (1943–1945)

CHAPTER ONE–TORN FROM EDEN

RAF Raydon, England, December 1, 1943–the day after the whole 357th Fighter Group arrives.

Paul and Ben sat in a pub with a fire smoldering in the corner, they cradled a tin mug of lukewarm coffee in one hand and a Lucky Strike in the other.

"Ben, have you ever thought about what happens if we don't come back?"

"Only when I look at my son."

Murphy exhaled, the smoke curling like vapor trails in a dogfight.

"You still keeping him secret from the brass?"

"You think they'd let me become a squadron leader with a newborn son and fly combat missions?"

"They let me fly, and I can't even keep a damn cactus alive."

The two men moved outside and sat on crates outside their quarters, jackets zipped high against the Suffolk chill. Their P-51s rested on the tarmac behind them, still gleaming with fresh paint and the vexing promise of victory or defeat.

It took several weeks to assemble the P-51s. It was a reflective time for Paul. Away from his new wife and desperate to find himself in this new setting of active battle.

"What's it like, Ben?"

"What?"

"Being... you know, righteous. Believing in something. God, family, nation. I mean, really believing."

"It's not about belief. It's about obligation. If I don't fight, Ariel and Joseph don't get to live free."

"And if you die?"

"Then at least I died giving them a future."

Murphy nodded, quieter than usual. Somewhere behind them, the mechanics turned over a Merlin engine. It coughed, spluttered, then roared to life.

"Katie's pregnant," he announced abruptly.

Green turned to him, eyes widening with honest joy.

"Mazal tov. When?"

"February, I think. We haven't told anyone. Hell, I wasn't sure it was real until yesterday."

"Then what are you doing here, man?"

"Same as you. Making sure there's still a world for our kids."

The silence hung like a prayer, unspoken but understood.

"We fly tomorrow," Ben finally breaking the silence.

"And we kill Nazis. God help us."

"He does," Ben whispered distantly as he closed the prayer book and tucked it into his jacket. "And I thank him for it every time we fly and come back breathing."

A sudden gust carried the scent of fuel and frost. Murphy stood up and stubbed his cigarette on the crate.

"Have you ever named your P-51?"

"Ariel," Ben continued without hesitation. "That way she's always with me."

"Figures. I was thinking 'Katie's Fury' or maybe 'God's Irish Problem.'"

"Always dramatic."

"Always the steady one."

They shared a laugh that turned into a coughing fit—cold air, stale coffee, and the nerves of impending combat.

***

Flashback: October 1943—Novato, California—Hamilton Army Airfield.

The screen door creaked as Ariel stepped out onto the porch. Joseph nestled tightly against her chest, a soft lullaby in Hebrew drifting from her lips. The baby cooed, blinking up at her as if memorizing her face.

Katie sat on the steps below; her lab uniform unbuttoned at the collar. She glanced up and grinned.

"Still singing?"

"Always. He sleeps best when I sing the Shema."

"I tried singing to Paul once. He told me I sounded
like a goat with a hangover."

"That sounds like Paul."

They both laughed—two women from different worlds, brought
together by war and the men rushing toward it.

"You think they'll make it back, Ariel?"

"I don't let myself wonder."

"You're always that strong?"

"No. I just pretend better than most."

Ariel adjusted Joseph's blanket as the wind off the Pacific swept over
the hills. Inside the house, Benjamin and Paul were packing their
duffels, laughing too loudly—forced laughter, loud enough to drown
out the ticking clock.

Katie examined her new friend's eyes, unsure of what to say. She
tried to gently redirect the attention away from the departure of their
husbands.

Katie noticed the sadness flicker in Ariel's gaze and offered a small,
reassuring smile, hoping to ease the tension of the situation.

"He's got your eyes, Ariel."

"And his father's stubborn jaw. He fights sleep like
it's the Luftwaffe."

"Guess he's already a fighter."

They sat in silence for a moment. Then Kathleen flicked away her
cigarette and stood.

"You ever get mad, Ariel?"

"Every day. But then I remind myself why he's
going."

"To fight Hitler?"

"To protect Joseph."

"Yes, the same reason Paul's going, now."

"Then they go together. And they come back together."

Back inside the house, Benjamin's fingers brushed the velvet cover of his siddur before slipping it into the side pocket of his duffel. Paul held up a black-and-white photo of Katie with her hands on her hips and a smirk on her face.

"This one'll keep me alive," he muttered.

"You should frame it for your Mustang."

"It's always with me."

"I'm thinking about finally painting her name on the nose of mine"

"Katie's Fury?"

"Of course."

Benjamin picked up Joseph's knitted cap—navy blue with a tiny white star. Ariel had made it during his final week of training.

"You sure about this?" Paul asked quietly.

"No. But I'm going anyway."

"What if we don't come back?"

"Then Ariel and Katie will raise sons who remember why we left."

The door opened. The men stepped outside. Uniforms sharp and crisp, their bags and hearts weighing heavy, and their flight jackets draped over their shoulders. Ariel handed Joseph to Benjamin. He held the child as if cradling the Torah—reverently, protectively.

"You're my legacy," he whispered to Joseph. "My covenant."

"Amen," Ariel whispered.

Paul and Katie embraced fiercely.

"No tears, my love."

Benjamin kissed Ariel's forehead. She reached into her coat and pressed a folded piece of parchment into his hand.

"Psalm 91 in Hebrew and English. Read it every time before you fly."

"I will."

"Promise me."

"I swear on our son."

And with that, they turned and walked toward the car that would take them to the airfield.

As the engine started, Ariel and Katie stood together on the porch, watching their husbands disappear down the gravel road, into war, and history.

"They'll be alright, Ariel"

"They have to be, Katie. It's not just us depending on them."

On the way to operations, Green handed Murphy a folded form.

"Sign this."

"What is it?"

"An allotment. Monthly pay to Katie. Rental allowance. Family allowance. If something happens, she won't have to fight the Army for it."

Murphy hesitated.

"Don't talk like that."

"Sign it."

Murphy scrawled his name without reading the fine print.

"Anything else I should know?"

Green met his eyes.

"If you get careless, she gets ten thousand dollars."

Murphy didn't answer. He folded the paper and handed it back.

CHAPTER TWO – THE SKY TURNS RED

RAF Leiston, England — March 3, 1944

The morning fog hung low and sour, like damp wool thrown across the airfield. Engines grumbled beneath tarpaulins, restless and impatient. Benjamin Green wiped a thin smear of oil from the edge of his prayer book, closed it carefully, and slid it into the inner pocket of his flight jacket. Across the tarmac, Lt. Paul Murphy tugged on his gloves and shook his head. "Another milk run," he muttered. "Easy escort to Leipzig. In and out. Back by tea." Green approached, fastening his sidearm. "You don't believe them?" Murphy snorted. "The last man who called it easy came back with a wing full of holes and someone else's blood in his cockpit." They held each other's gaze a moment. No bravado. No smiles. "Not today," Murphy declared. "Not today," Green agreed. They climbed into their aircraft.

Over Central Germany — 20,000 Feet

The sky was clear. Too clear. The B-17s droned ahead in rigid formation, silver bellies glinting in the cold light. Green flew tail-end Charlie on the right flank of Red Flight. Murphy sat steady off his wing. For a brief moment, it almost felt routine. Then the radio snapped alive. "Bandits. Nine o'clock high. Coming in hot." The Messerschmitts dropped out of the sun.

The sky shattered. Green rolled left as tracer fire cut through the formation. A P-51 ahead of them—Red-Four—erupted in flame before anyone finished calling his number. The canopy tore away. The aircraft disintegrated midair. "Was that Charlie?" Murphy shouted. "Stay with me!" Green barked. A 109 flashed across Murphy's nose. He broke hard, pulled into the climb, then rolled over the top.

The German filled his windscreen—close enough to see the shape of the pilot's helmet. Murphy squeezed the trigger. The Mustang shuddered. .50-caliber rounds stitched across the enemy's fuselage. Smoke. Then fire. The Messerschmitt snapped downward, spiraling. Murphy followed for a second too long—then saw it. A parachute blooming white against the earth below. He eased off. Green engaged seconds later. An Fw-190 broke toward the bombers.

Green climbed into position, steady hands, short burst. The 190 rolled inverted and vanished into cloud. No chute. The fight dissolved as quickly as it had begun. The remaining Mustangs regrouped around the bombers. Five American fighters failed to answer roll call. Two B-17s burned in the distance. Nobody said the words "milk run" again.

Back at Leiston, the intelligence officer asked for distances, angles, ammunition expended. Murphy answered automatically. Green wrote his report in careful block letters: one destroyed. No one celebrated. That night, Murphy sat on his bunk staring at his hands, flexing his fingers as if they still held the stick. He could still see the parachute. Green wrote to Ariel in silence. Neither man mentioned the kills. War had stopped being theory. It had become arithmetic.

CHAPTER THREE: IT'S JUST ANOTHER DAY

That night in the Officers' Mess at RAF Leiston, the whiskey was thin and the silence heavy. Benjamin stared at the glass in front of him without lifting it. Murphy sat beside him, collar open, sweat dried white against his undershirt.

"Charlie had a girl back home," Murphy muttered quietly. "He was gonna marry her after Easter."

Ben nodded. "He didn't make it through Friday."

They sat with that. Around them, men talked too loudly or not at all.

"You still believe in it?" Murphy asked after a while.

"In what?"

"God. This. Any of it."

Ben folded his hands on the table. "I believe in the reason. Not the outcome."

Murphy let out a short breath. "Feels like the outcome's doing all the talking."

Ben glanced toward the door. "I miss hearing Hebrew out loud. I miss Shabbat."

Murphy studied him. "What if we're just feeding the machine?"

Ben didn't answer immediately. The engines outside coughed to life in the darkness.

"Then we make sure it's not for nothing."

Murphy finally took a drink.

"That sky turned red today. I won't forget that."

"No," Ben replied. "Neither will I."

Outside, another aircraft rolled toward the runway.

Morning would come whether they were ready for it or not.

CHAPTER FOUR: FAITH IN THE FOXHOLE

RAF Leiston, Suffolk — Thursday Morning

Thursday brought another fighter sweep southeast of Kassel. Major William "Mickey" Lochstern delivered the briefing without flourish. Ammunition was standard. Altitude twenty-six thousand feet. Rendezvous over Bruges. Expected contact with 109Gs. Debrief mandatory. The routine no longer felt instructional. It felt inevitable. The sky over Germany was crowded before noon. Green led the second element of White Flight, Murphy steady off his wing. The 109s came in from above and behind, fast and disciplined.

Green broke right into a shallow dive, closing the distance before the German pilot realized he had been seen. His first burst struck the fuselage. The second stitched the wing roots. The Messerschmitt faltered, then rolled into a steep descent, smoke trailing. The canopy separated. A parachute opened at nine thousand feet and drifted into cloud. Green did not watch him land. Back at Leiston, his report was clinical. One Me-109 destroyed. Four hundred sixty-one rounds expended. Enemy pilot bailed. No significant evasive action after first burst. He signed it without comment. Later, in his diary, he wrote only: To be a Jew is to ask questions. To be a soldier is to follow orders. To be both is to live inside a contradiction.

RAF Leiston, Suffolk — Thursday Afternoon

The toolshed behind the hangars smelled faintly of oil and old timber. Green had swept it clean himself. Two candles flickered on a pair of dented brass holders, their light catching the rough grain of the boards. He whispered the blessings softly, Hebrew moving across his tongue with practiced restraint. The door creaked open.

"You hiding from the Luftwaffe?" Murphy asked quietly.

"Only from the noise." Murphy stepped inside, still in his flight jacket, streaked with grease.

He looked at the candles, then at Green. "You still do this? Even here?"

"Especially here."

Murphy leaned against the wall. "I haven't been to Mass in years."

"Faith isn't about attendance," Green replied.

Murphy studied the small flame. "You think God sees this?" Green considered the question. "I think we need Him to." Outside, engines coughed to life for the afternoon mission.

Captain Steven Jones—call sign "Balls"—handled the second briefing with easy confidence. The mission was nearly identical to the morning sweep. Same route. Same altitude. Same warnings. He spoke as if repetition guaranteed safety. It did not. They encountered ten 109s north of Kassel. Jones turned toward the Channel at the first sign of contact. The German formation pivoted as one and fell on him. His Mustang erupted in flame before a single American gun fired. There was no time to react. The sky dissolved into a furball.

Murphy broke right and climbed into the nearest pair of Messerschmitts. He fired once—too far. Corrected. Fired again. The first enemy aircraft exploded mid-dive. The second rolled hard left, but Murphy stayed with him, closing inside two hundred yards. His burst shattered the canopy. The German pilot bailed into the overcast below five thousand feet. Murphy felt the recoil and nothing else. By the time the remaining Mustangs reassembled, their mission commander was gone. The bombers pressed forward without them. Back at Leiston, Murphy signed his report in silence.

Two Me-109s destroyed. Six hundred five rounds expended. He did not comment on Jones. There was nothing to say. That night the wind rattled the tin roofs. Green sat on his bunk with his siddur open across his knees. Murphy lay above him, staring at the ceiling.

"Hey, Ben?"

"Yeah?"

"If I don't make it back next time... will you say something for me?"

"Of course."

"Even if I'm a lapsed Catholic bastard?"

"Even more so."

Murphy laughed softly.

"Just don't come back dead, Paul."

"That'll be best for us all." Outside, another aircraft rolled toward the runway. Morning would come again, indifferent to who answered it.

***

That night, Paul wrote his daily letter to Katie to tell her about the allotment, signing off with, "If you need more, just let me know and I'll find a way to send more. Sorry, my love, I should have attended to this earlier."

Katie and Paul married so fast that they never even had time to discuss finances. Before they had a chance, the war called and Paul was whisked away. Paul was suddenly concerned but knew Katie was so responsible and self-sufficient she'd probably never even ask about money. It would be beneath her somehow.

CHAPTER FIVE: FIRST FLIGHT OVER BERLIN

RAF Raydon – March 5, 1944

It would not be their last flight over Berlin, nor even the worst. But on that cold March morning in 1944, none of them knew what was still to come. This was the first time they would follow the bombers all the way to the heart of the Reich.

The briefing room was dark except for a single bulb over the map. Major Sloan tapped Berlin with a piece of chalk.

> "Direct run. Minimal diversion. Marshalling yards and
> heavy industry. First time the Mustangs go all the way in."

No one whistled this time. They had already learned better.

Frost silvered the wingtips. Faithless sat quiet and lethal in the gray light. Green ran his hand along the fuselage, feeling the cold through his glove.

> "How are you feeling?" Murphy asked.

> "Like history doesn't care whether we make it back."

Murphy nodded once. They climbed in.

The North Sea was deceptively calm. Forty bombers droned ahead, two dozen fighters guarding them like a tightening fist. Berlin appeared first as haze on the horizon. Then the flak began.

Black bursts climbed toward them in thick, deliberate walls. The formation shuddered. A Fortress lost two engines and slipped out of line, smoke pouring from its wing.

"Stay tight," Green ordered quietly.

The Luftwaffe hit moments later—190s and 109s diving in coordinated pairs. The sky became vertical.

Green rolled under a climbing bomber as tracers sliced past his canopy. A 190 overshot and tried to recover. Green closed and fired. The German aircraft bucked, wing shearing loose before it fell through the flak curtain below.

He did not look for a chute.

Murphy disappeared into cloud after a 109. For several seconds there was nothing but static. Then—

"I'm here."

A Fortress ahead of them exploded without warning. The wing separated cleanly, the fuselage tumbling end over end. Ten men vanished into smoke and fire. Neither pilot spoke.

The bombers held formation.

Bomb bay doors opened. Hundreds of bombs fell in disciplined silence, disappearing into the gray sprawl below. Smoke began to climb from the city in slow columns.

Flak intensified on the turn outbound. Faithless jolted as fragments tore through the left wing. Murphy's canopy cracked but held. Behind them, the sky burned.

Raydon—Debriefing Tent

They lost six fighters. More bombers than anyone wanted to count. The intelligence officer read names from a clipboard without looking up. Green removed his gloves slowly.

"They'll call it a success," Murphy spat defiantly.

Green stared at the mud on his boots.

"They always do."

Murphy leaned back in his chair.

"You think we made a difference?"

Green considered the question.

"We're still here," Green finally releasing his imprisoned thoughts. "That will have to be enough."

CHAPTER SIX: TWO ACES—TWO COMMANDERS

March 22, 1945
RAF Leiston

By early 1945, the war had begun devouring its own structure. Squadrons that once flew with seasoned commanders were now led by men who had simply survived longer than the rest. Experience was no longer something earned slowly—it was inherited in the instant another man failed to return.

That was how Green and Murphy found themselves standing at the front of briefing rooms. Promotion had come without ceremony. A handshake. A nod. A quiet understanding that leadership now meant watching younger pilots take the same risks they once had

The map on the wall showed the route in red chalk: Groningen to Hamburg to Berlin. Bombers would strike factories in the capital. Intelligence expected heavy resistance.

> "Same altitude," Green commanded evenly. "Twenty-six thousand feet. Stay tight on the bombers until engagement. Do not chase alone."

No one asked questions. The men in the room had learned what happened to those who did.

The sky over northern Germany was already hostile before they reached Hamburg. Flak rose in thick black blossoms, deliberate and methodical. At twenty miles out, it began finding them.

The first squadron commander vanished in a burst of orange flame. One moment his P-51 was holding formation; the next it simply came apart, struck through the fuselage. There was no spiral, no attempt at recovery. Just smoke and absence.

"No chute," someone whispered over the radio.

Moments later the second commander was lost. A pair of Focke-Wulfs dropped from high sun, cutting through the formation before anyone could react. The Mustang disintegrated under the burst.

Green saw it happen. There are sounds you never forget. The short metallic cough of .50-caliber guns. The hollow thud of flak. And the sickening silence after an aircraft disappears. Command transferred itself in the air.

Green broke right, climbing toward a formation of Me 109s hanging a thousand feet above. They turned down into a forty-degree dive. He followed, closing fast. At two hundred meters he fired. The first German aircraft erupted immediately, fragments peeling away like torn metal leaves.

He shifted to the second. Murphy was already there.

Murphy fired from closer range—one hundred seventy-five meters. Green watched strikes tear through fuselage and wing roots. Pieces flew off both enemy aircraft. Both German pilots bailed out, their parachutes snapping open against the gray sky. Murphy did not stop.

A Me 262 cut across their path, converging fast. Murphy rolled right and took a deflection shot at roughly four hundred meters. He held the trigger longer than Green liked, walking the rounds into the jet. Smoke bloomed. Fire followed. The canopy blew free and the German pilot ejected.

"Break left," Green ordered, but Murphy was already turning.

By the time the squadron reassembled, Berlin was burning beneath cloud cover.

Green had secured his twelfth confirmed kill that day. Murphy added three more—his thirteenth, fourteenth, and fifteenth. The numbers meant something to headquarters. —They meant nothing to the sky.

Back at Leiston, the debrief was mechanical.

Altitude. Distance. Ammunition expended. Enemy types encountered: Me 109s, Me 262s, Fw 190s. Weather: broken cumulus at eighteen thousand feet over target. Green signed his report in clean block letters. Murphy's hands were still trembling when he set down his pen.

That night, in the officers' quarters, neither man spoke for a long time.

"We lost both squadron commanders."

Green nodded once. "We did."

"They were good men."

"They were."

Murphy leaned back against the wall, staring at the ceiling.

"You realize what this means."

"Yes."

"We're it."

Green did not answer immediately. Command was not triumph. It was inheritance of risk. After a moment Murphy gave a dry half-smile.

"Three in one day," he muttered. "I should feel something."

Green looked at him carefully.

"You do," he muttered with a measured smile. "You just don't know what to call it."

Outside, the wind rattled the hangar doors. The war was almost over. Everyone said so. —But the sky had not received the message.

CHAPTER SEVEN: LAST FLIGHT OVER BERLIN

*"Tell her I'll be home before the spring breaks the snow. If not…
tell her I saw the sky once, and it was beautiful."*

—Final letter from Lt. James Carson, March 1944

April 18, 1945
Over Berlin — 26,000 Feet

Berlin no longer looked like a capital. It looked like a wound. Smoke rose in slow columns through broken cloud. The bombers pushed forward in disciplined formation, silver and deliberate, as if repetition alone could end the war.

Green flew lead element now. Murphy held steady off his wing. Carson was tucked in tight on the right, young enough that his confidence still came easily.

"Red Leader, confirm visual on Eagles One through Six," a voice called.

Green leaned forward against the straps, scanning through glare and haze. "Affirmative. Formation holding."

Flak arrived without warning. Black bursts climbed in staggered rhythm, walking toward the bombers with methodical patience. Faithless jolted hard enough to rattle Green's teeth. A Fortress ahead of them lost its tail assembly in a single violent flash. The fuselage tipped, hesitated, then began to fall.

"Chutes?" Murphy asked.

Green searched the space beneath the tumbling aircraft. "One… I see one."

There should have been ten. The radio snapped again. "Bandits. Three o'clock high. Multiple contacts."

They came in fast and coordinated—109s diving out of sun, 190s angling from below. The sky compressed into motion and noise. Green broke right and climbed to intercept. Murphy rolled inverted, then dove through the first pair as they cut toward the bombers. Carson accelerated straight ahead, chasing one that had slipped inside the screen.

"Carson, hold your altitude," Green ordered.

No reply.

Tracer fire stitched across Carson's left wing. His Mustang jerked violently. A second burst struck the fuselage. The canopy tore away in a spray of fragments and the aircraft yawed, engine coughing flame.

"Carson's hit!" Murphy shouted. "Carson's hit!"

Green saw the fire bloom along the cowling. The Mustang rolled onto its back and began to fall.

"Punch out, Jim!" Murphy yelled.

Two words cut across the radio, strained but clear. "Tell her—"

The transmission broke into static. The Mustang disappeared into smoke and cloud. No white blossom of silk followed. No chute.

Green turned back into the fight because there was nothing else to do. A 190 flashed across his nose. He fired one short, controlled burst and saw the wing root split. The German aircraft broke apart and dropped away. Murphy drove a 109 off a bomber's tail, forcing it into a steep dive. The Luftwaffe disengaged minutes later, as if satisfied with the damage already done.

The bombers held formation. Bomb bay doors opened in unison. The city absorbed the payload without flinching.

On the return leg, the radios stayed quiet. Men spoke only when they had to, as if words could make the losses more real.

RAF Leiston — Debriefing Tent

Helmets thudded onto tables. Gloves dropped. The intelligence officer waited with a clipboard and a face that had learned not to react.

"Losses?" he asked.

"Three fighters," someone answered. "Multiple bombers."

"Names?"

Green removed his gloves slowly. His fingers felt stiff, as if cold had gotten inside the bones. "Carson."

The officer wrote it down without looking up.

Later, in the barracks, Carson's bunk was already stripped. Regulations required it. Personal effects were packed into a cardboard box for shipment home—letters, a photograph, a small shaving kit, a book he'd never finished.

Murphy stood staring at the empty mattress.

"He had a ring," Murphy's voice solemn. "Carried it in his flight jacket. Said he'd propose in June."

Green sat on the lower bunk opposite him. "He won't."

Murphy's jaw tightened. "We kept telling him he was ready."

Green nodded once. "We did."

Murphy looked up. "What's the difference?"

Green took a moment before answering. "Readiness assumes risk," he declared finally. "Invincibility denies it."

The wind rattled the tin roof overhead. Somewhere outside, laughter broke briefly from another room—too loud, too forced—then disappeared.

After a while, Murphy spoke again. "You said your blessing today?"

Green stared at the floorboards between his boots.

"No."

Murphy waited.

"I forgot,"

The words landed between them and did not move.

Murphy shifted on the edge of the bunk. "That's not why he died."

Green did not answer. He knew that. He also knew the mind did not obey logic when it wanted a culprit. Leadership had begun to feel less like authority and more like accounting. Not for victories. For bodies.

Murphy picked up Carson's photograph from the box—a young woman in a summer dress, smiling awkwardly at the camera. He set it back down carefully, as if it might break.

"Someone should tell her the truth," Murphy sighed.

Green rose and moved to the window, looking out across the darkened field. The air smelled of fuel and wet grass.

"No one gets the truth," he murmured quietly. "They get something survivable."

Murphy turned toward him. "And what do we get?"

Green rested a hand against the cold glass. The runway lights sat in a straight line beyond the hangars, pale and patient.

"Tomorrow," he replied.

He reached into his jacket and removed his siddur. This time he did not whisper. He spoke the words aloud, voice steady, almost flat with exhaustion.

"Blessed are You, Lord our God, who gives strength to
the weary."

He paused. The room was silent except for the wind. His voice did not break. But something inside him had. Murphy bowed his head beside him.

Outside, engines turned over in the dark. The war was almost finished. No one felt victorious.

TWO SQUADRON COMMANDERS—LAST FLIGHT

Sometimes they began the morning with a song.

It wasn't official. It wasn't even particularly good. But it steadied the nerves.

Tuck away those flutes
Into their chutes
It's another day to fly today
It's another day to fly away
Put away your fear
Pack it in your gear
It's the perfect day to hit the sky
It's the perfect day—not to die

April 25, 1945
RAF Leiston

The engines started the same way they always had. There was no announcement that this might be the last time. No speech. No ceremony. Just ground crews moving quietly beneath gray English sky, hands blackened with oil, breath fogging in the cold.

Green stood with his helmet tucked beneath his arm. Murphy adjusted his gloves beside him.

"No one wants to be the last man killed."

Green nodded. "Which makes today dangerous."

They had both felt it building for weeks. The Reich was collapsing. Reports said Berlin was encircled. Some targets were already rubble before bombers reached them. But the missions continued. War did not stop simply because it was losing.

Lieutenant Chuck Yeager approached with his usual steadiness, younger than both of them, but untouched by hesitation.

"I'll take lead," Yeager declared.

Green studied him. There was no arrogance there. Only readiness.

"Keep them together," Green replied.

"Yes, sir."

The Mustangs lifted in sequence, climbing through broken cloud. Five to ten tenths at three thousand feet. Clear above. At altitude, the air felt strangely empty.

They crossed into Germany without the immediate violence they had grown used to. Flak rose eventually, but thinner now, sporadic. The sky no longer felt defended so much as stubborn. Green and Murphy flew high cover. Yeager led the forward element.

Over Steinhuder Lake, contrails formed ahead—Me 109s crossing from eleven o'clock. Twenty or more, but scattered, not disciplined. Not what they once had been. Yeager climbed gradually, patient. He waited for separation within the German formation, then dropped his tanks.

Green watched from above as Yeager slid into position. One German pilot broke early, bailing before a shot was fired. Another followed.

Murphy exhaled softly over the radio. "They see the end."

Yeager pressed forward. Short bursts. Controlled. One aircraft rolled inverted and fell. Another trailed smoke and spiraled away. A third tried to disengage but stalled in a tight turn. It was not chaos. It was unraveling.

Within minutes, the engagement was finished. The remaining German fighters dove east, toward territory that no longer promised safety. No one chased.

The bombers continued to target, releasing their payload over rail yards that had already been hit twice that week. Smoke rose again, though it was difficult to tell what was newly burning and what had simply never stopped.

On the return leg, the formation held quiet. No one joked. No one celebrated. Back at Leiston, mechanics moved toward the aircraft automatically. Pilots climbed down slower than usual. Yeager removed his helmet and walked toward Green and Murphy. There was no swagger in him.

"That should do it," Yeager was a man of few words.

Green looked at him carefully. "Yes," he replied. "It should."

Murphy clapped him once on the shoulder. "Five?"

Yeager nodded.

Murphy gave a half-smile. "Hell of a way to finish."

Yeager shrugged lightly. "Still breathing."

That seemed to be the only measure left.

The O-Club that night was subdued. No piano. No shouting. Just men sitting with drinks they did not finish. Someone mentioned Berlin might fall within days. Someone else said it already had. Green raised his glass but did not stand.

"To the ones who didn't see this"

The room echoed it quietly.

Murphy stared into his drink. "Feels strange," he muttered. "All that noise... and now this."

Green considered the silence around them. The way men kept glancing at the door as if waiting for another mission call that might not come.

"We trained for years to survive it," Green declared. "No one trained us to stop."

Murphy looked up. "You ready to?"

Green did not answer immediately. Outside, the airfield lights glowed across the dark grass. The Mustangs rested in rows, engines ticking as they cooled, as if reluctant to surrender their heat.

"I don't know who I am without it," Green stammered finally.

Murphy nodded once. "That's the trouble."

The war was not officially over. But something had already ended. And in the quiet that followed, survival felt less like victory and more like an unanswered question.

THE END AND THE BEGINNING—MAY 1945—MAY 1946

May 1945
RAF Leiston

The war did not end with a trumpet. It ended with paperwork.

Word reached the base in fragments. Berlin had fallen. Hitler was dead. Germany had surrendered. The mess hall erupted once—briefly—then settled into something closer to exhaustion than celebration.

Men shook hands without smiling. They had expected to feel something larger. Instead, there was only relief—and an odd, unsettled quiet. The points system was posted on the board outside operations within days. Months in service. Combat missions. Air medals. Distinguished Flying Cross. Confirmed victories. Every category converted into arithmetic. Every life reduced to tally.

Murphy stood with his hands locked behind his head, staring at the numbers.

"Seventy-six," he muttered. "Nine short."

Green studied his own total. High enough. High enough to go home. The war had required them. Peace did not.

"You'll rotate soon, Ben?"

Green nodded. "Looks that way."

Murphy kept staring at the board. "Funny."

"What?"

"We fought like hell to survive it. Now I'm disappointed."

Green understood.

Survival had been the objective for so long that it had become identity. Without missions, without briefing rooms, without flak bursts and tracer fire, there was an empty space where urgency had lived.

The airfield grew quieter by degrees. Fewer sorties. Fewer engines.

Aircraft were inspected, logged, prepared for shipment or reassignment. Some pilots were already gone, leaving behind bare bunks and folded blankets.

The younger men talked about home constantly now. About girls who had waited. About farms, storefronts, college plans. Green listened but did not join.

One afternoon he walked alone along the perimeter fence. Beyond it, Suffolk farmland stretched in orderly green rows, untouched by bombardment. Sheep grazed in silence. The world looked intact. He felt foreign in it. Murphy joined him eventually, hands in pockets.

"You thinking about Brooklyn?" Murphy asked.

"Yes."

"And?"

Green watched a farmer in the distance guiding a plow.

"I don't know how to arrive there as the same man."

Murphy nodded once. "We aren't."

They stood in silence.

After a while Murphy said, "Carson should be here."

Green swallowed. "He should."

"Lochstern. Sloan. All of them."

"Yes."

Murphy kicked at the dirt near his boot. "Feels wrong."

Green considered that before speaking.

"Maybe it's supposed to."

The official announcement of Victory in Europe came days later. Flags appeared. Someone found a bottle of champagne. A band tried to assemble in the mess hall, but the music faltered halfway through. There was cheering. There was also weeping. That night, Green returned to his quarters and opened his siddur. He did not read from it immediately. He simply held it.

He thought of Ariel. Of Joseph. Of candles burning in a Brooklyn apartment. Of letters folded into a wooden box. He thought of Carson's last words.

"Tell her—"

The phrase lingered unfinished in his mind.

Murphy knocked once before entering.

"You heading home soon," Murphy said, not a question.

"Yes."

Murphy leaned against the doorframe. "You scared?"

Green did not answer immediately.

Finally, he came clean. "Yes."

Murphy gave a small, tired smile. "Good. Means you still feel."

Outside, no engines started. The sky above Leiston was empty.

Green stepped to the window and looked out over the quiet field where Mustangs had once launched in disciplined sequence. Now they sat in neat rows, paint dulled, waiting for destinations no one had trained them for.

"We trained for years to fly into fire," Murphy spoke softly. "No one trained us to land."

Green closed the siddur and set it carefully on the table.

"We'll learn," he replied.

Murphy studied him for a moment. "You believe that?"

Green looked back out at the runway.

"I have to."

Somewhere in the dark, a distant church bell rang. The war was over. Morning would come.

And this time, they would not fly.

END OF PART I

INTERLUDE—LETTERS FROM ANOTHER LIFE

Brooklyn, New York—March 1945 – Shabbat evening

The envelope was creased at the corners and dotted with obvious fingerprints of men who treated war as ordinary paperwork. The censor's stamp smeared one corner. The return address—RAF Leiston, England—was written in neat, clear block letters in Hebrew beneath the U.S. Army Air Forces heading.

Ariel Green held the letter as if it were sacred scripture. In her lap, Joseph stirred, his small fists rising in his sleep, still pink and soft from infancy. She smiled unintentionally. The war had taken so much, but not this. Not yet.

She unsealed the envelope with a paring knife and unfolded the single page.

> March 18, 1945
> Leiston
>
> "My dearest Ariel,
>
> I dreamed of Jerusalem again.
>
> I was flying—not in a Mustang, but in something older and slower. There were no instruments, no machine guns. Only wind and sky. I could see the Dome of the Rock beneath me, and the sun rising over stone rooftops that looked like they hadn't changed in two thousand years.
>
> Then I saw you. You were on a balcony in the Old City, lighting candles. Joseph stood beside you with your father's tallit draped across his shoulders like a cape. You didn't see me. But I saw you. And I remembered why I fight."
>
> Ariel paused, pressing the letter to her chest. She could smell his soap in the folds—that cheap pine-scented bar he insisted on using, even when she bought the expensive French one from the market on Delancey Street.

She kept reading.

Murphy says we're all lunatics—writing letters as if we'll live long enough to mail them. But Murphy still writes Katie every day. He says religion is what you cling to when nothing else makes sense. I told him that's exactly right. It's also what teaches you to act when everything else says to sit still.

We lost a boy. Carson. He was barely twenty. I watched his Mustang go down like a comet over Berlin.

Some nights I feel like I'm already dead and just haven't been told yet. But then I think of your voice. The way you say my name during Havdalah. The way Joseph clutches my dog tags in his sleep. That is what keeps me flying."

Yours—until the sky falls,
Benjamin

Ariel folded the letter carefully—as if she were worried the ink might still smudge—and placed it in the carved wooden box that held all of his letters. Each one is a lifeline. Each one is a thread between two worlds.

She turned to Joseph, who had now woken and was blinking at her from the crib.

"Your Abba still believes in God," she whispered. "Even up there."

She lit the Shabbat candles, her hands trembling slightly, and whispered the ancient blessing. The flame danced and held.

"Now. I wonder who is coming home?"

PART II: TWO FLAGS, ONE BROTHERHOOD
(1946–1956)

CHAPTER EIGHT: AFTER THE SILENCE

*"Victory is a soundless thing. It arrives like fog—soft, ambiguous,
full of ghosts."*

—Excerpt from Murphy's notebook, May 1947

Brown's Hotel—33 Albemarle Street—Mayfair, London
August 1945

Ben and Murph were enjoying 30 days in London before they had to return
to their commands, now located in Germany. The war in the Pacific had just
ended, so the streets were alive with energy.

The ticker tape fluttered but to Paul it felt like shredded promises despite
their celebratory purpose. He stood in the middle of Trafalgar Square in his
Class A uniform, watching the crowds explode into joy. Strangers kissed in
the streets. Children waved flags from rooftops. The radio blared with news
from Tokyo Bay—Japan had surrendered. The war was over.

Katie had purchased two of the first commercial tickets available for
travel from New York to London. She had convinced Ariel to come with her
so that the four of them could have fun like they did before the boys went
off to war.

That night, the two couples relaxed in Paul and Katie's suite at Brown's
Hotel. Ben was uncomfortable with Katie having purchased Ariel's plane
ticket and these obscenely expensive hotel suites. He would have to pay her
back, and it bothered him that she had been so extravagant. He sat on the

floor with his back up against the gold upholstered couch with Ariel in his lap; she had just finished lighting a memorial candle, not for the war's end, but for what had been lost.

"They danced in the street today," Ariel's voice was distant and reflective as she lamented the deep losses of war.

"We're not dancing yet." Ben took the opportunity to deliver the bad news. "We're going back in."

Ariel looked at him with a knowing. She didn't want this, but Ben was Ben. There was no way to alter his course. His passion and commitment were undeniable.

"Auschwitz. Dachau. Treblinka. What we saw in Berlin was only smoke. The fire came later."

He gently lifted her with the same hands that had fired .50 caliber rounds into German aircraft.

"They need pilots, Ariel. In Palestine."

"I need a husband. Joseph needs a father."

Benjamin nodded, acknowledging the weight of both truths.

September 1945

Katie was waiting for Paul in their suite. She was dressed in a velvet robe with a silk slip that she had bought at John Lewis & Partners. It was only a 20-minute walk from Brown's, and she desperately needed the walk after her flight. Upon returning to the hotel, she had her maid draw her a bath, and after 30 minutes of relaxation, she prepared for Paul's arrival.

When Paul arrived and took the elevator up to the suite, he was excited but also anxious to see his Katie. War had a way of removing reality— separating it into another compartment. He was about to leave the field of battle and reenter a world that he was worried may not even exist anymore. He had so little time with Katie before they went to war and things can change with absence.

Paul need not have worried. Katie was obsessed with Paul—his courage, commitment, intellect, and passion. She could not contain herself and was waiting excitedly to present him his prize. She heard the elevator's faint ding in the hall and prepared to drop the velvet robe as soon as the door opened. The key slid into the lock. The robe dropped. The doorman helping Paul up to the room with his bags was hugely impressed by his welcome. But Katie didn't mind and made light of it, saying, "Oh well, nothing wrong with an audience after going to all this trouble but just to be clear, this is only for you," Katie announced with authority, pointing lovingly at Paul with a sexy smile and pose.

Paul hurried over, picked up the robe and threw it around her shoulders while seamlessly embracing her lovingly and laughing.

> "Darling, I do hope the hotel staff don't get the same treatment when they service the room."

> "Just you my love. You've been gone so long, I wanted to do something special and exciting. But I'm sure James the doorman will have a nice story to tell his girl. Or boy, as the case may be."

> "Hmm. Well let me take another look here." Unwrapping his gift with gusto.

Later that evening, Paul poured himself a whiskey and settled in. Katie saw that he was distracted and anxious.

> "What is it, darling? What's wrong? Are you okay?"

> "Everyone thinks it's over, but it's just… different now. The uniform comes off. The war doesn't."

She wrapped her arms around him. He didn't resist, but he didn't respond either. His body was there, but his soul still hung in the air somewhere above Berlin. Their time together in London was almost over, and Katie knew that was what was causing Paul's sour mood and dark, heavy presence.

> "Paul, we've got two days left in London in this beautiful hotel in this beautiful city. Let's spend that time in love and happiness. Let's celebrate each other and prepare for our time apart by creating beautiful memories to get us through."

Paul smiled and snapped right out of his mood. "I love you even more than I did yesterday, and I never imagined that was even possible. Thank you for being my wife and the love of my life."

Paul and Katie honored their agreement and had the time of their lives for their remaining days in London. They attended shows, took carriage rides, and dined in fascinating and extravagant places. They took a boat ride on the Thames and took bike rides through the city in the sunny and mild autumn weather. Then it was over. The hour always comes.

***

Ben proved to be right about being a squadron commander during peacetime, except he forgot to include preparing for the Inspector General inspections. The 357th Fighter Group remained at Neubiberg until it was inactivated on August 20, 1946. The week after the group disbanded, Paul traveled to the Port of Bremerhaven as his POE (Port of Embarkation). It took nearly a week to secure passage on a ship. He boarded the USS Europa (AP-177), a U.S. Navy troop transport ship that was initially a German ocean liner, and sailed from Bremerhaven, Germany, to New York City, arriving on September 5, 1946. Ben was worried about Israel, Haganah, and his extended religious family.

Correspondence—September 1946

Letter from Benjamin Green to Paul Murphy:

> Paul.
>
> They're training volunteers now. Americans, Canadians, Brits... even South Africans. They're smuggling in planes through Czechoslovakia. I've written to a man in Tel Aviv named Weizman. He says we'll be flying soon. After Dachau, how can I not? I apologize for not writing sooner. I needed time to breathe. Or to pretend I was breathing.
>
> Tell Katie I pray for you both.
>
> Ben

Murphy didn't write back. Not at first.

***

November 1946.

Benjamin's apartment was in darkness when Ariel arrived. She walked through, calling his name and asking why the lights were off. She soon found him at the window, staring out into the snow.

"Hi. When are you leaving?"

"I don't know."

"You already decided. I know your face."

"I'll come back."

"Will you?"

He turned to her, and in that moment, he looked more like the boy she married than the man who'd come home from war.

"Ariel, they are building a nation out of ashes. If I can give them air, I have to."

"Then promise me this: You fight to live. Not to die for them."

Murphy's letter to Benjamin — December 1946

Dear Ben,

I saw the stories. The camps, the gas chambers, the ovens. I understand now why you're going. I couldn't go with you. I have Katie. And soon—God help us— another child. You always had a conscience. I had the compass. Maybe now they finally point in different directions. If this is the last letter I send before you disappear into the desert skies, know this:
I love you, brother.

May G-d fly with you.

~Paul

CHAPTER NINE: NEW LIVES, NEW ORDERS

5 September 1946—The Eldorado—Central Park West.

Katie received word that Paul was finally returning from his service in Europe. She began thinking about how she would welcome him home, having known him for only three weeks before he was deployed and then their time in London last year. What a whirlwind romance. She was an honors student at Stanford University, and he was a new pilot in the 363rd Fighter Squadron. She was very proud that he was the youngest Major in the Army Air Corps.

He had done very well in Europe; he was promoted to Captain, then Major, and later became the Squadron Commander of the 363rd Fighter Squadron. He had written her a letter nearly every day. He was a devoted husband, and she believed he would be a dedicated father to their one-year-old son. What troubled her was what he didn't know.

He knew she was a high honors graduate from Stanford with both a Bachelor of Science Degree in Chemistry and a Master of Business Administration. She was also the valedictorian from both programs.

What he didn't realize was that her father had been the principal shareholder and CEO of Kidder & Co., making him one of the wealthiest men in the United States. Katie had inherited half of the family's wealth upon her mother's death and the other half when her father died earlier that year. Those events made her the wealthiest woman in the country. Paul didn't know where she lived and was unaware of her business, political, and charitable obligations. She was his wife, and she understood her role was to support him and his career. But what was he going to think?

At that moment, his cab pulled up to the building, which Katie called

The Eldorado. Major Murphy got out, grabbed his bags, and tried to get to the front door. After the journey, customs, and waiting for a cab, his uniform was clearly disheveled. When he finally reached the door, a man dressed in what appeared to be an unusual and pretentious uniform opened it and stood in front of it preventing his entry. He spoke down his nose in a condescending voice.

"Sir, what business do you have here?"

"I'm here to see my wife, Katie Murphy."

"Sir, there is obviously some mistake. There is no Mrs. Murphy here."

"Uhm—is this The Eldorado?"

"Nobody by that name lives here, Sir. Please move along."

"Are you sure? My wife gave me this specific address, called it The Eldorado, and said she lives here."

"Sir, I know every resident here. I know their guests, and their staff. There is no one here with that name. Do I need to contact the authorities?"

"Excuse me, I just got off a troop ship after spending too much time flying a fighter in combat. My wife Katie Murphy said this was her address. Would you please check for me? Actually, come to think of it, perhaps she's going by her maiden name. Her maiden name was McFarland. Miss Katherine McFarland!"

The man looked up like he had been shot, then looked like he was going to throw up, but slowly regained his composure. He thought about the mistake he had made. Mrs. McFarland, now Mrs. Murphy, while generally nice, could be highly assertive. He had made a real mistake. He apologized and said in a subservient voice.

"Sir, I humbly apologize. I am Robert, the doorman here at The Eldorado. Please let me inform Miss McFarland, umm, Mrs. Murphy that you have arrived."

The doorman made a call to the McFarland residence and informed the staff. He hung up the phone and immediately walked over to pick up Major Murphy's bags and led him over to the elevator—continuing to apologize for how he treated the new husband of his most important resident.

Robert then told the elevator operator—who was a woman dressed in equally odd attire—to take Major Murphy to Tower 2—7th floor. The elevator operator looked exasperated.

"Who is going to watch my elevator while I escort him to the second elevator bank?"

"If you would like to keep your job, I suggest you wriggle along."

Paul's first impression of the apartment building was that it looked very nice but it all seemed a bit overwhelming. He arrived at the top floor and stepped outside. He was surprised to find only one door with a single sign on it. PH, whatever that meant. "Maybe private house?" He thought to himself.

He walked over to the door and knocked. The door was quickly opened by another gentleman dressed in what appeared to be a costume. He introduced himself,

"Good afternoon, Sir. My name is James, and I am Miss McFarland's Butler. She said to say that she will be with you presently. May I take your bags to the master bedroom?"

"Ummm... Certainly," Paul offered in deepening bewilderment.

Katie appeared almost immediately, and Paul gasped,

"Oh my gosh, I'm married to the most beautiful woman in the world."

Katie smiled widely and jumped into Paul's arms and kissed him like it was their first time.

"I think I'm going to have to come home more often."

After the longest kiss of his life, Paul slowly came back to reality, gathered himself,

"Katie, is this place yours?"

"No, darling."

"Oh, thank God."

"It's ours. I'll explain everything now that you are here."

After settling in for a few minutes, Paul noticed that the living room featured a large fireplace.

"Katie where is the master bedroom?

"Oh, I see someone is eager to get down to business."

They both laughed and Katie led Paul to the farthest room from the front door taking them past the dining room, the breakfast room, the sitting room, the library, and two bedrooms on each side of the hallway.

"I think this is the nicest house I've ever been in."

He was going to enjoy his time here for as long as his leave lasted. Over the first week, Paul was starting to come to terms with the fact that Katie owned a sprawling five-bedroom, five-bath residence, complete with a fireplace, living room, sitting room, library, office, formal dining room, breakfast room, and numerous other rooms that Paul could barely keep track of.

When they met, she was a sophomore at Stanford, and he was a cadet pilot. At the time, Paul had no inkling of her considerable wealth. All he saw was a brilliant, captivating woman he quickly grew to love. Or perhaps it was lust at first. Either way, they had fallen fast, engaged quickly, married even faster, and then he was off to complete his flight training in Pennsylvania. After that, he was immediately deployed to Europe.

Their lives over the past few years had unfolded on separate, yet oddly parallel, tracks. Both had help, but of vastly different kinds. Paul had an orderly who occasionally fetched him coffee or brought a meal. Katie had an entire household staff of butlers, maids, and cooks to tend to her needs. And now, a nanny who cares for their young son.

Even with their month in London, they had not discussed their backgrounds, wealth, or possessions, they were so in love they just lived in each other's glow that isolated them from any reality.

With Benjamin now separated from the Army and devoted to his religious mission in the Middle East, Paul was facing decisions about his own future—decisions he'd have to make without Ben. He had no idea what the Army had in store for him, but aside from marrying Katie, he believed joining the service had been the best thing that had ever happened to him.

Just then, word came that his first piece of mail had arrived at the apartment. Unsurprisingly, it was from the Army. Paul couldn't help but wonder what orders—or surprises—they had in mind for him next.

***

Department of the Army

00000540

3 September 1946

Maj Paul Murphy
013238298 HOR
The Eldorado, 300 Central Park West PH, New York, NY 10024

Action: Permanent Change of Station
Reason: Operational
Effective Date: 15 September 1946
End Date: June 30, 1947
Report Date: 15 September 1946

Report to: United States Army Command and General Staff College
Position Number: U.S. Army Command and General Staff College
Student, Fort Leavenworth, KS
By Authority of the Department of the Army
Approved by: Col Lay, Art D.
202-555-1259

"Wow, I wonder what Katie is going to think about this," Paul reflected silently. "The only thing I know about Fort Leavenworth is that it has a federal prison. Is it in the middle of nowhere? I need to see if I can get this Colonel on the phone. I've more questions now than I've had at any other point since I joined the Army. Is it a hardship tour where my wife isn't permitted to accompany me? Or is it a regular reassignment where my whole family is allowed to join me? And who is this Colonel Lay guy? Perhaps an assignments officer?" he thought to himself. "That looks like a pretty high-ranking officer to be dealing with a lowly major. There's a phone number listed, so I suppose I should try it before involving Katie."

Following Katie's instructions on how to place a call, Paul picked up the phone and asked for a long-distance number. After giving the operator the number, she said that she had placed the call. A few seconds later, the phone started to ring. Almost immediately, Sergeant Major Jones, Field Grade Officer, Assignments, answered the call.

"Hello. This is Major Paul Murphy. Is the Colonel available?"

"No, he isn't. How may I help you, Sir?"

Paul immediately thought, "Well, it's clear I'm back in the Army now."

"I've received orders to go to Fort Leavenworth, Kansas. There's a position number for the Command and General Staff College as a student. I have a few questions about the assignment."

The Sergeant Major, slightly perplexed. "What kind of questions do you have, Sir?

"Well, for instance, is this a hardship tour? Am I allowed to bring my spouse? Am I permitted to ship household goods? Sergeant Major, I just returned from Europe, where I commanded a squadron in the 357th. I was brought on active duty in late 42, commissioned in early 43, and shipped to Europe as a Second Lieutenant pilot. I don't know anything about the assignment."

It seemed that the Sergeant Major's attitude changed almost immediately.

"Well, Sir, you're in for a treat. The Command and General Staff College is the first school where officers are selected who are deemed exceptional individuals, likely to rise to the senior ranks of the Army. So yes, you can bring your wife and children. I am personally aware of your credentials, Sir. You are one of the youngest Field Grade Officers in the Army. You may be the youngest officer to have ever been selected for Command & General Staff College, so I am here to assist you in making this assignment as easy as possible."

The Sergeant Major explained that transportation costs would be paid for by the Army. Additionally, household goods would be shipped to Fort Leavenworth. He noted that Fort Leavenworth is located outside of Kansas City, and most of the spouses enjoy traveling there for shopping. He informed Paul that the academics are rigorous, but not for someone like him, who has risen quickly enough to become a Field Grade Officer.

"Keep your nose to the grindstone for the nine months in the program, and when you leave, there's a good chance you'll become a Lieutenant Colonel."

"Thank you, Sergeant Major. I arrived from Europe recently, and the orders I received state that I must arrive at Fort Leavenworth no later than 15 September. That gives us just 10 days to pack, ship, and travel to Fort Leavenworth. Is there any way that my arrival date could be delayed?"

"Well, Sir, that won't work. You see, classes begin on the 16th, and missing any classes isn't permitted. It looks like I have a lot of arrangements to make to get you and the misses to Kansas on time. I'll need to contact the transportation officer for your household goods, the billeting officers at Fort Leavenworth, and arrange air travel from New York City to Kansas City. A driver will pick you and your wife up on the 12th. One question I know the reception department at Fort Leavenworth will ask is how many children you have and their ages. Additionally, they would like to know if you want temporary furniture in your quarters upon arrival."

"Well, Sergeant Major, thank you for your help. I think I'd better tell my wife about my orders. How about if I call you back in a little bit with answers to your questions?"

"That'll be fine, Major."

"Thank you for your help, Sergeant Major."

Katie and Paul sat down to talk about their upcoming move. When Paul told Katie they would be living in government housing, she responded:

"Absolutely not. I will quickly arrange to purchase a home at Fort Leavenworth, and someone from the bank will handle the details. Also, I see no reason to remove the furniture from this lovely apartment and move it to Fort Leavenworth. I will have a talented young lady from the bank fly to Kansas City to buy all the necessary furniture while we are stationed there. Once you complete your assignment, we will rent the house to another fortunate student who has been assigned to it. Our family has a rule that we never sell real estate; we simply rent it to suitable tenants. We have a department with a full complement of people to manage that. We will rent the house to another deserving field-grade officer. By the way, what exactly is a field-grade officer?"

"Field grade officers are a specific rank group within the officer corps. Major, Lieutenant Colonel, and Colonel. They bridge the gap between junior officers or otherwise named company grade officers and senior officers which are general or flag officers. They are known for their experience, leadership skills, and ability to manage larger, more complex units and operations.

"OK. So, we will rent to one of those."

Katie then noted that they would need two new cars.

"What kind of car do you want, Paul? as a dashing fighter pilot, one of those new MG TDs would 'fit the cut of your jib.' The bank will take care of it. Also, we will take one of the bank's planes to fly us directly to Ft. Leavenworth. It'll be quicker than flying commercially."

Paul was still not used to this level of wealth, even though Katie had shared every detail of her background with him. It still all felt a little surreal. Especially compared to how he had been living through wartime. Paul wondered what the Army would think of Katie. She is a beautiful, well-mannered, highly educated, and decisive woman. She was generally "conservative" with money, but she had more than most states, let alone individuals. Most people can't handle that.

That afternoon, Paul called Sergeant Major Jones back and informed him that they would not need quarters, furniture, or transportation to Leavenworth.

"Also, Sergeant Major, how would I go about registering our cars even though we haven't purchased either of them yet?"

The Sergeant Major sat in stunned silence before eventually speaking.

"Well, my, ...this is going to be interesting!"

September 8, 1946

That evening, Katie Murphy was very proud of herself. In two days, she had arranged everything at the apartment.

"So, when do we have to be there, Paul?"

"According to my orders, I'm required to be there on September 15th."

"I talked to the bank this morning. Our new address is 500 Pine Ridge Place, Leavenworth, Kansas. The bank said it will be completely furnished by tomorrow. The plane is scheduled to pick us up on the 10th, and our two cars will be ready on the same day."

"Well, I guess that covers everything. I will need to sign in upon arrival. I need to let the Sergeant Major at the Pentagon know our schedule and that you have covered everything. Is there anything that you would like shipped from here?"

"I'm glad you brought that up. What do you think about our boys' toys and some of my clothes? I can have all of them boxed and ready to go by tonight. That way, it won't slow us down when we are on our way."

"Great. Also, I was wondering what kind of airplane we will be flying in?"

"Why, Paul. Are you picky about our private planes?"

"No, my dear. It's just that, as a fighter pilot, I always like to know about the aircraft that we'll be flying in."

"Oh, I see. Well, the bank has a modified DC-3 and a Lockheed L-49 Constellation. I think it's called a Constellation, but some people call it a Connie. I've been told it's a big plane and that it's pressurized. I was told it's much faster and more spacious for us to travel in; we will just have to wait and see which ones are available tomorrow."

"Ok, but if you speak with them today, please ask if they know the plane's tail number, which should start with the letter N. We can land at Fort Leavenworth Airport, where fuel is cheaper; please coordinate this in advance if possible."

"Sure, I'll call them right now,"

"Ok, I'll call the Sergeant Major now. Thanks for all your work, darling, I love you."

"I love you too, my darling."

Paul went to his luxurious office and called Washington, D.C. After giving the operator the number, she said she had placed the call. After a few seconds.

"Sergeant Major James Jones, Field Grade Officer, Assignments. How may I help you?"

"Sergeant Major, this is Major Paul Murphy. First, I would like to thank you for all your assistance in identifying the tasks that need to be completed for me to attend my class at the Command and General Staff College. I wanted to let you know that my wife, Katie, has organized everything. We have purchased a home at 500 Pine Ridge Place, and all the furniture will be installed today, and our POVs will be delivered tomorrow afternoon. Our airplane will be arriving tomorrow in the late afternoon, and I was wondering if we could fly into Fort Leavenworth's airport."

The Sergeant Major then asked what the aircraft's tail number was, just as Katie slid a sheet of paper with the details on top of Paul's desk in front of him.

"Yes, it will be either a DC-3 tail number, November 502CH, or a Lockheed L-49 Constellation tail number, November 503CH."

"Well, Sir, that's mighty fine. You're the first officer I've met with two airplanes and a wife who is so efficient. I think I'll be able to take care of your request for landing at Fort Leavenworth. But Major, I believe you should be aware that this will all likely spark some discussion once you're there."

"Yes, Sergeant Major, you're right. My age and rank often raise questions, but probably nothing more than my wife buying a house, new furniture, and two new cars."

"Well, Sir, I'd really like to meet you. You clearly have a remarkable wife and a practical attitude. If you ever need a Sergeant Major, I'm available."

"Thank you, Sergeant Major, and good day."

The next morning, they all piled into a limo and headed to the marine terminal at LaGuardia Airport. Once there, they met their pilot, who introduced himself as Col. Steve Payton, USAAF (retired).

"Major, your bags have been loaded earlier this morning, and the DC-3 is ready to depart as soon as we board. Would you like to join me up front?"

"Thank you, Colonel, but my wife must live without me while I fly for a living, so it would be wise for me to stay with her while I can."

"Ah, you're a wise man, Major. Would you mind sharing with me how someone so young was able to achieve such a rank?"

"No, not at all, Colonel. I commanded the 363rd Fighter Squadron of the 357th Fighter Group, and I was a triple ace, so I guess that all added up to an early promotion."

He was shocked. "Well, I commanded a transport group during the war, but I must tell you I am both impressed and envious of your success. If I can offer a small piece of advice, keep a low profile at C&GSC because the West Point Protective Association might be out for you—you've surpassed all your classmates in terms of success."

"Yes, will do, Colonel."

Four hours later, Colonel Payton was calling the tower to ask for landing instructions. He was told that traffic was landing on runway 34 and that dignitaries were waiting to welcome the Major to Fort Leavenworth. The visitors included General Leonard T. Gerow, Commandant, his aide Colonel Charleton Smith, and SM Sonu.

"Well, Major Murphy, you are being met by the bigwigs. Just a heads up so you'll be prepared for company."

What a show. The former commander of the 15th Army was waiting to meet a lowly student who happened to be a major, a triple ace, and a former squadron commander. When the general saw Murphy's obviously young age, he slowed down and whispered to his aide, asking why the Sergeant Major at the Pentagon had informed the Fort Leavenworth duty officer to prepare a welcome party for a VIP. Paul immediately picked up on the confusion and stepped in.

"I apologize sincerely, General. I wasn't expecting a welcome party of such significance. Please meet my wife, Katie, and my son, Tommy."

"My pleasure, Mrs. Murphy, and nice to meet you, young man. Tell me, Mrs. Murphy, I was informed that you do not require us to provide accommodations. Is that correct?

"Yes, General. You see, this is my first time accompanying my husband to a military assignment, so, being such an auspicious occasion, I decided to use my own funds to buy a home for us at Fort Leavenworth. My family has always advised me to buy property every time I move to a new location. Then, when you move again, you rent the first house to a deserving married soldier. The family's rule is to never sell real estate. And I suppose that advice has proven itself as it seems to afford us the ability to do it."

The general stood in stunned silence, then finally broke the tension.

"Yes, well, very good. That's very good indeed. I bet my wife would love to meet you all. Let's plan to get together when you're settled."

After saluting, the general, his aide, and the Sergeant Major left. Paul, Katie, and Tommy headed to their new car waiting at the hangar. They drove to their new home at 500 Pine Ridge Place and spent the next two days unpacking and settling in.

On the 14th, Paul went to Fort Leavenworth and signed in for duty. As a new student, he was given a packet of information and told to report to his school for duty at 0730 on the 16th.

The school wasn't terrible; Paul learned a lot about ground forces, armor, staff studies, and other military subjects. Adjusting to the formality of a military school for officers wasn't hard, but it did take some acclimation. Most of his classmates were West Point graduates. They treated him with disdain, as if he were a low-life urchin. They were, without exception, the most condescending people he'd ever met.

Although that attitude never changed, it became easier to handle after his first test. Paul was ranked #1 among all the students in the class. That partly eased the public harassment, but it didn't alter their opinions. Being number one in the class earned him a dinner with the commanding general and his wife.

General Gerow and his wife, Kathryn, hosted Katie and Paul at their home after the first quarter of C&GSC. It was a wonderful dinner. When Mrs. Gerow learned that Paul and Katie had their own house in town, she said that if Paul remained number one in the class after the second quarter, they would have to host her and the General for dinner at their place. Paul saw that as a challenge. He worked his tail off—harder than anyone else in the class—and by the end of the second quarter, he was number one by a long shot. So, Paul and Katie were obliged to host the General and his wife, and Katie got to work.

First, Katie called the house in New York and requested that her butler, chef, maids, and servers come out for a special event dinner. She provided them with the following menu:

Menu

Soup

CREAMY CUCUMBER-AVOCADO SOUP

Salad

MIXED SPRING GREENS WITH
CANDIED WALNUTS, GOAT CHEESE, AND A HONEY VINAIGRETTE

Entrée

BEEF WELLINGTON
WITH MUSHROOM DUXELLES SERVED WITH MADEIRA SAUCE
BACON-WRAPPED ASPARAGUS
OVEN-ROASTED TOMATOES
MASHED POTATO PUFFS

Dessert

CHOCOLATE MOUSSE
A DARK AND WHITE CHOCOLATE SHELL WITH
CRÈME ANGLAISE AND FRESH ASSORTED BERRIES

Generals are used to that kind of service, but the Army has rarely seen a lowly major providing a dinner as magnificent as this one. They also weren't accustomed to a four-piece jazz band.

Mrs. Gerow was overwhelmed and suitably impressed. She praised the meal, the setting, and the music all evening. On her way home, she asked the general about Paul Murphy's success at such a young age and whether it was related to the family's apparent wealth.

"Major Murphy is probably the most talented young officer I've ever met. No one in the Army, much less Major Murphy's chain of command, knows anything about his financial situation, except that he and his wife are the wealthiest family serving the country. All they know is that he is extremely talented, a great leader, and one of the best combat commanders anyone had ever seen. Major Murphy will likely be awarded the rank of Lieutenant Colonel after graduation. That will probably make him the youngest peacetime Lieutenant Colonel in the Army this century.

"Well, in that case, I can't wait for the promotion party. If tonight's dinner is any indication, this would be a party for the ages."

Gen. Gerow quietly thought to himself. "In fact, Major Murphy's wife is probably the most talented wife I've ever met. She would be a fabulous resource for the Army."

***

When the ring knockers discovered Murphy was ranked number one in the class halfway through the program, they took action. They first contacted the head of the West Point Association of Graduates (WPAOG) at Fort Leavenworth. They complained about favoritism toward him, claiming it was impossible for a high school graduate to outperform nearly 200 West Point graduates. Then they began a lobbying effort. They had high-ranking army officers reach out to numerous C&GSC instructors, questioning their reasoning for grading a high school graduate so highly, however, the ring knockers' efforts eventually backfired on them. One of the instructors nearing retirement filed a complaint with the IG. The complaint claimed that students were inappropriately challenging the grading of an individual's work. That's when Paul discovered how deeply the RKs were trying to hurt him. However, this only motivated him to increase his study efforts even further. There was nothing above number one, but now his aim was to be the highest-ranked officer ever to attend C&GSC. He succeeded.

May 1947—Fort Leavenworth

Murphy impressed all his instructors. His interim reports noted that he was the most creative officer C&GSC's faculty could remember seeing. His instructors observed that Major Murphy did not seem to recognize his own exceptional skills; he was simply a good man, not trying to impress anyone. That trait made him a leader everyone wanted to follow.

At the end of the third quarter, Major Murphy was again number one and remained in that position for the entire year. The lead instructor noted that Major Murphy's scores were the highest ever recorded by any student at C&GSC.

Katie and Paul enjoyed their time at Fort Leavenworth. They made many new friends, and Katie was subtly introduced to the ways of an Army wife. She relished every moment. She also became pregnant during the first quarter of the school year. So, when the final grades were posted and Paul was ranked #1 in his class and selected for promotion to Lieutenant Colonel at age 24, it was time to celebrate.

The invitations went out. A luxurious celebration unfolded. Artillery punch, infantry punch, and martinis were served. After an hour, nearly everyone at the party had drunk one too many. The wives were all at the top of their game, however, the general's wife drank a little more than usual. All her inhibitions disappeared. The guests all sat down to a magnificent dinner and after dessert, Mrs. Gerow went to the kitchen to meet the chef and thank the servers. But, because of her intoxication, she began taking notes by drawing with crayons on the wall. Nothing more was expected from her that evening—the party continued.

After a while, it became clear that the only mammal who wasn't inebriated was Tiger, the German shepherd. However, Tiger had other talents that surfaced during the party. He had a great trick; he would run up behind you, stick his head between your legs, and lift it up. He expected you to pet him under the chin. Well, you can imagine the kerfuffle when he went to the general's wife to try her on. Unfortunately, he didn't quite get his head all the way through her skirt. So, when he lifted his wet nose, he startled her, which tipped her forward, tripping her foot on the fountain wall, and sending her headfirst into the water. Once it was established that she was not injured, aside from her pride, everyone began laughing, and the laughter turned into belly laughs. Everyone said they would remember that incident for the rest of their careers. Under other circumstances, it could have been a career-ending move for the laughers.

As the honor graduate, Paul would usually get to choose his assignment, but in this case, because of the incident at the party, he wasn't on the best of terms with the general. He knew he needed a flight assignment, but the general had him assigned to a desk job at the Pentagon, where he would have "political supervision." He was supposed to learn how to serve hors d'oeuvres at dinners and presidential receptions. The military recognized his potential, but they thought he might need to mature.

Paul knew that wouldn't work, and a few days after receiving that assignment, he told Katie all about the issues. After Katie understood what the West Point Protective Association and the over-the-hill general were up to, she developed a plan of action.

Katie called the U.S. Senator from New York and suggested that they meet with President Truman and discuss her being the lead investor in establishing a foundation focused on education and nurturing young leaders in public service. The Senator said he would immediately call the President and schedule a meeting. Katie went so far as to quietly establish the new Harry S. Truman Leadership Foundation, which aims to support education and develop young leaders in public service.

The meeting with the President was scheduled for the following week. Katie knew that the President was a former National Guard Colonel, so he was very familiar with the West Point Protective Association and how they mistreated reserve and National Guard officers. Therefore, Katie prepared her lunch with the President the following week.

During lunch, the President inquired about Katie's husband, the youngest lieutenant colonel in the US Army and U.S. Army Air Forces. Katie told the President about her husband's success at Command & General Staff College, where he graduated first in his class. She also mentioned his undesirable assignment to a non-flying role in Washington, D.C. She expressed her dissatisfaction with how the West Pointers were mistreating her husband and found that behavior completely unacceptable. While Katie didn't use inappropriate language with the President, she exerted some subtle political pressure, and the President recognized it for what it was.

People quickly realized what Katie was capable of when pushed to act. Right after she met with the President, Katie met with the senior Senators from New York, Kansas, and California. All three received the harshest tongue-lashing imaginable. Shortly afterward, the congressional liaison staff at the Pentagon received direct phone calls from all three Senators. As a result, Paul's assignment was changed, and the senior officers of the US military learned a lesson about Katie Murphy.

He quickly received the flying assignment: Director of Aviation for the American Mission for Aid to Greece, commanded by Lieutenant General Van Fleet. That would normally be an assignment for a full colonel. The General was very pleased to get an officer who had been number one in his class at Command & General Staff College. General Van Fleet was leading a highly covert operation to support the Greek government during the Greek Civil War and needed all the smart officers he could find. It was an excellent assignment to work for such a superb general, but it was also a challenging one because Paul would once again be away from his wife and son. The nice part of the assignment was that it would not start until January 8th, 1948.

CHAPTER TEN: EXODUS TO ZION

"We are not promised peace. We are promised purpose."

January 1947—Letter from Benjamin Green

Dear Paul.

Well, I'm finally out of the service. You know it took 14 months before they would let me out. They were convinced that my life would be better off, as they felt I would make a great Army Air Force officer. They assumed I would follow you to the Command and General Staff College. But that's not what my life is for. After learning about Auschwitz, Buchenwald, and the other hideous camps, I know that I must fight for freedom for my religious partners.

So, what are the next steps? My friends have told me that the Weston Trading Company has been purchasing ships and providing them to refugees to enter Palestine, which is part of the Aliyah Bet movement. So, I'm going to visit them to see what help they can provide. I know that the State Department has rules against American citizens participating in a foreign military operation. In some cases, the State Department has stated that participating in a foreign military operation is illegal, and they have attempted to prosecute some individuals. That will not stop me. I have a duty to defend members of my faith. That duty is just like the duty I had after the Japanese attacked Pearl Harbor to protect the United States. I will now defend Israel.

It was difficult to find the offices of the Weston Trading Company. It turns out that they have a one-room office on the Lower East Side of Manhattan. I couldn't find a phone number for the company, so I took a taxi to their location. When I arrived at their offices, no one was there. As you can imagine, my frustration level was elevated. But an individual in an adjacent office had the name of the company's president, Mr. Dewey D Stone, and his residential phone number. I must have resembled a supporter somehow.

My next step in the process to identify the correct way to get to Israel was meeting with Mr. Stone. He told me that the State Department is scrutinizing all travel attempts to Europe or Israel. He asked me if my passport was current, and I informed him that I had been travelling using my military ID card, and I didn't have a current passport.

Mr. Stone asked me what I had done in the military and whether I had served during the war. I told Mr. Stone that I had been a triple ace and that I commanded the 363rd Fighter Squadron, part of the 357th Fighter Group, the most effective fighter group during World War II. Furthermore, I told him that I flew P-51s during my entire combat service. After providing Mr. Stone with this information, he was quiet and contemplated his response. He then said, Ben, call me Dewey. You will be a very valuable member of Haganah and eventually our Air Force.

He let me know that that was the first step to obtain a passport and then purchase a plane ticket to Europe. He then stated that once I was in Europe, I should purchase a ticket to Jerusalem. He told me to return to see him as soon as I had obtained my passport and had purchased my plane ticket to Europe. He then informed me that someone would meet me upon my arrival in Europe and coordinate the rest of my travel to Israel.

Obtaining a passport proved to be much more challenging than I had expected. First, I had to obtain a certified copy of my birth certificate. Since I was born in California, I had to travel there to obtain the certified copy. Then, they requested a certified copy of my wedding certificate, so I had to travel to California to obtain it. Then they asked for proof of my military service. I had that, it was my DD214, but when I provided that document, they started asking questions about my religion and whether I was heading to Israel.

I informed them that I was returning to the location where my fighter squadron, which I commanded, had been stationed. I was going back to make sure that those individuals who had served the United States were being taken care of. I said it was my duty to take care of those who had taken care of us. So, they finally decided I could have a passport. I was beginning to wonder if I'd been fighting for the right side during World War II, or if I should have been fighting to eliminate our government's bureaucrats.

I then went to Pan American Airlines and purchased a ticket to Paris, France, for the following week. With the ticket in hand, I called Mr. Stone and arranged to meet him the next day. That evening, I took Ariel to dinner. I updated her on my plans and let her know that as soon as it was safe, she should plan on joining me in Israel.

The next day, I went to Weston Trading Company's offices to meet with Mr. Dewey Stone. When I arrived, in addition to Mr. Stone, there was a very abrupt man named Mr. Blank. Mr. Blank immediately searched me and confiscated all the documents and papers in my coat and pants pockets. Then he went through each piece of paper carefully. While he was doing that, he asked me a myriad of questions. Mr. Blank asked some of the questions three or four times, and he was constantly looking for any inconsistencies in my background or what I was telling him. After three hours of questioning, it became apparent that I had completed Mr. Blank's extensive questioning process.

Mr. Stone then started reviewing with me what would occur when my plane landed in Paris, France. He told me that an individual would approach me once I cleared immigration. He said that the individual would have a series of passwords and answers that I would use to verify his identity.
The first pair of words was:
    Challenge: Watermelon
    Response: Boise

We then went through who would make the statement and who would respond. Initially, the individual who identified themselves as my escort would state watermelon, after which I would then state Boise. If that was completed, I would then state my next challenge:

Challenge: Moscow
Response: Dog

If those were correctly completed, the escort would then conduct the third challenge, which was:

Challenge: Blitzen
Response: Lulu

Upon successful completion of the three challenges and responses, I was to ask the individual their name. The name was:

Response: Peter Pan

After that challenge was completed, he was to ask my name, and I was to respond:

Response: Donald

Assuming that the name challenges were properly completed, I was to follow him to his vehicle. He would then take me to a safe house in the heart of Paris. Once I was in the safe house, I would be briefed on the next steps in my transit towards Israel.

I was driven to a townhouse located at 69 Rue de la Roquette. After parking the car, we entered a lovely but plain townhouse.

During my time in the townhouse, I was briefed on the procedures for entering Israel. I was to be flown by a Haganah aircraft. I would be using forged papers that identified me as:

Paul McMurphy—call sign: Mensch. Instructions followed.

"Well, Mr. McMurphy, here are your papers. You need to memorize them immediately. You will not have a second chance when asked the question, 'What's your name?' A silly mistake like saying 'Ben' will get you, and everyone who accompanies you killed. This is not a Boy Scout camp; this is not a place where you get a second chance. You are responsible for yourself and everyone else who is risking their lives to get you to Israel. The promise that you offer—to lead our Air Force—— is worth the risk to the individuals who will be accompanying you. However, let me say again, it is a stupid mistake—like not remembering your name—that results in getting yourself killed, along with all the people who are helping you. In addition, it would be a significant blow to a free Israel. Do you understand?"

I immediately said yes, Sir, and I started my life as Paul McMurphy.

Best
Ben.

Israel March 1947

The airfield was crude, barely a runway—just a stretch of snow-packed dirt lined with crates. Benjamin Green stood beside a C-46 Commando transport, its tail marked only by hastily painted Hebrew letters: שירות אוויר — Sherut Avir. The Haganah's fledgling air service had no official standing, no insignia, and no promise of survival.

He carried no passport—only forged papers and conviction.

"Welcome to the shadows," a man whispered, extending a hand. "Call me Rubenfeld."

"Ben."

"American?"

"Jew."

They both understood the code.

Tel Aviv—Days later

The landing was brutal. Three hours of turbulence. Cargo: fuel drums, makeshift munitions, and salvaged plane parts from the Czechs. When they touched down at Sde Dov, a boy no older than 17 greeted them with a salute and a grin.

"You made it."

"No one shot at us."

"Yet."

Ben looked around—dust, barbed wire, and the sea in the distance.

***

Maxwell Field, Alabama—June 1947

Paul Murphy squinted through the Florida sunlight, clipboard in hand. Rows of young pilots stood at attention on the tarmac, boots too clean, eyes too eager. It reminded him of the old days… but he had work to do. As the youngest LTC in the military, he didn't have time for amateurs or the weight of their young lives on his conscience if they didn't fully respect the weight of imminent threat and the real danger of war for the inexperienced. A staffer approached from behind and handed him a cable. Murphy read it in silence.

From: Green, Benjamin
Location: "Somewhere Between Memory and Canaan"

Message:

Arrived safely. We're flying again. It's not Europe. It's dust and prophecy. Hope
you're well. Keep teaching them to survive.

Murphy folded the cable and tucked it into his jacket.

"Gentlemen, it's time to get to work and you're going to
need to listen closely, as if your life depends on it—because
I assure you, it does…"

***

Cairo intercept—February 1947

Benjamin flew low, hugging the coastline.

Cargo: communications equipment and emergency rations.

Mission: deliver to a Palmach outpost near the Negev before Egyptian scouts
intercepted the convoy.

The sun beat through the canopy. The Avia S-199 rattled in the
crosswind like it wanted to return to the graveyard it came from.

He thought of Ariel. Of Joseph. Then he remembered the synagogue in
Krakow he had seen bombed in '44—the faces at Dachau. The telegrams
from refugee ships turned away by every civilized nation.

"This is what I was born for," he muttered quietly to
himself.

The wheels touched sand. The arms were unloaded. He was airborne again
within twenty minutes.

Letter from Paul Murphy to Benjamin Green—June 1947

Ben

I just finished the Command and General Staff Course. It looks like I will graduate
number one in the class. The commanding general Gerow likes me, and Katie has

been a hit with both him and his wife. That may be one of the reasons that I have been selected for promotion to Lt Colonel. That was a surprise.

However, during my promotion party, the General's wife had a bit too much surplus inventory to drink, and Tiger goosed her. So much for a good assignment after C&GSC. I've been assigned as the Director of Air Operations in Greese, working for General Van Fleet. I've heard he's a good guy, but I'll be out of the mainstream again.

Katie's about to bless us with another child. I'm grounded, but not really. You know that feeling? Being in one place but always somewhere else? Sometimes I envy you. And of course, sometimes I think you've lost your damn mind.

But I'll always believe in you.

—Paul

Letter from Benjamin Green to Paul Murphy—April 1948

Paul

Ariel and Joseph are safe. I write her every week. Sometimes I lie to her. I tell her the missions are short. Uneventful. Routine. All the while, I'm flying a patched-up Messerschmitt through ancient skies like a madman with a death wish.

She writes back in half-truths. Tells me Joseph laughs in his sleep. That he's taken to calling every passing bird an "Abba plane."

I miss him so much, I feel it in my soul.

They call me "the old man" here. I'm just 26. But when I fly? I'm not tired. I'm not broken. I'm… home.

We're not soldiers, Paul. Not here. We're builders. Every crate we drop is a brick in something that's never existed before—a Jewish horizon.

—Ben

***

Cairo—intercepted British transmission, June 10, 1947

Subject: Unauthorized aircraft from "neutral" origin landed in Palestine. Suspected American-trained pilot. Investigation inconclusive. Suspected Aliyah Bet.

Such incidents were increasingly common as part of *Aliyah Bet*, the underground effort to bring Jewish refugees into Palestine despite British immigration bans. With legal avenues closed, Zionist networks turned to clandestine landings by sea and air, openly challenging the authority of the British Mandate.

***

Brooklyn—Ariel's Journal

I saw his face in the news today. Not by name. Just a photo. A man in a flight suit next to a Czech fighter painted with a Star of David.

I still set the Shabbat table for three. Joseph asks when his father will come down from the clouds.

June 1947 — Jan 1948

Paul completed the Command and General Staff College as the No. one honor graduate. After some follow-on assignments, he received notice of a new post—he was to work for General Van Fleet. However, his official orders indicated that the assignment wouldn't begin until January 1948, when General Van Fleet would depart for Greece. In the meantime, Paul needed to find something productive to occupy the next six months. Aware of what his friend Ben was working on, he considered conducting a staff study on the Air Forces' surplus inventory.

He reached out to General Van Fleet's aide and proposed the idea. The aide returned his call a day later with encouraging news: the general thought the staff study was an excellent initiative. Van Fleet believed the information would be particularly useful for the upcoming campaign, The American Mission for Aid to Greece. Motivated by the endorsement, Paul began his research. Quietly, he wondered whether the findings might be of use to Ben.

On September 26th, Paul received a formal order:

Secretary of Defense Transfer Order No. 1—September 26, 1947
Implementing provisions of the National Security Act of July 26, 1947.

> Effective immediately, all personnel of the Army Air Forces (including officers and enlisted) are hereby formally transferred from the Department of the Army to the Department of the Air Force, thereby establishing the USAF as an independent service branch.

Though Paul had been aware of the formation of the United States Air Force as a separate military branch, the official notice made it real—and complicated. He began to wonder how this shift would affect him. With orders to report to a three-star Army general, he wasn't sure how Air Force leadership might view his role. Still, the only opinion that truly mattered was General Van Fleet's. Paul focused his energy on producing the most comprehensive and insightful staff study possible on surplus and excess resources.

At the same time, he was enjoying a period of contentment with his wife

Katie and their children. The thought of leaving them again for the Greek assignment weighed on him, casting a shadow over what had otherwise been a joyful interlude.

A Secret Civil War—January 1948

Major General James A. Van Fleet arrived in Athens in early 1948 and was promoted to Lieutenant General. President Truman had sent him to Greece to lead the American Mission for Aid to Greece (AMAG) and serve as the executor of the Truman Doctrine. He received a warm welcome upon arrival.

General Van Fleet established his headquarters in Athens, with an advanced command post in Kastoria. Soon after settling in, he began visiting the dispersed Greek national forces operating in the mountains.

Lieutenant Colonel Paul Murphy departed Washington, D.C., on February 1st en route to Athens. His recently completed staff study on the Air Force's surplus inventory had drawn praise from General Van Fleet, who forwarded the report to both the Army Chief of Staff and the newly appointed Chief of Staff of the Air Force. Both men responded with letters of commendation, recognizing Murphy's exceptional work. The feedback reinforced Murphy's emerging reputation as a rare combination of decorated combat leader with the strategic mind of a first-rate staff officer.

The journey to Athens took nearly forty hours. It was another six hours from the airport before Murphy reached the Hotel Grande Bretagne, which served as General Van Fleet's headquarters. When he finally arrived, he was thoroughly disheveled and fatigued. His uniform was in disarray, and he looked anything but the polished officer he was. The first person he encountered was Major General Reuben Simons, Van Fleet's deputy chief of staff. The initial impression was less than ideal.

General Simons, unimpressed, questioned the presence of an Air Force officer in Athens and cast doubts on the Air Force's competence.

"What is your background as a staff officer, son?"

This prompted Murphy to reluctantly recount his authorship of the surplus inventory study and the commendations it had earned from the highest ranks of both the Army and Air Force. He also noted that he had graduated as the Distinguished Graduate (#1 in his class) from the U.S. Army's Command and General Staff College.

Skeptical but somewhat amused, Simons continued. "And what is it you've done to land such an assignment, may I ask?"

"Perhaps the Army has been punishing me for outperforming their own officers, Sir." Murphy quipped with a subtle heel click and a smirk.

The comment elicited a chuckle, breaking the ice. Simons instructed him to get some rest, have his uniforms pressed, and report back first thing in the morning.

"General Van Fleet is expected to return this evening, and he'll meet with you tomorrow."

"Yes, Sir."

Murphy saluted and turned on his heel. After grabbing a quick bite to eat, Murphy retired to his room for a much-needed nap. Later that evening, he ventured downstairs for dinner at the hotel's bar. There, he unexpectedly ran into Allen Dulles, a senior figure within the newly formed Central Intelligence Agency. Dulles introduced himself and offered to buy Murphy a drink, which Murphy accepted without hesitation.

As they spoke, Dulles asked what Murphy's role would be as Director of Air Operations under General Van Fleet. Murphy replied candidly that he wasn't entirely sure. He explained that he had received the assignment while still an Army officer and that it appeared to include both flying and staff duties. Dulles inquired about aircraft availability, and once again, Murphy admitted he had no idea.

Dulles offered a solution—he had access to a late-model P-51 Mustang and proposed making it available for Murphy's use, in exchange for occasional assistance with agency missions. Murphy promised to bring the offer to General Van Fleet's attention during their meeting the next morning.

At 7:30 a.m. the next day, General Simons informed Murphy that Van Fleet would meet with him at 11:00 a.m. With time to prepare, Murphy dressed in his Class A uniform adorned with his full ribbon rack. At just twenty-five years old, he looked every bit the accomplished lieutenant colonel. Van Fleet, already aware of Murphy's academic and commendation record, seemed surprised to learn that the young officer was also a decorated pilot—wearing a Distinguished Service Cross, Distinguished Flying Cross, and holding a prior command with the 357th Squadron Group.

Reporting formally to General Van Fleet, Murphy introduced himself and stood at attention. Van Fleet took stock of his decorations and qualifications, then asked a pointed question: What did a Director of Flight Operations do when there were no aircraft in the theater? Murphy responded honestly, noting the unusual nature of the assignment and referencing his recent meeting with Allen Dulles, who had offered the use of a P-51 Mustang. He suggested that, although he wasn't aware of Dulles's specific mission in the region, their objectives might align.

Van Fleet was impressed. He commented that Murphy had wasted no time "penetrating a tough target" and asked if Murphy held Top Secret clearance. Murphy confirmed that he did. The general then instructed him to reconnect with Dulles to determine what support the CIA needed. Murphy agreed immediately and set off to follow his orders.

It took several hours before Murphy was able to reconnect with Dulles, who suggested they discuss details over drinks that evening. During their meeting, Dulles explained that he needed close air support provided to Greek military units. Murphy clarified that such missions would require General Van Fleet's direct approval.

The following day, Murphy briefed Van Fleet, who authorized the missions on the condition that they remain secret—even from General Simons. Van Fleet also requested the acquisition of a B-25 aircraft, retrofitted as an executive transport, for his staff's use. He was confident that Dulles could make the arrangement.

That night, Murphy met with Dulles again and agreed to undertake the missions on the condition that the B-25 be delivered. Dulles briefed him on the aircraft's location and operational protocols.

Soon after, Murphy was flying combat support missions once more— this time in the rugged mountains of Greece, backing the government's anti-communist forces. He found himself fully immersed in the fight again—and loving every minute of it.

CHAPTER ELEVEN: DUST AND DESTINY

"We flew relics against empires. Outnumbered. Outgunned. But not outwilled."

—Benjamin Green, oral testimony to the IAF Historical Division, 1972

Tel Nof Airbase — May 28, 1948
D+14: Two weeks after the Declaration of the State of Israel

The airfield smelled of rust, death, and miracles. Piles of scavenged engines lay next to crates of ammunition wrapped in burlap and prayer. Mechanics spoke in Czech, Yiddish, Arabic, and clipped British English. It was Babel with bombers.

Benjamin Green stood next to his aircraft: an Avia S-199, a Czech-built bastardized version of the German Me-109. The guys called them "Messershits" for a reason—they were underpowered, poorly balanced, and deadly to both the enemy and their pilots.

Still, it bore a Star of David on its fuselage. That changed everything.

Squadron Briefing—101st Squadron

"This isn't the USAAF," barked Lou Lenart, squadron leader and ex-Marine Corps pilot. "This is survival with wings. Today, you're intercepting an Egyptian armored column north of Isdud. You'll have four minutes over target. Then fuel becomes your enemy."

Benjamin raised his hand.

"Is there anti-aircraft fire?"

"I guess you'll find out soon enough."

Over Isdud—Midday

The flight of four aircraft screamed in low from the southeast. Dust rose like smoke from the Sinai. Below: tanks, trucks, and men—thousands of them pushing north toward Tel Aviv.

Benjamin flew third in line. His bombs were mounted crooked. His cockpit canopy was barely sealed.

"Target visual. Beginning run."

"Copy. Stay tight. Watch for flak."

"God be with us."

They dove. The world narrowed. He released at 200 feet—two 70-kilogram bombs slamming into the rear of the Egyptian convoy. Fire bloomed behind him as he pulled up into a hail of tracer fire. To his left, a Messerschmitt exploded mid-climb.

"We lost Eddie!"

"Triple A hit—repeat, Triple A hit!"

"Pull out! Everyone, pull out now!"

Benjamin rolled hard, skimming a rooftop, then climbed as the anti-aircraft fire thickened.

When he landed back at Tel Nof, only two planes made it. His landing gear failed, and he skidded off the makeshift runway into a pile of sandbags. The ground crew erupted in cheers. Not because the mission was a success. Because they were still alive.

Later that night – Tel Aviv, Yarden Hotel bar

Green nursed a bruised shoulder and a whiskey that tasted like lighter fluid. He didn't care a lick.

Across the room, Ezer Weizman—still a teenager—was laughing with Rubenfeld, recounting the story of Milton parachuting into a kibbutz and shouting "Shabbes! Gefilte fish!" to prove he was Jewish.

"We're lunatics," Green muttered.

"No," Lenart despaired beside him. "We're founders."

"We lost two pilots today."

"And saved twenty thousand civilians. That's not arithmetic—it's faith. It's the great cost of protection. It's what we do."

Green nodded, but his eyes drifted to the window, where the lights of Tel Aviv sparkled with promise.

Letter from Benjamin Green to Paul Murphy—June 1, 1948

Paul

We flew our first strike mission. Four of us went in. Two came back.

The Egyptians didn't expect an Air Force. Neither did we.

I don't know how many lives we saved. But I know this: a people with no country are a shadow. And today, we cast light.

Tel Aviv still stands.

Tell your children I hope they see it someday.

—Ben

***

U. S. Air Forces in Europe Wiesbaden, Germany—April 1948

General Curtis E. LeMay Commanding.

"I need some real staff officers now," blared General LeMay. Why is this so hard for anyone to understand? For example, who the fuck was our highest graduate in the 1947 class of C&GSC? That's not a tricky question to answer. Find out, and find out Now!"

A few minutes later, Col Theodore R. Milton reported to General LeMay that LTC Paul Murphy was the Distinguished Graduate in question. He then noted that he was assigned to the American Mission for Aid to Greece as the Director of Air Operations under the command of LTG Van Fleet. During the war, he earned the DSC among other awards and commanded the 363rd Squadron of the 357th Fighter Group. Additionally, he was a triple ace. That was too much for General LeMay.

"What the Fuck is one of our best Field-Grade Officers in the U.S. Air Force doing in Greece, working for an Army REMF? Transfer his ass here pronto!"

Colonel Milton immediately called Air Force Field Grade Personnel Assignments and spoke with Sergeant Major Jones, Field Grade Officer, Assignments. He questioned Sergeant Major Jones and asked about his rank.

"Is your rank correct, Sergeant Major Jones? I thought you would be a Chief Master Sergeant."

"No, Sir, we haven't transitioned to the Air Force yet."

"Is that why LTC. Paul Murphy is in such a backward assignment?"

"No, sir, we were just trying to hide one of our best officers, sir."

"Well, that's not going to work anymore. Have him reassigned to headquarters, United States Air Force Europe Command, immediately. VIP travel for him, his wife, and their family. General LeMay wants him here tomorrow. Do you understand?"

Sergeant Major Jones, soon to be Chief Master Sergeant Jones, responded with enthusiasm, "Sir, that will be a pleasure," and hung up.

During the call, Lieutenant Colonel Murphy was flying his P-51 straight into a firefight with a communist unit in support of a Greek military command. Sergeant Major Jones immediately tried to contact LTC Murphy by phone, and when that failed, he attempted to call General Van Fleet. When that also didn't work, he asked for General Simons. Sergeant Major Jones then promptly informed General Simons that Colonel Murphy was on urgent orders to report to General LeMay in Wiesbaden, Germany. He also asked if General Simons would personally deliver the orders to Lieutenant Colonel Murphy, knowing that Colonel Murphy would want to leave his difficult assignment immediately and would want to know about his new assignment so he could be with his family. General Simons—aware of the situation— immediately said he would find Colonel Murphy and have him on the next plane to Europe.

General Simons made a mad dash to the Athens airport to meet his most promising field grade officer. He had great news for him. He was on the next flight to Germany, where he would meet with his wife and his two children. The end of a hardship tour. What could be better for him and his family?

When he got to the airport, he saw a P-51 Mustang entering the pattern, returning from their mission. Paul was about to take command of a group of fighters that would be transitioning to jets shortly. As a result, he needed to be as proficient as possible when he took command of the new unit. It's taken a lot of work for two army generals to convince the Air Force leadership that Paul should be chosen for that command.

Paul completed a perfect landing and taxied to the ramp. When he arrived, General Simons noticed that it looked as if the P-51's 50-caliber machine guns had been firing. There also seemed to be bomb pylons that wouldn't be necessary for training flights. When Paul exited the P-51, General Simons confronted him.

"What kind of flight was this? Were you firing your 50-caliber machine guns? Did you drop bombs?"

Paul took a deep breath. "Sir, I apologize, but you do not need to know the answers to those questions."

General Simons lost his temper. "Murphy, I came here to tell you that you are on orders to report immediately to Wiesbaden, Germany. That is no longer the case. Lieutenant Colonel Murphy, you're to consider yourself under arrest pending investigation for intentional violation of standing orders."

"General Simons, request permission to speak."

"Denied," screamed General Simons.

"Sir, I'm afraid you do not have the authority to issue that order," Paul firmly stated in a measured voice. "Sir, I request that you immediately call General Van Fleet and discuss this matter with him in person only. If General Van Fleet is not available, I request that you speak with Mr. Dulles who will be speaking on behalf of the national command authority. Do I make myself clear, Sir?"

"Who the actual fuck do you think you are, son? You're completely out of control, officer."

"Sir, I know my mission, I know my authority, I understand the classifications of the matter before us, and I know that you are not aware of any of those matters. I had hoped to avoid this confrontation, which now seems to be on the verge of spiraling out of control. Sir, I implore you, do not say another word until you've had the chance to talk with General Van Fleet or Secretary Dulles."

"LTC Murphy, you don't give orders to a General Officer. You are under arrest."

"Sir, I am afraid you are under arrest and will be held so until General Van Fleet, Secretary Dulles, or a court judge is willing to hear your case."

At that moment, three individuals who had been impersonating Air Force mechanics approached the general and placed him under arrest.

GENERAL CURTIS E. LEMAY COMMANDING

USAF Command Briefing, Germany, March 15, 1948

Murphy sat in an auditorium full of brass. It was his first staff call. He hated these briefings.

The subject: Soviet troop movements in Eastern Europe.

The question: How quickly could America respond if Stalin moved into Berlin?

At the conclusion of the briefing and Q and A, the J3 (operations officer) for U.S. Air Force Europe asked if there were any other questions

Murphy raised his hand.

"What about Palestine?"

"It's not our concern," the general replied. "Israel will rise or fall on its own."

Murphy lowered his hand, jaw tight. He thought of Ben.

General LeMay then took charge of the meeting. Standing:

"That concludes this briefing. Murphy, I would like to see you immediately after this meeting."

Paul remained standing as all the remaining staff exited the facility. Once the room was cleared, General LeMay began:

"Murph, the Director of the CIA for Europe, the Chief of Staff for the Air Force, and the Chairman of the Joint Chiefs, has approved assigning you responsibility for a project implementing the European Recovery Program. Your project, classified TS/SCI, is known as Project Moose 2. Your mission is to take the necessary steps to ensure that (1) the significant foreign aid we invest in war-torn Europe and (2) the non-military covert operations we are prepared to deploy will reshape war-torn Europe in America's image. Murph, my aide-de-camp will provide you with an SF-312 to execute after we finish this meeting and a second meeting. Remember, he, like General Simons, does not have a need to know about your assignment or what you are doing. You may not realize how you were selected for this assignment. Remember when General Van Fleet assigned you a TS/SCI task that prohibited you from informing or telling General Simons about what you were doing? It also required you to use all necessary efforts to keep the project's secrecy, including the use of deadly force if needed."

"Yes, sir," replied LTC Murphy.

Scan the code to read the SF 312—Classified Information Nondisclosure Agreement for Lieutenant Colonel Paul W. Murphy

"Well, Murph—that was a test. Simons put on a convincing performance when he confronted you, and you handled it exactly as you were supposed to. You passed.

From this point forward, you'll be entrusted with some of our most sensitive information. On your initial assignment, you were authorized to say that only General Van Fleet, Secretary Dulles, and the National Command Authority were aware of your mission—who approved it, and any actions taken by you or anyone connected to you in carrying it out. You followed those orders precisely.

Those instructions remain unchanged, except that my name now replaces General Van Fleet's. Do you understand?"

"Yes Sir. Permission to ask two questions, sir."

"Granted."

"First, you said the National Command Authority. Sir, is that who I think it is?"

"Murph, some questions are better off left unanswered."

"Yes Sir. Sir, as you may know, my wife is highly intelligent, creative, curiously inquisitive, and has unlimited resources."

"Get to the point, son," General LeMay, running out of patience.

"Sir, do you have any ideas on how I should address this security issue?"

"My God, a couple who can keep professional, political, and military secrets from each other? It's not a problem; she has a TS/SCI clearance and has been read in for this mission. Did you think we would overlook such a thing? We're not stupid, son. Now, let me tell you your mission. You will be assigned the position of Commanding Officer of the 86th Fighter Group, part of the 86th Fighter Wing. Your XO is a highly competent officer who is an LTC and was assigned to your Wing during WWII. He knows that (1) you are always in command, and (2) you have other missions that will take you away from your day-to-day assignment as CO. He also knows that an excellent officer's efficiency report from you will get him promoted to full Colonel. Understand?"

"Yes, Sir."

"Your true mission, the operation, and the resources of Project Moose 2 will stay hidden in plain sight. While covert operations may occur as you and your team pursue your objectives, you should avoid any actions that could attract public or, more importantly, media attention. Additionally, you are authorized to conduct operations that may divert either the public's or the media's focus from your primary mission. Is that understood?"

"Yes, Sir."

"Murph, I am assigning you responsibility for taking the necessary steps to ensure that the significant foreign aid we invest in war-torn Europe and the non-military covert operations we are prepared to deploy will reshape the region. Here's how: Joint Planning with the US, UK, and French State Departments to form a new German state from their respective zones of occupation. Effective June 1948, US and British policymakers will introduce a new currency, the Deutschmark, to their zones, including West Berlin, without informing the Soviets. This move is aimed at regaining economic control from Russia and integrating Germany into the Marshall Plan. We anticipate that the Soviet forces will block all road and rail traffic into West Berlin, initiating a blockade. If the Soviet forces initiate a blockade, the US will launch *Operation Vittles*, to supply the city by air. A CIA Intelligence Memorandum, which you will now go and review, has warned President Truman that the Soviets would likely use obstruction and harassment to force the Western Allies out of Berlin. The CIA analysis and State Department communications corroborate this assessment. You will have access to all these communications. Finally, you will be responsible for planning Operation Vittles which is now nothing more than a term."

"Understood, Sir."

"US military leaders recognized the numerical superiority of the Soviet Red Army in conventional forces, making a ground-based military solution to overcome the blockade highly risky and potentially escalating into a larger conflict. Faced with the blockade, the Truman Administration has opted for an airlift as a non-military solution to sustain the city and demonstrate American resolve. We believe that Operation Vittles will avert a military confrontation and ultimately force the Soviets to lift the blockade. Your responsibilities are to coordinate all these matters and develop the infrastructure necessary to see that the overall objective—the reshaping of Europe—Is achieved. During Project Moose 2, you will report directly to me and no one else. Murph, I'm saying it twice. You report directly to me and only to me. Understand?"

"Sir, yes, Sir."

"The only individuals you may communicate with regarding this matter are listed on Exhibit A of the SF-312."

General LeMay's aide then handed the new Colonel Murphy a sealed envelope containing a fully completed copy of Form SF-312.

"Do you have any other questions, Murph?"

Paul thought an appropriate question was, "WTF were they thinking when they assigned this to me?" But before he could ask that, General LeMay reached into his pocket. He then called for his aide-de-camp, a photographer, and the rest of the 'gaggle.' At that point, his aide, the photographer, the command's S1, and Mrs. Katie Murphy entered his office.

With the group assembled. LeMay barked his last instructions.

"Congratulations, let's get on with it, S1, publish the orders."

***

Department of the Air Force Headquarters—United States Air Forces, Europe

Special Orders No. 5011
March 15, 1948

1. By order of the Secretary of the Air Force, and in accordance with the following Department of Defense Instruction (DODI) 1334.02, the officer named below has been selected for promotion from the grade of Lieutenant Colonel by the United States Air Force promotion board. The United States Senate has confirmed the promotion, and the officer is hereby frocked to the grade of Colonel.

2. Paul Wesley Murphy
    Lieutenant Colonel

3.   The effective date of Paul Wesley Murphy will be the date his promotion is published in the Air Force's official records. The date when Paul Wesley Murphy will be entitled to all pay and allowances of the grade of Colonel will be the date specified in the previous sentence.

4.   The Secretary of the Air Force has placed special trust and confidence in the patriotism, valor, fidelity, and professional excellence of Lieutenant Colonel Paul Wesley Murphy. Due to these qualities and his demonstrated leadership potential, Paul Wesley Murphy is promoted to the rank of Colonel, United States Air Force, in recognition of his leadership and dedicated service to the United States Air Force.

_____________-S-___________________

LTC Paul Wesley Murphy

"Mrs. Murphy, this is the first time you'll be pinning on your husband's new rank."

General LeMay reached out and took her hand.

"I have no doubt that it will happen four more times. Here is one of the Eagles, and I hold the other one. The photographer will take a picture of me pinning one on your husband's uniform, and you will pin the other. We will each, at separate times, remove one of your husband's silver leaves and replace it with the eagle. The photographer will be taking pictures and giving orders to a General and a new Colonel during the ceremony. He loves doing that. At the end of the pinning ceremony, we will have refreshments in my office. Now, let's get the promotion to the child Colonel finished before we all change our minds."

Katie smiled genuinely at the General and shook her head in agreement.

"Yes, Sir."

A week before his 26th birthday, Paul Wesley Murphy achieved the rank of full Colonel in the United States Air Force. "What were they thinking?" Paul whispered while smiling to himself.

OUR REUNION—APRIL 1, 1948

Paul sat at his desk, reviewing projections for food, fuel, supplies, wheeled vehicles, tracked vehicles, and all the financial data, when his Scrambler Telephone started ringing. It was the first time his secure phone had rung, so he tried to remember the proper way to answer it.

> "Headquarters U.S. Air Force Europe, Col Murphy speaking. This line is not secure."

> "This is Mensch calling."

> "Ben? Mensch, I hear you five by five."

> "How about lunch in your O Club?"

Officers' Club Wiesbaden, Germany 1948

One advantage of being a "Senior Officer" is that the O Club always has a private room or a screened table available for you. No reservations are needed. It's a small perk that comes with the rank. When Paul parked his car, he remembered that there were very nice reserved parking spots for Colonels, so that's where he parked his new Mercedes.

Walking through the front door, Paul was bewildered to run into a uniformed Air Force Lieutenant Colonel that looked exactly like his old friend, Ben Green. Why was his best friend—who had left the U.S. Air Force the previous year—wearing the uniform of an Air Force Lieutenant Colonel?

> "Mensch, embrace me. What in the world are you doing in uniform?"

> "I'm a Lieutenant Colonel in the Air Force Reserve."

Still shocked and flanking his head like a dog that wasn't quite sure what was going on, Paul led Ben to a private room for lunch. /They sat down, and Mensch got into it without delay.

> "Allen Dulles is fully aware of what I'm doing. Secretary Dulles had given me a copy of your report on surplus inventory and excess resources."

Paul was surprised, even though when creating the study, he thought of Ben often.

"That report is classified Top Secret…"

Ben saw Paul's reaction and immediately started analyzing the issues he had learned due to his connection with Haganah.

"There are three issues you need to become comfortable with. They are: 1. US Neutrality and Recognition Declaration; 2. The impact of the Foreign Agents Registration Act or FARA, and 3. Whether the officer's role could have created conflicts of interest with their military affiliation and potential loyalty concerns. Paul, here are all the potential legal issues. Let's review your concerns. First, I have been authorized by Allen Dulles to discuss this with you. He understands all the issues and has confirmed there's no violation of the law. Second, Israel is not considered a Foreign Principal. Israel currently does not exist. Furthermore, I work for Haganah, which operates independently of any government agency. As a result, I am not required to register at this time. It could become necessary in the future, and then I may need to comply with the act; however, for now, there is no issue. Finally, my interests, Israel's interests, and our country's interests are aligned. We all want the same thing: the creation of Israel and a peaceful Palestine.

"Ok, Ben, you never had trouble getting to the point. Why are you here and what do you need?"

"Well Paul, I've reviewed your paper. I see there's surplus inventory; Israel needs it. We are currently purchasing airplanes being built in the Czech Republic, along with heavy weapons and training. These assets are operating at a basic level. I've been assigned to oversee these acquisitions. Money isn't an issue; we have the resources and materials."

"I know you're passionate about the Holocaust, Ben. It was horrific, and we must never allow something like that to happen again. But you're here today wearing the uniform of a Lieutenant Colonel in the United States Air Force. I will follow my orders regarding my duties and what's best for the United States; you are obligated to do the same."

"Look, my old friend, I need planes, trains, and automobiles. I also require combat-trained pilots who served in WWII but whose obligation has expired. Palestinian Arabs are currently attacking areas within the Jewish regions outlined in the United Nations Partition Plan. We believe that a military force is forming that includes Palestinian Arabs and troops from Lebanon, Syria, Iraq, Egypt, and Saudi Arabia, loosely led by an Egyptian command. These groups have already launched small attacks on Jewish cities, settlements, and armed forces. The Jewish forces, consisting of the Haganah—the underground militia of the Jewish community in Palestine—and two small irregular groups, the Irgun and LEHI, have so far managed to hold their positions. Additionally, our agents have discovered that the Egyptians are in the process of bombing Tel Aviv. We are flying German Messerschmitt Bf 109Gs and pre-war Spitfire fighters that are either being built or rebuilt in the Czech Republic. We urgently need a transport aircraft. Our pilots come from all over the world—U.S., South Africa, and Britain among others. Over 60 percent of our pilots flew for the Allies during WWII. Paul, will you help us?"

"Ben," Paul paused for a moment while he considered his request as his first impulse was to refuse but something made him change tact. "Yes, of course, Ben. I'll at least try, OK? I give you my word."

"That's all I can ask, my friend."

"Meanwhile, tonight, we're making a wonderful American dinner for you. Katie has prepared roasted steak, potatoes, salad, and a delicious dessert. Allen Dulles will also be there. I'm sure he'll have some thoughts about this whole surprise package."

"Sounds amazing, my friend. How is 7PM?"

"Perfect. Katie is looking forward to seeing you."

***

Ben and Allen arrived at 1900, and Paul wondered if they had come together and were working together. Heck, they may be one of Secretary Dulles' teams operating at various levels on different projects. Since Katie was read into Project Moose 2, they were immediately able to start discussions on Ben's requirements.

The group started discussing the Marshall Plan and the disposal of the surplus equipment that Paul had listed in his memorandum. The question of how that related to the Marshall Plan then came up. Paul quickly explained that the Marshall Plan helped facilitate the transfer of equipment and resources that might be seen as "surplus." Still, its real goal was to make sure that the significant foreign aid the US invested in war-torn Europe—and the covert operations the US was ready to carry out—would reshape war-torn Europe in America's image.

After a brief pause, Ben began.

"On May 14, 1948, David Ben-Gurion, the leader of the Jewish Agency, declared the creation of the State of Israel. President Truman recognized the new country on the same day. The next day, the Egyptian Army invaded Israel. As a result, I became busy arranging planes, weapons, and artillery. There is just never enough guns, bullets, bandages or general supplies. The excess or surplus equipment could be given to European countries, and they could sell it to 'good development companies.' Wouldn't that cash make these European countries more likely to be reshaped as desired?"

"Isn't there a wonderful American phrase that 'a little bit of cash can go a long way?'" Allen Dulles murmured rhetorically.

Katie sensed it was time for a woman's voice.

"So, Ben, when are you starting your development company?"

"I'm all in, Katie. I've already started putting things together."

That was the end of the first major issue supplying Israel. Allen reminded the team that the second issue that needed to be discussed was the merger of the British, French, and United States occupation zones and the development of a common currency. Allen stepped in with an important question.

"What currency should the US and the other non-communist states issue to their citizens?"

His organization believed that the non-communist parts of Germany should have a single currency. Allen then reminded Paul that, in addition to running his Wing, he was responsible for ensuring that once Germany was transformed from a nation that had been ravaged by war and Nazism, it would become a peaceful and democratic society in the image of the United States. Allen reminded the team that this involved a complex mix of political, economic, and social reforms, all while dealing with the growing tensions of the emerging Cold War, and they had an unlimited budget to ensure their objectives were met.

And so, the next morning, Ben would establish the *Tikkun Olam Tools Development Company* with a motto of *Aligning with the Principles of Social Responsibility and Repairing the World.*

"Who could object to doing business with a company with that motto?" mused Allen Dulles.

On April 3, 1948, President Truman signed the Economic Recovery Act of 1948. It became known as the Marshall Plan, named for Secretary of State George Marshall

On May 15, 1948, Israel established its diplomatic mission to Germany. According to a statement by Israel's Consul General, Benjamin Green, "the mission's goal was to support the emigration of survivors to Israel." However, its secret purpose, which was well known across Europe, was to work alongside its efforts in Warsaw to acquire surplus planes, trains, and automobiles from the United States. Ben was also the owner and general manager of the Tikkun Olam Tools Development Company.

While Ben was busy with his acquisitions business, Paul also focused on developing contingency plans. The area where they were most vulnerable was

Berlin. If they passed the consolidation and the new currency plan, they could expect the Russians to react.

Paul continued with Operation Vittles. The plan initially involved using Douglas C-47s and then transitioning to C-54s. He requested that two Groups of C-47s be immediately relocated to Germany. He also anticipated the need for additional runways and had extensive earth-moving and concrete production equipment stationed in Berlin.

Throughout this time, the Allied Military Governments (US, British, and French) were also active in developing plans to merge the occupation zones. They also prepared to pass the law on monetary reform that led to the introduction of the Deutsche Mark to replace the old Reichsmark, which the Soviets had devalued. They then began planning to reindustrialize and rebuild the German economy.

June 19, 1948:

Paul, home from the airport, told Katie,

> "I never expected to be in Germany running both a fighter wing and a covert operation for the CIA. Much less doing that with my bride."

> "Would you have it any other way?" quipped Katie.

And so, the team consisting of Katie, Paul, Allen, and Ben became known as Team Moose 2. Then Paul told Katie that General LeMay had just complimented him on "his outstanding contingency plan, Operation Vittles."

Allen Dulles was busy working with the Allied Military government, and on June 20 and 21, 1948, the government implemented a comprehensive reform. This reform unified the three Western occupation zones into a single economic region called the Trizone. It also introduced the Deutsche Mark (DM), replacing the Reichsmark and Rentenmark as the sole legal currency. The reform was a crucial step toward West Germany's economic recovery after World War II, paving the way for Marshall Plan aid and the subsequent Economic Miracle.

June 24, 1948.

"Well, the Russians instituted a blockade of all of the rail, road, and water access to the Allied-controlled areas of Berlin today," announced Paul."

"Isn't that what your Operation Vittles anticipated? Oh and did you get all the C-47s that you requested last month?" Katie retorted.

"Yes, and yes, Paul exclaimed. I believe that everything is under control, and we will beat them again. We will start delivering massive amounts of food beginning June 26th. They surely don't anticipate that."

September 29, 1948.

As the Israeli Embassy opened in Warsaw, Ben was the Mossad head of station, in addition to being Israel's Consulate General at the Munich Consulate Office—one of the earliest Israeli consular offices established abroad. One might say he had his hands full.

December 14, 1948

Paul's secure phone rang again, "Headquarters U.S. Air Force Europe, Col Murphy Speaking, Sir this line is not secure."

"Paul, this is Mensch. Do you have time to meet at the O-Club again?"

"For you, of course, always."

An hour later, Paul arrived at the O-Club reception room. Accompanying Mensch was a familiar woman in uniform. Being out of context it took Paul a few seconds to realize it was Ariel.

Mensch got into the substance without delay.

"I was hoping that Allen would be here for our meeting."

Paul interrupted, "Ben, we have been lifelong friends. Is it possible that we spend a few minutes talking about our families? Like, why is your wife in uniform?"

"Of course, Ben. That's actually one of the topics I wanted to discuss. Please meet Maj. Ariel Green"

"Ariel. It's so good to see you again. Katie will be dying to see you. But what's with the title and the uniform?"

"Paul, Ariel is a senior member of Mossad. You see, every Jew living in Israel must serve in our armed forces. Because of her language skills and her understanding of Israel's needs for planes, trains, and automobiles, she was asked to join Mossad several years ago. We have been a two-person team. Now that I must return to Israel to command a fighter wing, she will be replacing me as Mossad Head of Station in Warsaw. In addition, she will serve as Israel's Consul General at the Munich Consulate Office with the same mission I had."

"So, Ariel, who is watching the kids in… and what city do you live in? There is obviously a lot I don't know" Paul laughed at the situation.

"We have a wonderful home in Tel Aviv," explained Ariel with a smile. "We have an amazing couple who live in our guest house and are available, full-time, to see to the kids' needs."

"Well, I guess our team is now five, Katie, Ariel, Ben, Allen, and me. And we are all, except Katie, field grade officers now. Ben, we can also give our wives orders because we outrank them—every man's dream."

Ariel hid her distaste for Paul's comment convincingly as they started discussing the team's objectives to help Israel meet its goals:

- To legally support the emigration of survivors to Israel, and: obtain:

1. Subsistence
2. Class III: Petroleum, Oils, and Lubricants (POL)
3. Class V: Ammunition:
4. Class VII: Major End Items: tanks, trucks, planes
5. Class VIII: Medical Supplies and Equipment:
6. Class IX: Repair Parts and Components

- That Israel's representatives will assist the USA's representatives to ensure they take the necessary steps to guarantee that the significant foreign aid that the US invests in war-torn Europe and the non-military covert operations they are prepared to deploy will reshape Europe in America's image. Israel will use its embedded individuals to provide information to Team Moose 2.

THE RUSSIAN CORRIDOR

On the morning of June 27th, General LeMay's aide de camp reported that Col. Murphy had been flying a P-47 to Berlin. This caused a great deal of concern in the country because of the hostile activities by communist troops and Russian aircraft.

"What is that crazy 26-year-old Colonel up to? If he's shot down by those commie bastards, I'll kill him myself!" Yelled LeMay to the air.

Russian Guard Tower:

"Unknown aircraft, this is Soviet Control, you are entering restricted Soviet airspace. Identify yourself immediately. State your intentions."

"Soviet Control this is P-47, callsign Mensch 2, assigned to the United States Air Force. The aircraft is operating in the established Allied Air Corridor to Berlin. Maintaining course and altitude within the agreed-upon air corridor."

"Air corridor is temporarily closed for maneuvers. Deviation from current heading required."

"Negative, Soviet Control. This is an internationally recognized air corridor and authorized for operation. The mission is reconnaissance. State intentions."

A hesitant pause.

"Soviet Control the air corridor appears open on my charts. This is a recognized international air corridor."

"Your charts are not updated. Air corridor closed. Immediate deviation required, or intercept will be authorized."

"Soviet Control, authorized to operate within this corridor under existing agreements. Maintaining flight plan."

"Mensch 2," the Russian guard tower is now frustrated and shouting, "This is your final warning. Turn immediately or face consequences."

"Soviet Control, copy your message. Maintaining course. Further clarification on the supposed closure is requested."

Silence built the tension for a few moments, then, with a thick, forceful Russian accent;

"Mensch 2, be advised, your presence is unwelcome. We will be monitoring your every move."

"Understood, Soviet Control. Mensch 2 out."

During the next 30 minutes, Paul enjoyed a peaceful flight. His only call was to Berlin's Tempelhof Airport.

"Tempelhof Tower. This is Army Mensch 2, an Army P-47 with a Code 6 on board requesting a low approach, Runway 9 or the Option. For Runway 9, I am with you on 118."

"Sir, are you nuts? Have you heard that those crazy commies have, and I quote: 'closed the air corridor temporarily for maneuvers.'"

"Son, I advise you that you either permit or deny my low pass or the Option. Otherwise, in 5 minutes I will be crawling up your static."

"Army Mensch 2, you are cleared for the Option on Runway 9. Advise on the completion of the Option regarding your intentions."

About three minutes later: "Tempelhof Tower, Mensch 2 has completed the Option. Please advise Wiesbaden Approach that Mensch 2 will be contacting them in about 20 minutes. Inform them that I will be flying the corridor and will maintain the agreed-upon course and altitude within the air corridor. Please ensure the alert aircraft are warmed up and fully loaded. Mensch 2 out.

"WILCO, Tempelhof Tower Out."

While this was going on, General LeMay's patience was running out. He had sent for his worthless J1, Colonel Jones. He was perplexed as to why all the personnel officers couldn't keep their shoes tied or eat lunch at the club without dropping food on their clothes?

"Yes, sir," boomed Colonel Jones.

"Please go find Col. Murphy, I think he is on a training flight. I need him yesterday."

"Yes, sir."

Two minutes later—Russian Guard Tower:

"Unknown aircraft, this is Soviet Control, you are entering restricted Soviet airspace. Identify yourself immediately. State your intentions."

"Soviet Control, this is a United States Air Force P-47, callsign Mensch 2. The aircraft is operating within the established Allied Air Corridor to Berlin. Maintaining course and altitude within the agreed-upon air corridor."

"Mensch 2, you were advised by Soviet Control 30 minutes ago that the Air Corridor is temporarily closed for maneuvers. Deviation from current heading is immediately required."

"Negative, Soviet Control. This is an internationally recognized air corridor and is authorized for operation. The mission is reconnaissance. State intentions."

A slight pause with an air of hesitation.

"Soviet Control, the Air Corridor appears open on my charts. This is a recognized international air corridor."

"Your charts are not updated. Air Corridor closed. You have been advised by me and by Tempelhof Tower 5 minutes ago. Immediate deviation required, or intercept will be authorized. Your Behavior is reckless."

"Soviet Control, all allied aircraft are authorized to operate within this corridor under existing agreements. I am maintaining my flight plan, which you have a copy of. If you have a problem, contact, Marshal of the Soviet Union, Vasily Sokolovsky. Tell Vasily that I will send him the pictures he requested last night after the party at Hotel Adlon."

"Mensch 2," barked the now bewildered and irate tower chief. "He will have you shot. This is your final warning. Turn immediately or face consequences."

"Soviet Control, copy your message. Maintaining course. Further clarification on the supposed closure is requested. I always thought that Vasily was a nice guy. I don't think he would shoot anyone."

Silence…

"Mensch 2, be advised, your presence is unwelcome. We will be monitoring your every move."

"Understood. Mensch 2 out."

Twenty minutes later, Paul was contemplating the challenges of running Operation Vittles. He had originally ordered two groups of C-47s, and they were in position. He was worried that there wouldn't be enough. He had arranged for 100 C-47s and as many C-54s as could be available. They were in place yesterday. He had also arranged for two complete flight and maintenance crews for each aircraft, and they were all in place. At that moment, his radio glared:

"Army Mensch 2, this is Wiesbaden Approach on 120.8 winds 250 at 8, pressure 29.92, landing and departing runway 25, tower is 30.1MHz. Upon landing, you will be met by Col. Robert Jones, the General's A-1"

"Please advise the nice Colonel that I have a Code 6 on board and the Code 6 will meet him at the dining room for the 86th Fighter Wing. Mensch 2 out."

"Please inform the out-of-control Colonel that General LeMay sent for him at 0700 this morning, and it's now 12:30. LeMay sent me—his chief personnel officer—to fetch Colonel Murphy, and I'll be damned if I'll go fetch him at the mess hall."

A few minutes later.

"Mensch 2, this is Wiesbaden Approach. Mensch 2 calling Wiesbaden Approach."

"Mensch 2, be advised that the J1 for U.S. Air Force Europe has been sent to fetch you for the CG. He is requiring that you meet him here at the tower. Over."

"Wiesbaden, please advise the leg Colonel that our O6 advised me he will see the J1 20 minutes after he parks his aircraft, after his shower, and after he gets something to drink at his Wing. Out"

As the J3 during the Berlin Airlift and the commander of the 86th Fighter Wing, he was once again amongst it. He was back in the Air Force. His flight today was a real reconnaissance mission, protecting the pilots of his wing.

Taxiing in from his Berlin trip, Paul wondered what General LeMay wanted from him. Boy, did the shower feel great. He knew General LeMay was getting angry, but he had to be in a presentable uniform when he showed up.

"Sir, Colonel Murphy reporting to General LeMay as ordered."

"Where the hell have you been, Murphy?"

"Sir, I flew to Berlin after flying The Corridor this morning and just returned. I then took a shower and got into a presentable uniform, Sir. I didn't want to stink up the General's office, Sir."

"Have you eaten today, Paul?

"No, sir, and I am famished."

General LeMay looked at Col Jones with some disdain and told him to fetch Col. Murphy and him a BLT and some iced tea. Col. Jones thought better of commenting that he wasn't a maid or secretary.

"Paul,"

General LeMay lay back in his chair,

"What were you up to this morning?"

"Sir, as you know, the Russians started the blockade on June 24. I waited a week before I undertook this reconnaissance mission. I gave the Russians almost a week to get their SOPs in place before I took this flight. I did that to gauge their reactions to a US fighter conducting a reconnaissance mission to test the Soviet Union's responses to flying a fighter along the Berlin corridor and then returning. I found that no matter how aggressively I behaved, the Russians did not interfere with my flight. The Russians would not interfere with allied air traffic that remained within the corridor, even if that traffic was conducting reconnaissance. This suggested that, at least for now, the Soviet Union was unlikely to attack any of the allies' aircraft if they stayed inside the corridor."

General LeMay thought for a few seconds and then asked Col Jones to excuse himself. General LeMay then started by telling Paul that in September, he would be assigned as the Commanding Officer of the Strategic Air Command. He asked Paul to consider giving up his Wing command and becoming the commander of one of SAC's wings. He asked Paul not to respond now, but to think about the question; they had plenty of time to consider the issue.

Paul listened to General LeMay while reflecting on the day's adventure. It was an interesting flight; the pressure was higher than usual for most days. The whole time, he had been waiting to be intercepted by a group of Russian pilots flying their Yak-9 fighters, which were some of Russia's best fighters. Luckily, they didn't bother him, and as a result, he learned something.

"General, I believe they will leave us alone if we stay in the corridor. Now, how many C-47s can we fly every hour, and what is the minimum separation?"

In the back of his mind, Paul wondered what Katie would think about his reasoning.

After the meeting with General LeMay, Paul went home for dinner with Katie and the children. Paul told Katie he wanted to discuss what he saw during his flight and get her opinion. He explained that he wanted to make sure he wasn't missing anything. Katie also had two topics she wanted to discuss: her investments and a dinner she had to attend in Washington.

Paul told Katie about his flight through the corridor to Berlin and that since the first flights of the Berlin Airlift began on June 29th, he wanted to see what would happen if he flew inside the corridor and ignored Soviet Control's instructions. He told her that although Soviet Control was very instructive and threatening verbally, they did nothing to respond. He hit Berlin, did a touch-and-go, and returned. No aircraft were sent toward the corridor, and he did not see any Russian aircraft during either his trip to Berlin or his return.

"Before July 1, the pilots of the 86th Fighter Wing flew missions and carved holes in the sky. However, everything changed when we activated Operation Vittles. The 86th was tasked effective June 1st with providing air defense for the Berlin Airlift cargo flights. Generally, they did not fly on the Corridor, but it seems that nothing prevents them from doing so.

"Fascinating." Katie was now completely engaged and deep in thought. "Can the U.S. have 120 planes fly to Tempelhof every hour for an indefinite period?"

"I am pretty sure we can," Paul retorted.

"I believe that this is more of a maintenance issue than it is a flight scheduling issue," she mused.

"I've always found the Air Force to be exceptionally well organized and the transport pilots to be highly skilled professionals. I don't, however, know much about the mechanics, and that was my concern. I have some ideas…"

PART III—A FAMILY AFFAIR

CHAPTER TWELVE—A WHOLE NEW DAY

Paul had been promoted months earlier, but his star might not come for years. In Greece, he had excelled—General Van Fleet had seen to it that he pinned on his chickens. He had delivered again for General LeMay. The problem was Germany.

His assignment as a Wing Commander had been a TS/SCI intelligence post. Officially, he commanded aircraft. Unofficially, he was reshaping war-torn Europe in America's image. No citation would ever mention that. No board would ever read it.

Nor would they read about the quiet transfer of surplus equipment that flowed through Europe and into Israel—known only to five people by its code name. Heroics that cannot be written do not advance careers. Katie understood that.

As the wealthiest woman in the United States, Katie was worried about not addressing these matters, especially considering her new role in the CIA. She said she believed she should hire the former director of investments at her late father's bank to manage the assets. She understood that this would mean hiring about ten professionals and a staff for them. As always, Paul trusted Katie's instinct and insight.

"Katie, you are the most competent person I have ever met. If you believe it's in your best interest to hire a professional staff and set up an office to handle your investments, I believe that is exactly what you should do. As you know, I have Wes, who runs the ranches. If it weren't for Wes, I would have to leave the military. I'm spoiled, and I want you to be as well. If you think the gentleman who managed investments for your father is the most capable person to handle your investments, you should get on a plane and go hire him."

"Ok, I will do that and handle one more matter while I am in D.C. "By the way, I was thinking of buying a home in D.C. You will inevitably be assigned there for some long periods. This way, we won't have to rush into something to buy."

Tel Aviv, Israel

When Ben joined the IAF, he was initially seen as a Machal (Hebrew: מח״ל), which means a foreign fighter. However, after a few months, the leadership believed he was a true immigrant. They then started calling him a Ma'apilim (מעפילים), a Hebrew term—used by the Jewish community in Palestine (the Yishuv). This was the term used for clandestine immigrants who arrived through Aliyah Bet—the secret, or "illegal," immigration of Jews to Palestine under British Mandate rule between 1920 and 1948.

Being a member of the pre-independence paramilitary organizations Haganah and Irgun through 1947, he was considered a true "soldier" for the country and a person to be honored.

During the War of Independence, Ben reminded Paul during an earlier call that most of the IAF's pilots during the entire War of Independence—about 70 percent—were overseas volunteers from 15 different countries. They served with distinction as pilots, navigators, radio operators, bombardiers, air gunners, aerial photographers, and bomb-chuckers, without rank or uniform. Of the 205 WWII pilots in the IAF over the same period, 181 were Machal.

During the Israeli War of Independence, Ben served as the commanding officer of Israel's Sde Dov Airport and Squadron 101, both of which were undermanned and under-armed. During the conflict, he and most of the IAF pilots flew Mustangs, Spitfires, and German aircraft that Czechoslovakia called S-199s, which were rebuilt German fighters from World War II. Despite these limitations, they succeeded.

Ben's additional duty was to locate these aircraft and gather as many repair parts as possible.

***

The next morning, Paul flew to Berlin, landed at Tempelhof, and was scheduled to spend the next three days inspecting assets available to support his Wing. The wall wasn't up yet. But the divisions were already drawn in breath and barbed wire.

Paul walked past Soviet guards who stared through him like ghosts. He was in full dress uniform—USAF insignia sharp, cap brim low. Around him, Berlin limped through winter, fractured and occupied. It reeked of ash and hunger.

He entered Tempelhof Air Base, where American C-47s came in hourly as part of the Berlin Airlift. A different kind of war now. Not with bombs—but with bread and fuel. Paul began his inspection.

"Colonel Murphy," an aide said, approaching with a sealed envelope. "Telegram for you, Sir. Marked urgent nonmilitary."

"From where?"

"France."

Paris—Two days later

Benjamin Green stood beneath the clock at Gare du Nord, in civilian clothes that didn't quite fit. His left eye was bloodshot from an old concussion. His knuckles still bore oil stains from repairing his Avia S-199 with his bare hands and a little luck.

Murphy stepped onto the platform and saw him instantly. They didn't embrace. Just a nod. A long, aching nod.

"You look older, Ben"

I sleep in sandbags these days, Paul"

They found a café off Rue des Martyrs. Quiet Jazz played in the background. No one there cared who they were.

"I hear you're a legend now in Israel, my friend"

"Of junkyard planes and teenage aces. We make miracles out of junk and leftovers."

"How long can that last?"

"As long as we believe it has to."

Murphy lit a cigarette, then remembered Benjamin wouldn't take one.

"You still doing Shabbat prayers in foxholes?"

"Every Friday. Sometimes with a Czech. Once with a Catholic Arab from Haifa."

"That's an interesting minyan."

"No," Ben uttered quietly. "That's a country being born."

Later that evening, outside the café, they walked in silence toward the Seine. The city was still alive with memory and music.

"Are you coming back, Ben?"

"No."

"There isn't any reason to visit?"

"There's nothing there for me now other than one of our parents. Not until Israel is real enough that I can bring Joseph and Ariel back to the States. You now know what Ariel is doing."

Murphy nodded. Then, after a pause:

"You know, I still dream about Carson."

"So do I."

"He was our best."

"We never were boys again after that day."

They stood on the Pont des Arts, the lights of Paris reflecting off the water. Green pulled out a small black notebook and handed it to Murphy.

"What's this?"

"Flight logs. Coordinates. IAF is building an archive. I want someone outside to know the truth if it ever disappears."

Murphy slipped it into his coat.

"You trust me with this?"

"You're still my brother, Paul. Even if we fight different wars."

***

Letter from Paul Murphy to Ariel Green—October 1948

Ariel, He won't tell you, but your husband is something like a prophet over here. They call him "Ha-Namer"—the Panther.

I watched him walk through Paris like he was still flying. Unafraid of gravity. Full of ghosts.

Keep your son close. The world may burn again, and he'll need to know that his father didn't just fight. He helped create.

—Paul

Jerusalem—Ariel's prayer journal

He didn't say goodbye. Just kissed Joseph's head and walked into the night like Elijah. If he survives this war, it won't be luck. It will be because G-d still believes we deserve men like him.

MRS MURPHY GOES TO TOWN

The morning that Paul had flown to Berlin, Katie boarded an American Overseas Airlines flight from Frankfurt to Washington, D.C. When she landed in D.C., she was no longer part of Team Moose 2. She was Katie McFarland, the wealthiest woman in the United States. As soon as she arrived at the Willard, she leased an apartment to last through the Cold War.

After cleaning up, she called Senator Wagner, the Senior Senator from New York. When the Senator's office answered, they said the senator was "Unavailable." That was enough for the tired Katie, who was also a Bird Colonel's wife.

"Get that lazy kraut on the phone now she said… I am not in the mood to be messed with, and I said now… "

About 5 minutes later, Senator Wagner answered the phone. "Katie, is that you? It's been a couple of years since we talked… Where are you?"

"Well, that hasn't stopped you from cashing my checks, has it? I need a favor. I'm in my apartment at the Willard; when can you get here… oh, and bring Sheridan with you?"

"Do you mean Senator Sheridan Downey from California?"

"Of course, I mean that commie try hard from California—who else?"

"Well, Katie, I must say, you've fundamentally changed your communication habits… "

"I have indeed, and if you don't want me to support someone else in the primary, you'll be here within the hour."
She hung up.

It was about an hour later when her new D.C. butler, Charles Johnson, answered the door and then announced to Ms. McFarland that Senators Wagner and Downey were there. They say they are expected, Ma'am."
Katie was dressed in a Chanel suit with a matching navy-blue boucle

skirt and jacket, paired with a white blouse and a beautiful strand of pearls. A picture of elegant simplicity. Katie stepped out and gently shook their hands. It was a handshake that conveyed strength, not a typical feminine gesture—delicate but powerful.

"How have you gentlemen been since our last meeting?"

"We're fine, fine" they attentively answered simultaneously.

"What can we do for you, Mrs. Murphy?" Senator Wagner asked with enthusiasm.

"We are old friends when we're in this kind of setting. Please call me Katie."

The two senators didn't know how to reply after the way they had been called to the carpet, and that was exactly the reaction Katie wanted.

"What do you two know about the Berlin Airlift? For instance, did you know that a wing commander flew down the Berlin Corridor in a Fighter yesterday without any repercussions? Flew solo without any advance notice to the Russians? How would you interpret that?"

The two senators sat there in shock. It confirmed Katie's assumption that neither of them was the brightest crayon in the box. However, Katie had to remind herself that she was the valedictorian from Stanford's 1944 undergraduate class with a BS in Organic Chemistry, and she also held an MBA with high honors from Stanford. She wasn't just an extraordinarily beautiful member of the lucky sperm club.

"Do you think this might mean that the Soviet Union is all bark and no bite? Are they focusing their efforts elsewhere? If so, where might that be?"

The two Senators just looked at each other without answering the questions. Katie assumed she knew why.

"Do either of you know my security clearance and my code word access?"

This confused the two Senators. Again, they didn't say a word.

"I have approval from Secretary Dulles to read you in on the following information. A runner will bring you a document from the CIA for you to execute once you get back to your office. It's an SF-312; I know you have completed them before. This one will be about the activities of Team Moose 2. Will you sign the form?"

Both Senators just nodded in the affirmative, and Katie continued,

"Good. Thank you. Although, you know I wasn't really asking. Team Moose 2 is a U.S. military, CIA, and Israeli team that has been collaborating in Germany and other countries in war-torn parts of Europe for the past several years. I am a member of that team and hold a TS/SCI clearance.

The shock could not have been greater. The two Senators each tried to say something but could not. Katie barreled on.

"So, with all this in mind, do you think this might mean that the Soviet Union is all bark and no bite? Are they focusing their efforts elsewhere? If so, where might that be? You are both members of the Intelligence Committee. Think, Gentlemen. Have you considered any other potential hot spots? Where might the Russians be focusing? Where should we be preparing our military to support U.S. interests? Come on, Senators, think. I don't want this conversation to descend into the same level of discussion as our last meeting. Think! Katie barked again. Think Senators"

The Senators were at a loss for words. They had expected a meeting with an attractive donor, but instead, they found themselves being cross-examined by the wealthiest woman in the U.S., who happened to be married to one of the smartest Army officers—and, unknown to them until this moment, a prominent CIA operative.

She also seemed somehow more beautiful than she had been at their last meeting. As they stared mesmerized, Katie loudly repeated the word "Think!" three times, each time more forcefully than the last. After observing their dumbfounded faces, she asked,

"How hard would it be to get me a meeting or lunch with Truman in the next two weeks?"

"That shouldn't be a problem with the contribution you made to his Leadership Foundation."

"Thank you, Senator Wagner. Please make it happen, just let my assistant in New York and Charles, my new butler here, know."

"Goodbye, gentlemen."

The senators both recoiled; they had just been dismissed like truant high school students leaving the principal's office. They didn't know what to say except yes and thank you. They certainly both understood that they had better get that meeting with President Truman scheduled promptly.

After that initial meeting at the Willard, Katie went to work finalizing her meeting with her father's director of investments and finding a real estate broker. Her first meeting was with Robert A. Johnson, CPA, and a founding member of the board of the Investment Company Institute. Her father had always spoken so highly of Robbie. It was for that reason that he was the first-person Katie called about managing her significant wealth.

"Robbie, it's so great to see you. Thanks for taking the time to visit with me. It's been way too long, and I really need your advice on a couple of topics."

Robbie, known for his directness, just got right into it.

"Of course, Miss McFarland, appologies, Mrs Murphy. Tell me the story."

"Thank you, Robbie. Always straight to the point. My husband, Colonel Paul Murphy has his own net worth of significance a significant net worth from ranching and her, was traveling all over the world. Additionally, she had a role with the CIA. Considering these factors, I believed I need to formalize my assets and financial holdings. To have them managed by professionals, and develop a family business to increase the family's net worth is responsible and takes it off my plate so I can focus on what I'm doing to better the world. The right person would be entitled to a significant portion of the earnings and, over time, the assets.

Robbie, never one to hold back, "What do you estimate your net worth to be, and what do you estimate your total assets to be?"

That was an easy question for Katie. She lived with it daily. "My assets are just over 1.2 billion, and my personal net worth exceeds $1.0 billion."

"Whew, impressive, Mrs. Murphy"

"It's okay for you to know that, but no one else, Robbie. If I find out any of the staff leak that information, I will fire them, sue them, and turn them over to the FBI, and that's if my people don't take care of them first. Because of the classified information that will be in that office, everyone will have to sign an SF-312 acknowledging they are handling classified information."

Robbie then proceeded to wrap up their business meeting with his usual efficacy.

"I'll need about a week to research, draw up a business plan, create a working capital framework. Would you be available next week to further strategize?"

"Yes of course, Robbie. How is next Friday."

"Perfect. Katie, one more question. Do you think Paul would be willing to discuss his family's wealth, how large their assets are, and how much debt they have? It would just give me a more complete understanding of the situation."

"Yes, I'll ask. See you next week."

***

Buying a house in a city where she had only visited the business district would be a very daunting task for most people. That wasn't the case for Katie. Having grown up in New York City, visiting the Hamptons each summer, and going to Martha's Vineyard each weekend as a young child gave Katie many chances to grow.

She called Shannon & Luchs Real Estate Brokerage. The firm was the longest-standing brokerage serving the multinational embassies on Embassy Row. She knew that she wanted an Embassy Row home on Massachusetts Ave. Heights. "This shouldn't be hard," Katie thought to herself. "Find out what's for sale in the neighborhood and buy it." What she didn't anticipate was that her passion for anonymity might reduce the inventory of houses she could buy.

So, she had the concierge call Robert Smithfield, the leading agent at Shannon & Luchs, and set an appointment for that afternoon. When her butler let her know that Mr. Smithfield had arrived, she was pleased.

When he was announced and entered her presence, however, she was somewhat taken aback by his brash and candid approach.

> "A pleasure, Ma'am. Tell me, not to be blunt, but it will certainly speed things up considerably if you would share how much you are considering spending to acquire a property.

> "Well, Mr. Robert Smithfield of Shannon & Luchs, that depends on what is available and how willing you are to work with an unlimited budget."

> "Oh, come now, madam. Only the Vanderbilts have unlimited budgets, and you aren't one of them. So, let's get real."

Katie was so taken aback she asked to be excused for a minute. She went into another room and immediately placed a call to Robbie. She asked him:

> "Robbie, how do I handle this pompous jerk. Supposedly, I must deal with him. He is the only person who has access to the type of homes that I would be interested in, and I don't want to tell him what I own. If I did, every gossip in this town would be told about me in minutes. That's not acceptable."

"Katie, I'll take care of this. Go back in and make small talk. It should take about 15 minutes. This is an example of why having a family business will solve problems for you."

Sure enough, only 15 minutes later, her butler, Charles, swooped into the room and announced that Russell C. Leffingwell, Chairman and CEO of JP Morgan, was on the phone and asked if Katie was available for a quick call. Katie said yes. Charles brought in the phone.

"Bill it's nice to hear from you."

"Katie, do me a favor and put that pompous jerk on the phone.

"Certainly, Bill."

"Mr. Smithfield do you have a moment for Mr. Leffingwell."

Stuttering, "of course."

"You are a lucky man, Smithfield. If Katie hadn't called her CFO and asked how to best deal with you, you would have been fired today. For your information and your information only, she can buy any piece of real estate available for sale in D.C, Virginia, or Maryland for cash, including the damn White House, should it become available. Furthermore, if a breath, much less a word about this call or Katie's resources, becomes known to anyone—and I mean anyone—you will be sued within an inch of your life, should you even survive the aftermath. Is that clear?"

"Yes, Sir."

As the call ended, he realized he could hear a dial tone and feel a warm sensation down his leg. "Shit," he had truly pissed himself.

"Ma'am, might I be directed to the restroom?"

Upon his exit, Katie snickered to herself, wondering what delightful insights Mr. Leffingwell had shared with the admonished Mr. Smithfield. When Smithfield finally returned, his demeanor had somewhat shifted.

"Mrs. Murphy, now that I am aligned with your expectations and your clear position, would you be so kind as to describe your needs for your new home? I assure you; we can accommodate anything."

"Oh come now, Mr. Smithfield. God himself can accommodate anything, but you're hardly one of those," Katie smirked cheekily.

"Touché, Ma'am, touché. Shall we get to work?

"I believe that a warm, pleasant, and unpretentious home on Embassy Row, if such a thing exists, will suffice. I will occasionally throw a formal or even an informal dinner. We would usually have a small jazz band. You get the picture. Evidently, confidentiality is a concern, so any house that I do purchase will be purchased in a company name and not associated with my or my husband's name. Is that clear?"

"Yes, I do believe I can accommodate your wishes. In fact, I believe I have just what you want."

"What do you think?" Mr. Smithfield asked. "It has a medium-sized ballroom, five bedrooms, six full bathrooms, and two half baths. The Kitchen is a full commercial outfit. It is also on five acres in town and stands behind a double row of trees."

"It sounds perfect, Mr. Smithfield. Is there any chance I could see it today?"

The Murphy Home—Embassy Row—Washington, D.C.

Katie sends a letter to Paul after securing the house.

Paul, we have an executive to manage the assets and incorporate our consolidated family business, and we have a house under contract in D.C. The house needs some work, but it's in a perfect location. Assuming you like the pictures, the company can close on the acquisition next week. I have picked an architect, builder, and decorator. I will be flying back as soon as I have lunch with a VIP."

Love Katie.

"Mr. President, thank you so much for taking the time to see me. I hope your staff will be permitted to keep this meeting confidential." Katie spoke with eloquence and grace as she walked into her private lunch meeting with President Truman.

"Why of course, Katie, and when we are in a private meeting, please call me Harry."

"Yes, Mr. President."

"Let's get lunch served and then you can tell me what you want me to know."

"Mr. President…"

"I told you to call me Harry!"

"Yes, Sir. Sir, I need to inform you that I am an unpaid operative and a member of a team called Moose 2. Sir, are you aware of this team?"

"No, I am not."

"Well, let me start by telling you who the members of the team are. Allen Dulles, Paul Murphy—Col U.S. Air Force, me—the unpaid operative, Ben Green—former LTC U.S. Air Force & Current Col IAF, Ariel Green—Major IDF & Mossad operative. Mr. Truman, I am sure you are somewhat surprised about this team, but furthermore, this is the reason I want no record of our meeting."

"I see… Ok, now that I understand the overview, pray tell, what on Earth have you been up to?"

"Well, firstly, I apologize for the length of this response. There is nothing in writing, and there won't be unless you order me to put it in writing."

"That won't be necessary, Katie."

"About two years ago, while Paul was waiting for an assignment to mature, he wrote an extensive report on excess WWII inventory and resources."

"I'm familiar with that report," stated the President.

"Somehow that report found its way into Haganah's hands, and before long it was in Ben Green's possession. It soon became a shopping list for Israel."

"Ben sought the help of Allen Douglas in 'legally' acquiring those assets that were in Europe. In a meeting that Paul, Ben, and I attended, we discussed several ideas. However, Paul had a mission to reshape war-torn Europe in America's image by using the significant foreign aid we will invest in the region and the non-military covert operations we are prepared to undertake.

"Using all of these tools to achieve Paul's overall objective, we determined that if we (1) transferred surplus inventory to various European governments, (2) those governments determined they didn't need that surplus inventory, (3) those governments could declare the surplus inventory excess inventory (4) the excess inventory could be transferred to local businesses owned by certain officials (5) the local businesses could sell the inventory to a local company owned by Israel's representatives (6) the excess inventory would be shipped to Israel and (7) the proceeds from the sale of the excess inventory would be transferred to the local government officials. This accomplishes two wonderful objectives. The local officials would reshape their war-torn countries in America's image (By the way, if they don't, we'll have proof of their corruption) and second, Israel would get the tools they needed to build their military and economy."

"Sir, I apologize for the length of that response but there is one more thing I would like to discuss."

"Go ahead."

"As cover for this meeting, if it comes out.

"And it better not, it was Winston that said, "Never in history have so few women done so much to protect so many... or something along those lines."

"I believe we should announce that Company A is so impressed with the Foundation's performance that it will donate $1.0 million. What do you think?

"Who, dare I ask, is Company A?"

"It's my new family business. I am moving most, if not all, of my assets into a business and hiring professional management. The CEO is my father's former Director of Investments. He knows the need for confidentiality."

"I think you might want to make Company A separate from your other assets, Katie. And you should engage a wonderful and colorful Board of Directors that doesn't have any idea that you or your family owns the Company. The Company's only job is to make anonymous charitable contributions. That way, even if it is investigated, no one will know the gifts are from you or your family business. Build layers on layers to provide privacy for the donors."

"Agreed, Sir. I will let Robbie know. Knowing Robbie, he may have some additional privacy ideas."

"Thank you, Katie, I would very much like to meet your husband the next time you are in the States. I believe you two are a team that is making a silent but significant contribution to our country."

"Sir, all we are doing is serving our country. We are just complying with our duty and hopefully doing it in an Honorable way. Until we meet again Mr. President."

"Katie?"

"Yes, Sir?"

"Harry!"

"Yes, Harry. Sir."

***

Paul didn't know when Katie would be getting back, and he had a lot on his mind. One item was his annual report. In his position, it would be normal for the DCG U.S. Air Force Europe to write his report and have it endorsed, hopefully by the Commanding General of U.S. Air Force Europe. When he got home that evening, Katie had returned from her trip.

One of the wonderful things about their relationship was their welcome-home activities. When Paul opened the door, Katie jumped into his arms and treated him to the gold standard of hugs and kisses.

"My love, when did you get in?" asked the breathless Paul.

"Well, I landed at Wiesbaden Airport about four hours ago. It was an amazing trip. I found a beautiful house, signed a deal with Robbie to manage the consolidated family business, and had a bunch of wonderful meetings. Robbie has already proven his worth".

"Oh, and I must tell you about the effeminate real estate agent I had to work with. He was so obnoxious and difficult I thought I was going to have to call you to deal with him. So, I excused myself from the meeting with Mr. Jerk and called Robbie to ask what I should do. Robbie, totally understanding, told me to go back in the meeting and keep my cool. He said I would get an unexpected call in about 15 minutes, which I did, and it was the CEO of John Morgan and Co. He asked to speak with the real estate salesman who was so terrified that the obnoxious real estate guy wet his pants—I mean, he actually peed himself. I pretended I didn't notice when he excused himself. He came back about 15 minutes later, all smiles about our new house"

"After he left, the CEO called with Robbie on the phone, and we all had a good laugh. How has your week been?"

"Well, a lot happened today," Paul announced happily. I got a call from Colonel, the A1 of Headquarters U.S. Air

Force Europe, who told me that General LeMay wanted to meet with me for the entire afternoon. As you know, I am not too fond of him."

"I see. Not a nice surprise. How did it go?"

"No, not one of my favorites. I got to his office at 1300, and he announced that he had my OER that he wanted to review with me. He then asked me to take time to review it, and when I finished, to let the J1 know, and he would come back in and discuss it with me. He then told me to take a seat at his desk and walked out."

"Strange, don't you think?"

"Oh indeed. So, I walked behind his desk, and there was a letter to the flag officer promotion board that was unsigned. The letter says five things need to happen: (1) that I should be promoted to Brigadier General ASAP, (2) that I should be selected for attendance to the Army War College, (3) that Ben Green should be selected for attendance at the Army War College, (4) Allen Dulles should be selected to be either a visiting professor or a student at the Army War College, and (5) during my attendance at the Army War College I should be allowed to Graduate from Norwich."

"When did you tell him about taking the bootleg classes at Norwich?" Katie bursts out as the excitement becomes too much.

"That's one of the many things I haven't done. Anyway, after reading the draft letter, I looked at my OER. Normally, he would be the endorser, not the rater, but he was the rater. He is the rater, so I now have a four-Star rater, which means that I don't have an endorser. That's generally a privilege that only a three-Star or four-Star general gets. In his review, he stated that, 'In my entire military career, he is the only officer whom I thought I should be working for, not the other way around! Are you fucking kidding me? I am a 27-year-old Colonel, and he is a four-star who oversees the Strategic Air

Command. What he said is just nuts. So, the good news is that we are moving back to the States, to Carlyle Barracks, for me to attend the Army War College to finish my bachelor's degree, and Ben and Ariel will be stationed there too. He has reconstituted Team Turtle 2. That will give us a year to work on a strategic plan for US–IAF military cooperation. I believe I can finish my BSBA by the end of the year. But classes start in Early August this year."

Katie burst into laughter.

"Another 10 days' notice to move, at least we are used to it. What about Allen, and what about your star?"

"Well, the general and I discussed his thoughts contained in his Letter to the Secretary of Defense. He decided to push for everything. He said Allen would be there. He also said that he believed that I would need the star in my next job, which would initially be Deputy Director of Operations for SAC. I could expect to be selected for Major General when I became Director of Operations. He thought the new position would activate in about a year to 18 months. He also said that he wanted every West Point fucking ring knocker to know that I was better than all of them. I'm not sure how I felt about that."

"Well, you are a superstar, my darling. You deserve it all. I know you won't accept it because of your humility, but you are truly remarkable. I don't just hang out with anyone, you know. Let alone marry them and let them father my children."

"Katie, as amazing as you are, and as much as you see me through rose colored glasses, don't you think he's pushing for too much? If he gets his way, I will be a 27-year-old BG. The last BG that young, may have been during WWII. Herbert Galusha Pennypacker was a 20-year-old when he was promoted to Brigadier General during the Revolutionary War. I am an old guy compared to Chesley G. Peterson, who was the youngest colonel in the US Air Force at the age of 23. That said, a Brigadier General at 27 or 28 is very young."

"There's no need to look this gift horse in the mouth, darling. You're worthy, you deserve it all. So, what's next?"

"I guess we find some boxes and put this show on the road. Again."

CHAPTER THIRTEEN—ARMY WAR COLLEGE

Carlisle Barracks, Pennsylvania—August 1948

The late-summer air in Carlisle hung heavy with humidity and discipline. Red-brick Georgian buildings stood in rigid formation along tree-lined streets, their white trim sharp against a sky bleached pale by the August sun. Somewhere beyond the parade field, a bugle cut through the stillness, crisp and ceremonial, while cicadas hummed in the tall oaks like static over a distant radio.

When the Green and Murphy families drove through the gates, past sentries in pressed khaki and perfectly edged grass, they realized immediately that this was not Europe, not Tel Aviv, not Wiesbaden. This was institutional America—orderly, symmetrical, and unapologetically conventional.

Their assigned duplexes stood side by side along a quiet row of officers' housing—brick, balanced, and indistinguishable from the rest. Each half offered four bedrooms, four baths, a formal living room, dining room, den, study, and a detached two-car garage. Functional. Respectable. Predictable. It was clearly not what Katie expected.

Katie stood in the doorway longer than necessary, surveying the symmetry of it all. Identical brick. Identical shutters. Identical lawns clipped to regulation length. Across the narrow driveway, Ariel's windows mirrored her own like a reflection she hadn't chosen.

She had grown up in penthouses and summer estates where architects competed to surprise her. Here, surprise had been engineered out of the equation. This was institutional America—efficient, respectable, small.

She said nothing. But in her silence lived a realization: power in this country did not always reside in grand rooms. Sometimes it hid in brick duplexes behind parade fields. And if this was the stage they had been given, she would learn to command it.

Classes started on August 15th. Ben was appointed as the commanding officer at Israel's Sde Dov Airport. During the Arab-Israeli war, the IAF flew Mustangs, Spitfires, and German fighters that Czechoslovakia called S-199s. Ben's additional duty was to locate these aircraft and repair as many as possible. He also received help from Ariel—now an undocumented foreign agent—to assist with his academic work, among other tasks.

The duplexes may have been modest, but the lives inside them were anything but. By day, the men would sit in seminar rooms discussing grand strategy, logistics, and the future architecture of American power. By night, maps of Europe and the Middle East would quietly reappear on dining room tables once cleared of roast chicken and children's toys. Carlisle was meant to be a year of reflection and theory. For the Greens and the Murphys, it was something else entirely—a command post disguised as academia.

At one of their first joint dinners, Ben let everyone know that he was still commanding Squadron 101 and responsible for Procurement for the IAF. Ben wanted everyone to be clear that he had a lot on his plate and may have to go to Israel at any time his Squadron needed him.

"Has anyone heard if Allen will be joining us and, if so, when?" Ariel spoke with thinly veiled impatience.

No one responded, so Ariel continued. "I will call his office in the morning. If that doesn't work, I will try to reach him through General LeMay. Does anyone have any other ideas?"

Katie refilled Ariel's glass before answering.

"You're anxious," Katie whispered lightly.

"I prefer informed," Ariel replied.

The table fell quiet for a beat too long.

Both women understood that Allen's presence meant decisions—decisions about travel, secrecy, and whose husband would leave first. Ariel's war was immediate and visible. Katie's was layered beneath committees and currency reform. Neither believed her battlefield was smaller.

"We'll find him," Katie affirmed calmly. "And when we do, we'll decide what moves next."

Ariel nodded once. It wasn't agreement. It was acknowledgment.

At that moment, the doorbell rang. Paul, well lubricated from wine at dinner, boomed, "Enter." A few seconds later, they heard Allen's distinctive voice.

"Where's the Pappy? Paul, guess what. You know that you are the senior military officer and President of your class of the Army War College? That means you assign duties, approve optional class assignments, and a load of other things. It also gives you a lot of freedom."

"Allen, I can't be the class commander. There are other Colonels here who have date of rank."

"But they don't have a (P) after their rank, Mr. Murphy," Allen handed over the announcement.

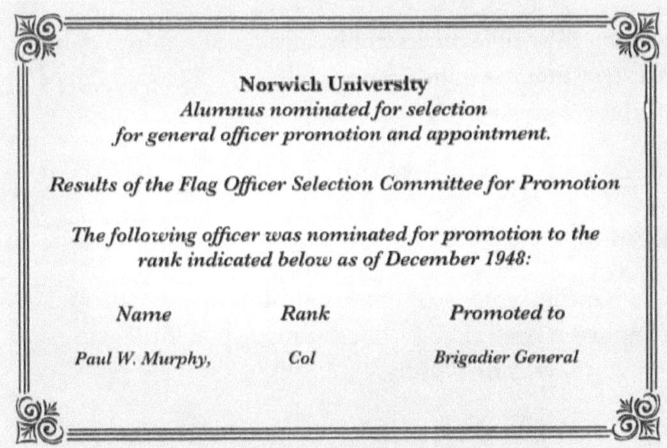

Norwich University

Alumnus nominated for selection for general officer promotion and appointment.

Results of the Flag Officer Selection Committee for Promotion

The following officer was nominated for promotion to the rank indicated below as of December 1948:

Name	Rank	Promoted to
Paul W. Murphy,	*Col*	*Brigadier General*

"Congratulations, Paul. You are now the class President and the prime target of all the members of the West Point Protective Association. By the way, when the fuck did you attend Norwich?"

Ben was laughing heartily at hearing Paul's new role. Allen joined him and then continued.

"So, Ben, you think that's funny, huh? Well, I guess you haven't heard that you are the senior International Fellow, and as a result, you have the same duties with the international students as Paul does with the U.S. students."

"Congratulations, Ben," Katie's tone got lower and more serious. "Paul, Ben, it may be hard for you to keep your numerous responsibilities under wraps. We should discuss strategy."

Allen did the math quickly. Visibility was the real enemy now. A 28-year-old brigadier general at the War College would draw attention. But attention could be redirected.

As soon as Paul's star was official, he would rate high enough to justify an aide. The aide would not simply carry papers. He would carry access.

Allen already knew the right officer—Air Force on paper, Company-trained in practice.

That night, he sent a short message to LeMay:

Confirm assignment effective upon War College completion. No explanation required.

The following morning the full team assembled again at the Murphy home. Paul had created a chart to define roles and responsibilities. He folded the paper and slid it back into his breast pocket.

"I've created a chart for clarity but here's how I see it"

He looked first at Ariel.

"You handle Israel's operational lifeline. Squadron 101. Aircraft. Spare parts. If they need wings, you find wings. If they need guns, you find guns."

Ariel gave a single nod. "And if they need pilots?"

"They'll have them."

Paul turned to Ben.

"You keep the channels open. Procurement, logistics, back-end coordination. You make sure what Ariel secures actually moves."

Ben leaned back. "And if it doesn't?"

"Then we move it another way."

Paul's eyes shifted to Katie.

"You work the atmosphere."

She smiled faintly. "Europe."

"Yes. Ensure the governments we're rebuilding don't drift. Remind them who is funding reconstruction. And remind Congress who is funding campaigns."

Allen watched the exchange, saying nothing.

"And me?" Paul finished. "I maintain flight status. I hold this class together. I make sure the official machine keeps running while the unofficial one does its work."

Allen continued to consider each team member's responsibilities and outline in more detail.

"The political issues surrounding US–Israel relations are sensitive topics that each team member must address. The transfer of excess equipment to European countries needs to be handled by Paul. Ben should be able to ensure that Israel is obtaining all the necessary weapons and spare parts. The purchasing of the surplus equipment from these European countries should be supervised by Ben but managed by Ariel. With the new house in D.C., Katie could manage all social events for both the Israeli delegation and the European nations. It would be easy for Katie to remind European dignitaries of how they are benefiting from the US provision of surplus equipment to their countries and how the US needs their countries to be reshaped. It should be clear to European dignitaries that the United States is aware of how both European countries and European dignitaries are financially benefiting from these transactions. Moreover, with Katie's wealth and U.S. citizenship, she needs to host fundraising events for Democratic Senators and House Members who support the President's agenda. She could also remind the other members of both the Senate and House what it takes to get her support. The next step is to get Congress to repeal the US embargo on selling military equipment to Israel."

While Katie was wildly processing her global to-do list, she realized she needed to consider Ariel in her plans for the children's care.

"Ariel, don't you think that now that the boys are rambunctious five-year-olds, it's about time they started fighting each other instead of fighting us?"

"When and where?"

"How about having Joseph, or do you call him Joe, come over after breakfast and play with Tom for the rest of the morning?"

"It's, Joe, unless we are in Israel, where it's יוֹסֵף (Yosef), and I would cherish that time."

"Well, in our house, it will always be Yosef. And I'll see you in the morning. I can't wait for the boys to really get to know each other. Oh, and one more thing, Ariel."

"Yes"

"With all our responsibilities, I was thinking of hiring a housekeeper/babysitter. I'm sure Allen could find us someone who would meet both of our needs."

"Allen... Allen," yelled Katie.

"Yes, ma'am," replied Allen sarcastically.

"Allen, with everything you're asking Ariel and me to do, I think we'll need help just like Paul has. Specifically, we'll need assistance with Tommy and Yosef. I believe that the helper will also need training in Personal Protective Detail services. It will have to be very discreet. What do you think?"

"I couldn't agree more. Additionally, they need to come from the Company. They should not have an Army background. We should have one to support you and one to help Ariel. That way, they can cover for each other and have a reasonable life. Let me work with the Directorate of Support to get their ideas and ensure all three positions are staffed as soon as possible."

That night, Allen reached out to Paul.

"Paul, I apologize for the late call. However, I didn't want your new aide-de-camp to surprise you in the morning. It's Captain Paul Clayton, previously he commanded a team of Pathfinders and currently holds the title of Special Tactics Officer. He will arrive tomorrow morning at about 1000 hours. Any questions?"

"No, Sir."

"Well, you should have questions, like how a Colonel (P) has a Captain as an Aide. Those WPPA jerks would ask that question. Come on, Paul, think. Yesterday, you were appointed Deputy Director of Operations for SAC, understand?"

"Sir, I understand, and by the way, it is 3:00 a.m. after three martinis."

"I know, I was there too, and I'm still working. Since you have such a low tolerance to booze, maybe you should permanently lay off the Martinis."

Paul laughed loudly, still mostly asleep.

"Yes, sir, I will take that under consideration. Thanks for calling. Goodnight."

Paul rolled over and resumed his beautiful sleep from which Allen's call violently yanked him. The next morning, Paul had a meeting scheduled with BG Philip B. Peyton, Commandant, U.S. Army War College, regarding Paul's new role as class president. General Peyton began.

"Please tell me about your new SAC title, aide, and promotion."

"Well, General Peyton,"

"Paul, please call me Phil. We're both generals now, and I want us to be on a first-name basis."

"Certainly, Phil. Well, I can't say that I am not surprised by this chain of events. Fifteen days ago, Gen. LeMay called me and told me to pack my bags; both my former wingman, who was also a squadron commander during WWII, Ben Green—and I were going to the Army War College. We were both promoted to Major and Squadron Commander of our squadrons toward the end of the war. Ben is Jewish, and after the war, he was deeply affected by the Holocaust. So, he left the Air Force and joined the IAF. Since he was appointed the commander of IAF Squadron 101, Israel's only operational fighter squadron, I have been unofficially assigned by the National Command Authority to support his efforts.

"The National Command Authority?"

"Yes, Sir. It's crazy but fits with the orders I've received for other assignments. The plan for me after completing the War College was to join General LeMay at SAC. It was implied that my position would be Deputy Director of Operations, and I needed to spend the year preparing for that role. This included qualifying as Pilot in Command of the newest bomber in the SAC fleet. I was shocked last night by a phone call appointing me to that position, effective immediately. I was also told that a SAC veteran, Captain Paul Payton, would be immediately assigned as my Aide."

"You got a senior Captain as your aide? That's a first for me," exclaimed General Payton. "It's impossible for me even to get a First Lieutenant as my aide."

"Phil, I got a call about my new position and my aide at 0300 this morning after an informal promotion party and having over imbibed in the supply cupboard. I'm still getting used to the concept of the SAC appointment, and I haven't met my aide yet. I'm sure he will have orders for me."

"I think you'll appreciate having an aide to handle all the administrative responsibilities as the class president and Deputy Director of Operations for SAC. Is that an O8 position? That would explain the captain for an aide."

"I'm not sure, Phil. I don't think that could be correct. I am only 28 years old. I understand the promotions from Lieutenant to Major, it was just a matter of survival. When an existing Squadron Commander died, was shot down, or became incapacitated, it was next man up. I was a triple ace and had a date of rank, so I became a Major and a Squadron Commander.

After the war, I was sent to C&GSC because of my performance as a Squadron Commander. I then finished number one in the class, so I received the automatic promotion to LTC.

While waiting to lead an organization during the Greek Civil War, I wrote a paper on the uses of surplus and excess equipment from WWII. General Van Fleet forwarded the paper to the new Chief of the Air Force and the current Chief of Staff of the Army. They were extremely pleased with the report; both sent me a letter of commendation, and I received my first green hornet. Between the memo, what I accomplished during the Greek Civil War, my contingency planning for a Russian Blockade of Berlin, and my command of the 86th Fighter Wing, I was selected below the zone for O6 at the young age of 27. I believe you know the rest of the story, Phil. I am exhausted just repeating it."

"You have a few other awards, don't you?"

"Certainly, from my Army Air Force days, I have a DSC and a Silver Star, plus a bunch of minor awards.

"Paul, I can now easily understand why you're a promotable Colonel. You are one of the rare few officers who are exceptional as both a combat commander and a staff officer. It's an honor to meet you!"

"Sir, the honor is mine."

THE SITTERS

October 1948—War College

The two new aides arrived at Katie's and Ariel's homes shortly after 1000 hours that morning. They both seemed unusual. The first to arrive, Beth McLean, came dressed in a Hardy Amies women's suit, which was made by a very high-end London women's fashion designer. It was certainly not what Katie expected her to be wearing. She also arrived with three suitcases and asked which room and bathroom were for her. Immediately after Katie got Ms. McLean situated, Ariel called.

"Which bedroom did you assign to your helper?"

"I gave her the upstairs bedroom next to Tom's."

"Did you see the weapons they were wearing when they arrived? They seem to be both nurturing and highly skilled with their guns. Is that what we asked for?"

"We have someone thinking for us. I didn't expect that the staff would be members of the Personal Protective Detail, but I'm glad they are. Ariel, you know how to protect yourself, being a Mossad Major. I don't have a clue. Having Beth, and what's your staff woman's name?"

"Kathy McLean."

"Her surname is McLean, too? Mine is Beth McLean."

"Oh, well, I guess Beth and Kathy will have to do."

"Right, well having these two here with us will allow us both to focus on our other responsibilities. I will host a reception for several senators on October 15. I think they will play a key role in repealing the Israeli arms embargo."

"Of course."

***

Captain Paul P. Payton arrived at Katie's house and introduced himself as Colonel Murphy's new aide.

"Ma'am, do you know where the Colonel is? I have some critical and time-sensitive information for him."

"He'll be along. I see you're carrying the M1911 45, Captain. If you don't mind, I don't want my son to see weapons around the house at his age. He's very curious. One question for you: Do you have quarters yet?"

"No ma'am."

"Well, go get your suitcase. I assume you're on TDY and that my husband will want access to you 24/7. Tonight, you'll be staying here until you get quarters. Is that ok with you?"

"Yes, ma'am. That is very nice of you."

After finishing his meeting with General Peyton, Paul discussed the findings with Allen and Ben. The three men talked about how to continue funding the European Leaders while also providing Israel with the equipment, planes, and ammunition it needed to maintain their independence. After a while, Ben enquired.

"Is it possible for your new aide, Captain Payton, to travel extensively on a diplomatic passport? If so, I believe we have found the solution to our problem."

"How so, Ben?"

"Simple, Paul; in Europe's current state, who would question the activities of a State Department Officer with the rank of Minister-Counselor? That rank is low enough that not everyone would recognize the title, yet high enough that no one would doubt him. I believe one of us should introduce him to our main contact in each country, including Israel. Also, since he has temporary quarters with Paul, it would be easy for him to brief us on any return trips. Allen, how difficult would it be for him to obtain the proper credentials?"

"No problem at all, Ben. I believe you have chosen the right rank for the right reasons. The only thing we need to do is ask him if he's willing to take on this job."

"He's willing, he works for me!"

"If that's the case, Allen, can you arrange his transportation? And would he require security?"

"Those are very complicated questions. A Minister-Counselor is a senior U.S. Department of State ranking equivalent to a two-star general. The decision to provide security would be based on a comprehensive risk assessment tailored to the specific circumstances of the travel and the environment of the war-torn region. Since his mission will be deemed critical to U.S. interests by the National Command Authority, heightened security would be more likely. Furthermore, I believe that he will need a blanket European and Israeli travel authority issued by the Secretary of State. We need to get that very quietly and then notify all European and Israeli ambassadors of that travel authority."

Allen paused mid-sentence.

"There is one complication."

The room stilled.

"The State Department will require a file. Even a quiet one. Minister-Counselor rank does not materialize out of thin air. Someone will ask where he has served."

Ben leaned forward. "And?"

"And we will have to give them something believable."

Paul exhaled. "A temporary reconstruction advisory post?"

"Exactly," Allen replied. "Economic stabilization liaison. Marshall Plan technical observer. Vague enough to be useful. Documented enough to survive inquiry."

Ariel's eyes narrowed. "And if someone pulls the thread?"

"Then we make sure," Allen declared, "that the thread leads somewhere we control."

The obstacle did not derail the plan. It made it real.

The following morning, Allen, Paul, and Ben headed over and sat down with Paul's new aide to brief him on the plan.

"Captain, welcome to this outstanding assignment. I promise that your rater will be General LeMay. I won't jeopardize a captain's future by having him rated by a mere colonel (P). I assume you weren't given any time to prepare for this assignment." Paul caught himself making assumptions and stopped himself to clarify. "Goodness, I apologize. Are you married? Do you have any children? What was I thinking?"

"Sir, first, I would appreciate your evaluation. You are the youngest flag officer in nearly 50 years. Second, we shouldn't bother General LeMay with such a minor issue. Third, I am single and have no known children. And Sir, I have been awaiting this assignment for over a month. I have completed Personal Protective Detail training. I hope that addresses your immediate questions."

"A few more; do you have a diplomatic passport, and who will be providing you with security?"

Allen chipped in, "Have you gone through Diplomatic Officer training?"

"Sir, why would I do that? I will be the General's aide."

"I just needed a third question," Allen remarked with a smile to Paul.

Ben, having heard enough, was eager to get into the guts of things.

"I believe that we should be getting down to business. Captain, unless you have your heart set on passing hors d'oeuvres at Katie Murphy's dinner parties, we have a better job offer for you. Using tonight's counting protocol, here goes: First, you will be named a Minister-Counselor, a senior U.S. Department of State officer ranking equivalent to a two-star general. Second, you will receive a diplomatic passport, and third, you will receive a blanket travel authorization for Europe and Israel issued by the Secretary of State. Fourth, you will receive a TS/SCI clearance. Fifth, your mission has been 'found' to be critical to U.S. national security interests by the National Command Authority. Sixth, you will join a multinational covert team with TS/SCI clearances. Seventh, the TS/SCI cleared team will be responsible for handling the most sensitive data relating to the United States, European countries, and a Middle Eastern country. Eighth, you will be assigned a Personal Protective Detail of your choice, ideally consisting of just one person, to keep you safe and your mission completely secret and compartmentalized. That means it will be invisible to anyone not on this team. What do you say, Captain Payton?"

"Sir, I don't know your name, rank, or position, but I have only one thing to ask: where is the Standard Form 312 for me to sign?"

After Captain Payton signed the SF 312, Allen stepped forward with his hand extended.

"Welcome to Team Moose 2, Paul. I mean Captain Payton. I see this is going to be confusing. Captain, we're going to need a different name for you, or else we'll keep confusing you and the soon-to-be general."

"How about Paul the second? Or P2, laughed Ariel, who had just joined the meeting. "

"Can we just not?" Captain Payton was not amused.

"Where did you go to college?"

"The University of Florida. It's where General Van Fleet was both the football coach and a professor. He coached at Florida twice, totaling five years. He was also the Professor of Military Science. I was raised in Florida, and The University of Florida is the best public university in the South. Go Gators."

"Gator!" Paul announced calmly with an air of authority.

"How about Allen? It was my dad's first name." Captain Payton was not in a playful mood.

"That won't work either. You're 'Gator,' and you are now the sixth member of Team Moose 2. Now, let's get to work. One of our two main missions is to ensure that the money the US government is spending on Europe's rebuilding and restructuring results in governments that resemble a US democracy. We do this by supporting the governments in this chart." Paul produced a chart from his inner breast pocket and shared it with the group. "One special country is Czechoslovakia because they have been providing Israel with S-199 aircraft and spare parts. That relates to our second mission.

Developing a deeper relationship with Israel by complying with the embargo on the US selling weapons to Israel, but ensuring they obtain everything they need to succeed as a country. The process involves identifying all the equipment and weapons the chart outlines, then adding everything Israel needs to the list, and finally informing Israel where they can buy what they desire. This way, Israel can purchase all it needs from the listed countries, ensuring that those countries receive payment. Gator, you'll work with each of the other members to build relationships with the leaders of these countries. We don't ask anyone questions about the money. That's their business. What we need to know, Ben will tell us. Understood?"

"Yes, Sir," Gator stamped his foot to accentuate his best infantry officer's parade ground voice.

"You need to meet with each team member tomorrow, choose your security office, and hit the road the day after. All your documents should be delivered by tomorrow afternoon. There's no need for you to spend any money on an apartment; the extra upstairs bedroom is yours. Finally, you will be on TDY for the entire duration of your assignment. Don't blow all that money in one place,"

Paul tapped Gator's shoulder with a smile. "I expect a telephonic report once a week from a secure phone, and we will set the time for the next call during each conversation. Any questions?"

"No, Sir"

"Then, as your first act as a member of this team," Paul announced quietly, "understand this: nothing we are doing here will stay here."

The room held that thought.

Outside, the cicadas buzzed over the parade field. Carlisle slept peacefully, unaware that inside two neighboring duplexes, the architecture of postwar power was being rearranged.

Gator reached for the glasses. No one toasted.

Moose 2 European Strategy Map

Country	Leader	Position	Political Orientation	Key Challenges	Team Member
United Kingdom	Clement Attlee	Prime Minister	Labour/ Sociallst	Economic crisis, decolonalzation	Katie
France	Charles de Gaulle	Head of Provisional Gov	Gaulist	National reconstruction, political unity	Paul
Italy	Ferruccio Parri	Prime Minister	Christian Democrat	Republic establish-ment, Cold War	Paul
Denmark	King Christian X	Const-Monarch	Monarchist	Post-occupation recovery	Katie
Czech-	Edvard Beneš	President	Democratic	Coalition, comm-unist pressure	Katie
Germany	Military Governors	Occupation Administration	Allied control	Division Division denazification	Ben
Austria	Karl Renner	Chancellor - President	Social Democcat	Four-power occupation	Ariel
Greece	Various		Competing Factions	Civil War, for-eign intervention	Ben

CHAPTER FOURTEEN—OCTOBER FUNDRAISER

By mid-September, Katie understood something clearly: persuasion was inefficient. Money moved faster.

Congress would not lift the embargo because it was moral. It would lift it because it was practical.

On September 15th, she instructed her Washington butler to get either Senator Wagner or Senator Downey on the phone.

A few minutes later:

"Ma'am, Senator Downey is on the line."

"Clarence," Katie began warmly, "how is your day?"

"Never better, Ms. Katie. What can I do for you?"

"Well, I hope it improves further. You haven't seen the new house yet, have you?"

"No, ma'am."

"We've completed the first phase of renovations. I was wondering if I might persuade you and Senator Wagner to come to dinner tonight. I believe you'll find support for an idea that benefits both your reelection campaigns."

There was a pause—calculation, not hesitation.

"I'll be there. I'll call Bob. What time?"

"Seven for drinks and hors d'oeuvres."

The library felt different once filled with power.

"Gentlemen," Katie began, not bothering with pleasantries, "the Corrupt Practices Act limits you to $25,000 plus state allowances. Meanwhile, the unions operate through PACs with near impunity. I've decided to create one of my own."

Neither senator spoke.

"It will be compliant," she added evenly. "Entirely lawful. We will simply be… thorough."

Clarence broke first. "I think it's a fine idea."

"Then we begin tonight."

The McFarland PAC

The inaugural fundraiser exceeded expectation.

With an initial seeding of $250,000, the evening generated an additional $1 million. Contributions continued to flow in quietly over the next several weeks. By October's end, the McFarland PAC held just over $2 million—the largest war chest available to candidates willing to support two priorities:

1. Ending the Israeli arms embargo.

2. Funding European reconstruction aligned with American governance principles.

Katie's first call was to Allen.

"We raised just over two million. Clean. Non-partisan. Discreet."

"That," Allen replied from somewhere in Europe, "is what leverage sounds like. Congratulations. Congress will want to remain on your good side."

"I intend to ensure they do."

THE INSTA-GATOR

Thanksgiving Week

Gator stood at the head of the table, now entirely comfortable in his borrowed gravitas.

"Minister-Counselor at Large," Paul announced lightly, tapping a crystal glass with a spoon. "The floor is yours."

Gator inclined his head.

"The title matters. 'At Large' signals mobility. Authority. Decision-making capacity. Leaders respond accordingly."

He moved through his assessment with clarity and compression.

United Kingdom: Attlee remains reliable. Equipment transfers have been efficient and discreet.

France: Distrustful. Politically distracted. Not worth additional capital.

Italy: Cooperative. Prime Minister De Gasperi understands alignment.

Czechoslovakia: A critical window remains open before Soviet dominance fully hardens. Continue leveraging aircraft supply.

Finland: Quietly formidable. Worth sustained investment.

Germany: Central to long-term European stability. Reliable in surplus transfers. Motivated.

He paused.

"In Prague, one minister asked who had authorized my commitments. I told him the same people who authorized the Marshall Plan. He stopped asking questions. But we should not assume that answer will always suffice."

The room absorbed that.

"And State?" Paul asked.

"Professional. Helpful. Treasury officials, less so. Curious."

"Did anyone request oversight?"

"No. I was received at protocol level normally reserved for ambassadors."

Paul studied him. "Would you consider a permanent State Department role?"

Gator smiled faintly. "I believe I'm doing good work exactly where I am."

Paul let the moment breathe.

"Colonel Payton."

Gator blinked. "Colonel?"

"Your promotion packet moved quickly."

Silence.

"Very quickly."

Gator exhaled once. "I appreciate the confidence."

"Stay with us," Paul pleaded. "The mission isn't finished."

New Orders—Same Mission

The following morning was less diplomatic.

A siren shrieked through the duplexes—Israel's scramble alert. Ariel appeared in the doorway first.

"Where did you get that recording?"

Ben followed. "Paul, if this isn't urgent—"

"It is."

Allen entered last, calm as always.

"Congratulations," he began, nodding to Paul and Ben. "Your War College performance continues to exceed expectations."

Paul cut gently to the point. "Israel needs Ben back."

Allen nodded. "Agreed. The question is timing."

Katie spoke carefully. "We have roughly three weeks before Christmas recess. If we push now, we may secure embargo repeal before year's end."

Silence.

Ben finally answered. "If supply lines are stable, I can return. But I finish the course first."

Allen inclined his head. "Done."

STRATEGY SESSION

Sunday evening.

The women met first. Six Rheingold beers chilled beside a decanter of wine. Steaks marinated. The children upstairs. They reviewed their talking points for Congress.

1. Support from the American Jewish community.
2. Israel's right to self-defense.
3. Imbalanced embargo effects favoring Arab states.
4. Moral responsibility post-Holocaust.
5. Democratic self-determination.
6. Financial alignment.

Allen arrived midway through their review.

"The first five," he explained calmly, "are arguments."

He tapped the paper once.

"Number Six is leverage."

Katie nodded. "I suspected as much."

"We don't need to convince them morally," Allen continued. "We need to make alignment rational."

The men joined shortly after. Paul took control.

"By Sunday after Thanksgiving, each of you will refine five public talking points. We'll consolidate and deploy."

Allen's tone sharpened briefly. "Time is our enemy."

Then he caught himself.

"It's good to take stock," Paul offered evenly. "We've made progress."

Allen's shoulders relaxed.

"Yes," he conceded. "We have."

Upstairs, the boys slept. Downstairs, steak smoke curled toward the ceiling while strategy reshaped continents.

The embargo would fall—not because history demanded it, but because pressure would make it untenable.

Outside, the Pennsylvania air was cold and still. No one in Washington yet understood how quickly money could turn into policy.

CHAPTER FIFTEEN—THE HOLIDAY PARTY OF HOLIDAY PARTIES

It was not usually Paul's instinct to plan parties and usually left this sort of thing to Katie but he wanted a novel way to introduce his new rank with subtlety. He called for the families to gather at the Green home to plan the affair.

> "Katie, I've been thinking about a holiday party at our D.C. house. It might be a great opportunity for Ben to meet several Senators and Congressmen."

> "Why, my thoughtful husband, I am surprised you should suggest such a thing. It just so happens…"

Katie then handed out a previously prepared and mailed invitation to their holiday Party.

The room erupted with laughter and Ariel turned to Paul.

"Paul, when will you ever figure out that you married above your station?"

"Maybe so, Ariel, but just so you are aware, I too can plan a party"

Paul then handed out his version of the invitation.

Katie scanned the invitation and immediately noticed her husbands rank quietly included.

"Paul, oh my goodness, when did this happen? How could I have missed it? Did I miss the promotion ceremony?"

"All in good time, my dear. You know I don't like to toot my own horn."

555 Massachusetts Avenue
Washington D.C
December 15, 1948

"Good afternoon, this is Katie Murphy for Allen Dulles."

"Just a moment, ma'am.

"Katie, how are you doing?"

"I am amazingly well and ready for both the promotion ceremony and the party tonight."

"I understand, but I don't think that I have ever heard you voice this positive and animated"

"Then you haven't seen our confirmed guest list for tonight

"Why, who's coming?

"Allen you wouldn't believe it. We have the entire leadership of the democratic house including the ranking member, the minority whip, and all of the newly elected democratic senators. Allen, I will have a copy list here for you when you arrive for the promotion ceremony."

"Thank you, Katie. I can't wait to see it. I'll see you in about an hour."

***

"Allen, here is the guest list. You have my permission to be impressed."

- Carl Vinson (Georgia): As the ranking Democratic member on the House Armed Services Committee
- John F. Kennedy (Massachusetts): First house term.
- Lyndon B. Johnson (Texas): Just won his Senate seat
- John W. McCormack (Massachusetts): Serving as the House Minority Whip
- Sam Rayburn (Texas): As the House Minority Leader,
- Herbert O'Conor of Maryland successfully retained his Senate seat after a contested election case which was resolved in May 1948.
- Dennis Chavez of New Mexico also successfully retained his seat after a contested election case, according to the U.S. Senate.
- Scott Lucas of Illinois won his Senate seat.
- Elmer Thomas of Oklahoma won his Senate seat.
- Francis J. Myers of Pennsylvania won his Senate seat.
- Olin D. Johnston of South Carolina won his Senate seat.
- Elbert D. Thomas of Utah won his Senate seat.
- Warren G. Magnuson of Washington won his Senate seat.

"Katie, no one will ever doubt Paul's early selection for Flag rank if all he ever did was make the decision to marry you. I believe this attendee list will significantly increase our chances to end the embargo. Congratulations."

By the spring of 1949, the embargo no longer functioned. There was no vote to celebrate. No dramatic repeal. It simply became impractical to enforce. Israel purchased what it needed. Europe received what it wanted. Congress received what it required. And the party at 555 Massachusetts Avenue became the night everyone later claimed to have attended.

Katie was spending more and more time in D.C. as she became increasingly politically charged and motivated. She was splitting her time between Carlisle Barracks and 555 Massachusetts Ave. It was hard being apart from Paul and the boys, but Katie would often have Beth travel with her and bring the boys along when she wasn't going to be too consumed with her duties and activities.

CHAPTER SIXTEEN—BACK TO WAR

Tel Aviv—January 1949

When Ben Green stepped back onto the tarmac at Hatzor, the wind coming off the Mediterranean carried dust and cordite. Squadron 101 assembled without ceremony. They did not cheer. They stood straighter. Word had traveled ahead of him—War College graduate. European negotiator. Architect of supply lines. Triple ace returned from America with more than medals.

Ben looked across the line of pilots—Israelis, Canadians, Americans—young men who had already seen too much.

"Rav Nagad Levy," he ordered quietly, "bring the squadron to attention."

"Havaana." (Understood and will comply)

"Tayeset" (attention!)

Boots locked. Chins lifted. Ben let the silence stretch.

Operation Horev was entering its final phase. Egyptian forces were withdrawing, but not yet beaten. Convoys still burned. Aircraft still prowled. And somewhere between Sinai and politics, the war was shifting shape.

> Ben held the weight of the moment. "We support ground forces. We protect the convoys. We break whatever air capability remains. Clear?"

No one asked questions—they rarely did.

The Incident

Three days earlier, on January 7th, a patrol had gone south in the late afternoon. A truce was scheduled for 1600 hours. War has a way of filling the space before ceasefires.

Two Spitfires lifted from Qastina. A Mustang was meant to provide top cover but was declared unserviceable at the last minute. So it was just the two. Forty miles south of Faluja they saw smoke—three columns rising from what looked like a burning convoy. Israeli. They descended. Then shapes appeared in the haze. Spitfires. Low. Fast. No visible markings in the glare and dust.

> "Bogies," came the warning.

The fight began before clarity did. The Israeli pilots dove. Cannons flashed. Metal tore. One aircraft exploded in fragments. Another rolled inverted, trailing smoke. The sky became a scissors engagement—tight, brutal, instinctive. One pilot would later say he recognized the roundel only after firing Blue and red. Royal Air Force. By then it was too late. Five RAF Spitfires fell from the sky that afternoon. Two British pilots were killed. Two were captured. One escaped. The Israeli aircraft returned home intact.

They performed victory rolls over the airfield. Only after landing did the realization settle in. They had not shot down Egyptians. They had shot down Britain.

The Telegram

The next morning, someone in 101 Squadron sent a message to 208 Squadron RAF in Cyprus:

"Sorry about yesterday. You were on the wrong side of the fence. Come over for a drink sometime. You will see many familiar faces.'"

It was gallows humor. It did not prevent the diplomatic explosion.

The Summons

On Ben's first full day back in command, a runner intercepted him outside the briefing room.

"Colonel Green, immediate summons to Tel Aviv."

Signed personally by David Ben-Gurion. Ben stared at the signature. He did not need to ask why.

"Prepare a Spitfire," he ordered with sorrow. "And gather every after-action report."

Twenty minutes later, he was airborne.

Tel Aviv

The Prime Minister, the President, and the Chief of General Staff were waiting. The room smelled faintly of tobacco and fried eggplant—someone had sent for sabich while they waited. Ben saluted. Ben-Gurion studied him for a long moment.

"You return from America," the Prime Minister began, "and within seventy-two hours Britain is furious."

Ben did not smile.

"Sir, it was mistaken identity. Our pilots believed they were engaging Egyptian aircraft over a burning Israeli convoy. The RAF did not coordinate their presence in a live combat zone."

Yaakov Dori leaned forward.

"Were our pilots reckless?"

"No, sir. They were disciplined. They fought to protect ground forces."

Silence.

Ben-Gurion nodded once.

"Britain is protesting. Washington is uneasy. The timing is delicate."

"Sir," Ben retorted carefully, "if British aircraft operate over our front lines without coordination, incidents will happen again."
That was not defiance. It was reality. The Prime Minister stood and walked to the window.

"Britain promised a homeland," pontificating quietly. "Then detained survivors behind barbed wire. History between us is… layered."

He turned back.

"But we need the West. We cannot fight the British Empire."

"No, sir."

Dori spoke next.

"Colonel, today proved something. Our Air Force cannot remain merely tactical. It must become strategic."

Ben felt the weight shift.

"What are you proposing?"

"A development assignment. Strategic Air Command. Offutt Air Force Base. Nebraska."

Ben blinked.

"You want me… in America?"

"Temporarily. You are too valuable to lose in a cockpit. Learn how they think. Learn how they build power. Then return."

President Weizmann added softly, "We must protect you. Our survival depends on men who understand both war and industry."

Ben understood immediately. This was not a promotion. It was extraction.

The Prime Minister returned to the table.

"On a classified basis," he said, "you will be named Director of Strategic Plans and Acquisitions. Study their systems. Study scientific management. Study how they turn resources into dominance."

"And if Egypt resumes hostilities?"

"They won't," Ben-Gurion declared defiantly. "Not after yesterday."

The meeting ended without ceremony.

Night

Back in his quarters, Ben lay awake staring at the ceiling. Five RAF aircraft. An international incident. And now Nebraska. He reached for the field telephone.

"Ariel? It's me."

The line crackled.

"I heard something happened."

"It's being handled."

Pause.

"I may be reassigned. Possibly back to the States."

Longer pause.

"For how long?"

"I don't know."

"And Squadron 101?"

"They won't keep me in a cockpit much longer."

She understood what that meant. The more indispensable he became, the less control he would have over where he stood.

"I was thinking it would be safe for you and Yosef to come here, but with this latest news, you better stay put until we know what the war has in store for us."

"I suspected as much."

"I'll know more soon."

The line hummed between them.

"I love you."

"I know, and I you, my love. Come back to us intact."

After the line went dead, Ben stared into the darkness. He had returned to war. But the war was no longer in the sky. It was in strategy. And he was being moved to the center of it.

CHAPTER SEVENTEEN—MOVING ON UP

Yaakov Dori stood at the window of his office at HaKirya, looking out over Tel Aviv. The war had been won in the field, but wars were not secured on battlefields alone. They were secured in offices, in doctrine, in decisions made quietly and without applause.

"Miriam," he barked without turning, "arrange a secure call with General Curtis LeMay."

"Yes, Chief."

"And schedule Colonel Benjamin Green to see me this afternoon."

When she left, Dori remained still for a long moment. There were officers who won battles. There were officers who built institutions. Ben Green was becoming the latter. That made him indispensable.

Across the Atlantic at Offutt Air Force Base, Colonel Franklin stood outside Curtis LeMay's office reviewing his notes one last time. One did not enter that office unprepared.

"Sir," he began once admitted, "Chief Yaakov Dori of the Israeli General Staff requests a secure call regarding

Colonel Benjamin Green. We are informed he will soon be promoted to Brigadier."

LeMay did not immediately respond. He finished reading the document in his hands before setting it down.

"I know who Ben Green is."

"Yes, sir."

"Schedule the call. Block two hours."

"Yes, sir."

"And Franklin—clear the rest of the morning."

The following day, the encrypted circuit hummed to life.

"Dan," LeMay chimed as the secure line locked in.

"Iron Ass," Dori replied evenly. "It's good to hear your voice."

There was history in that exchange—Europe, reconstruction, decisions that would never be written into official histories.

"Congratulations on the armistice," LeMay smirked. "Britain isn't pleased."

"Britain rarely is," Dori replied.

A quiet pause followed.

"Ben Green," Dori began, "you know his value."

"I do," LeMay declared without hesitation. "He and Murphy are the two finest strategic minds I've seen operate together. Combat leaders who understand systems."

"We are concerned about two things," Dori continued. "His safety. And his growth."

"You want him under my roof."

"Yes. Two or three years."

LeMay leaned back in his chair.

"He'll work directly with Murphy. Strategic planning. Acquisition doctrine. Organizational structure."

"That is precisely why I am calling."

"Does he know?"

"Not yet."

LeMay allowed himself the faintest smile.

"He'll accept."

"If I do not call you within forty-eight hours, assume the answer is yes."

"Done."

The line went quiet. A man had just been moved across continents without being consulted.

That afternoon at HaKirya, Miriam appeared in Dori's doorway.

"Chief, Colonel Green is waiting."

"And General Remez?"

"On his way."

"Prepare the promotion team."

Her expression did not change, but her eyes brightened. "Yes, Chief."

When Ben entered the office at 17:15, he came to attention out of habit.

"Colonel Benjamin Green reporting as ordered."

Dori studied him for a moment. He still carried himself like a squadron commander—direct, practical, grounded in the immediacy of flight operations.

"Ben, before we discuss your future, there is something overdue."

The door opened behind him.

Boots entered the room. Uniforms. A small orchestra ensemble compressing into a space clearly not designed for ceremony.

"Attention to Orders."

Ben turned slowly.

Brigadier Mazah began reading. The words washed over him at first—commendation, service, valor, contribution—until the rank was spoken clearly and unmistakably.

Tat Aluf.
Brigadier General.

When the reading concluded, Lt. Gen. Yigael Yadin stepped forward and removed Ben's shoulder boards. Dori replaced them with the insignia of an Israeli brigadier.

The room applauded—brief, controlled, professional.

Ben felt the physical weight of the new insignia settle on his shoulders. Promotions during the war had come in urgency and loss. This one felt different. Deliberate. Permanent.

After the room cleared, only Dori and General Remez remained.

"General Green," Dori said, allowing the rank to settle, "the Prime Minister has directed that your safety — and that of your family — is to be treated as a national priority."

Ben remained silent.

"I spoke this morning with General LeMay."

That caught his attention.

"You will join Strategic Air Command as a foreign exchange officer. You will serve alongside Brigadier Paul Murphy. Your responsibilities will focus on strategic planning and acquisitions."

Ben absorbed the words carefully. Not Sinai. Not Squadron 101. Nebraska.

"You are being moved," Dori continued, "from tactical command to institutional design. Israel must learn to build air power, not merely fly it."

Ben nodded once. "My family?"

"They will join you."

There was a long pause.

"My first impression, sir?" Ben asked.

"Yes."

"It is the right move."

Remez smiled faintly.

"Ezer Weizman will assume command of Squadron 101."

The finality of that statement landed harder than the promotion had.

"Understood."

Later that evening, back in his quarters at Hatzor, Ben lifted the phone.

"Paul."

"Well," came the familiar voice from Nebraska, "how does it feel to be Brigadier General Green?"

Ben allowed himself a brief laugh. "Word travels quickly."

"I work for LeMay," Paul replied.

"You're coming to Offutt," Paul continued.

"Yes."

"We're building something here."

"I know."

"Five officers waiting for you to review."

Ben sat on the edge of his bunk. Just weeks earlier he had stood in Sinai dust briefing pilots before combat. Now he was being repositioned into the machinery that would define air power for decades.

"When do you land?" Paul asked.

"Tomorrow."

"Good."

The line clicked dead.

Ben looked around the small quarters—functional, temporary. Squadron 101 was no longer his. The war in the air had shifted into something larger and less visible.

He began to pack.

CHAPTER EIGHTEEN—HOMECOMING

Katie was extremely pleased with Robbie's operation of The Family Company. There was full transparency regarding the financial stability, operations, and earnings. It marked a significant improvement. Robbie had recently called and attempted to schedule a meeting with Katie to discuss these matters. Katie recognized that she needed to become more involved in the family's financial affairs. However, that meant she would have to start discussing Paul's businesses since his mother's health was declining.

She had never seen the ranch operation's financial statements. She knew that the ranch was just printing money.

She had met Wes a few years earlier and knew he was very impressive. The ranch operation was by far the largest business either of them was involved in. Wes had continued the strategy of acquiring more land, and she believed that the ranch now covered nearly a million acres. She thought that with Paul's increased duties, it would make sense for Robbie to have some involvement with the ranch. She also believed she should discuss this with Paul as soon as possible. With that in mind, she placed a call to Robbie.

"Robbie, I think we should have an in-person meeting to discuss operations for each business and financial reporting. I'm trying to figure out how to exclude the ranch from that meeting. Please give that some thought. You might find this hard to believe, but we're moving again. We're relocating to an Air Force Base near Omaha, NE. Paul is the new director of operations for the Strategic Air Command. I'm planning to buy a house or two there and would like to use the plane to get from Carlisle Barracks to Omaha in the next few days."

"That's fine, Katie, I'll arrange for the plane to be sent to you today. We have the same pilots with the same phone numbers. I'll inform your assistant of where they can be reached once they land. Just let me know when you would you like to have the meeting."

Katie thought to herself. "Reuniting the two families at a new assignment was wonderful. It was also great that General LeMay allowed them to live off base."

Once again, Katie faced a familiar dilemma. Paul was entirely focused on his military service. He had never paid much attention to his family's business, and he was the sole heir to the entire fortune. He felt responsible for the ranch, Wes, all his employees, and their families. The question was how she could get him to focus on that duty. She wondered what reports he received from Wes. She received detailed monthly financial reports on her family company from Robbie, but she wasn't sure if Paul received similar reports from Wes.

She needed to find a way to discuss this with Paul. Perhaps the best way to start the conversation was for Paul to join her session with Robbie. She decided to bring it up with Robbie during her next call. Now it was time to pick up Ariel and fly to Omaha on her new plane. Robbie had arranged to buy a C-69 from the Army and had it converted for personal use. It was fantastic—three and a half hours in a plane with a bedroom and a shower. She made a mental note to thank Robbie.

Ariel and Katie arrived at the airport to board the plane to Omaha to look for houses.

"Ariel, I am feeling bad about being away from the kids for so long and now we are getting on another flight to find yet another new place to live. Are Kathy and Beth okay with taking the kids for an extended time while we go house hunting?"

"Yes, they have everything under control back at the barracks, Katie—and the thing is, this move is going to centralize us again for a time. Who knows how long. But we take what we can get with these men we married and the lives we have chosen. By the way, have you heard anything from Allen? I wonder if we will be able to take Beth and Kathy with us to Omaha. Do you have any idea about that?"

"No, but I am sure that General LeMay is still working with Allen, even if just on a very casual basis."

"Katie, is that your plane? What the actual... I mean, Oh, my goodness. I have never been on a plane like that. How many seats does it have?

"Oh, I believe it has a crew of over ten. In a commercial setting, I think it could seat about 80. It's quite luxurious—one of the few indulgences I allow myself for efficiency's sake."

"Katie, I love your luxuries. I've benefited from them way too much."

When they boarded the Connie, named Katie's Joy, they were greeted by Col. Steve Payton (retired), who flew Katie and Paul on their first trip to Fort Leavenworth, Kansas.

"Katie, it is so great to see you again. I have a surprise for you. Robbie joined us for this flight. He hopes to provide you with a brief financial report and has another topic to discuss with you. One other surprise, we will be landing at Offutt Air Force Base. They have the best support facilities and insisted that I land there when they heard you were on the aircraft. I hope that's okay."

"You said that Robbie is on the plane. That's wonderful. Where is he?"

"I'm right here, Katie. While we are on the flight I wanted to review several things with you. Let's take a seat in the conference area and get started."

"Wow, this area is a nice improvement. Robbie, who did this work?"

"Our internal shop completed it in a week. I hope this is a good venue to review the Family's operations. I wanted to give you a quick overview of the increase in your asset value since we began. We've grown from $1.2 billion to $1.8 billion in four years. After fees. With liquidity. We're outperforming the Dow. I'd also like to discuss the ranch. Wes is an exceptional operator—both a businessman and a ranch manager—and Paul and his mother are fortunate to have him. Where the operation could improve is in capital management. That's our strength. The ranches are cyclical, and we have excess liquidity. Frankly, it's difficult to find well-run businesses worth acquiring, and this is exactly the kind of asset we want. I believe there's a strong case for The Family Company to bring the ranch under its umbrella. Before we move further, I'd like your initial reaction."

Katie was intrigued.

"And how would that transaction be taxed, Robbie?"

"Our tax team said there would be no tax on the contribution of the assets. Our accounting firm confirmed that analysis; Arthur Andersen & Co. confirmed that Paul and his mother would receive an equity interest in The Family Company in a tax-free exchange. The issue is how we would value the respective businesses."

"And how would we do that?"

"Well, there are several ways to value the respective businesses. We could get independent appraisals of both. Paul already owns half of The Family Company, and you own half of his interest in the ranches. Therefore, the relative valuation process won't change the ownership structure, with 50% belonging to Paul and his mother, and 50% to you. What do you think?"

"Well, it seems straightforward to me, Robbie. It all depends on what Paul thinks, but unless I am missing anything this sounds like a solid plan."

"Ok, pending Paul's approval, we should establish a preliminary budget for acquisitions in Idaho, Wyoming, and Montana. I believe our goal should be to become the largest ranch owner in each state. It wouldn't hurt to be the largest landholder in three states."

"How can I bring up the subject with Paul, Robbie, that's the only thing that makes me slightly uncomfortable."

"You already suggested holding an annual Family Company meeting. That is the correct protocol. Invite Paul, Wes, and Paul's Mom. During the meeting, someone will probably suggest that we spend too much money on separate accountants and lawyers. They might then ask if it makes sense to combine the businesses. After being asked that and seeing the $100 million of excess working capital we have, someone will likely propose merging the businesses. We all know that both families own 50% of each business. If Wes and Paul agree to the idea, then the deal could move forward."

"Ok, that's fine. How long do you need to prepare?"

"It will take us a couple of weeks to prepare the presentations. Just find us a date after two weeks from now, and we'll be ready to go. Is that okay?"

"Yes, Robbie, I will find out when Paul and his mother are available for the joint meeting. Thank you so much for the report. Very impressive progress."

"Ariel, I'm sorry for making you sit through all this, but it is so seldom that Robbie and I get together."

"Of course, Katie. The strategy seems very sound to me. Is it okay if we start talking about housing?"

"The top Omaha real estate brokerage is Payne & Sons Company. Harold Payne is the current president of the Omaha Board of Realtors®. Are you happy for us to work with him?"

"Of course, have you set up a meeting with him yet?"

"Robbie, do you know if your assistant or mine scheduled an appointment? I don't want a repeat of that self-righteous little man in D.C."

"Yes, you have an appointment in 90 minutes. He has been cleared onto the base. General LeMay's aide has arranged for you to stay in the VIP quarters. Mr. Payne is scheduled to visit you there, and he has been appropriately briefed."

General Officer Visiting Officers' Quarters

"Thank you, Robbie. As always, you are ahead of everything."

"You are most welcome, Katie."

"Robbie, I would like to discuss with you whether we should establish a separate business, apart from The Family Company, that will offer others the same resources you've been providing us. It's something to consider."

"Interesting. I've been thinking about that, Katie. Additional capital would give us even greater leverage in certain deals. Let's talk about it tonight after dinner. Tomorrow night, both of you are having dinner with General LeMay."

"Ariel, I don't know about you, but I would like to freshen up. We have about 80 minutes before Mr. Payne shows up. Robbie, how are we going to get to quarters with our luggage?"

"I have hired a car and driver. He has already loaded your bags and is ready to take you to the quarters."

They all deplaned and walked over to the waiting car while staff transferred the luggage. The ladies sighed with relief, laid back, and closed their eyes. They were exhausted at the pace of it all. Buying another house—and moving again this fall—weighed heavily on them. They were both well asleep when the car gently pulled into their destination. It felt like they had only just closed their eyes, but it was a 90-minute car ride. The door opened and a tall man stood at the ready.

"My name is Michael. I live here in Omaha, and it is my pleasure to help you with anything you need while you are visiting."

"Michael, it's a pleasure to meet you. I'm Katie and this is Ariel. Do you know if they have any snacks in this beautiful house?

"Yes, ma'am, they do. We were furnished a list of everything that you may need a few days ago, and the house is well stocked."

An hour later, Mr. Payne arrived at the house and immediately presented a list of houses—along with renderings—that he thought would meet Katie and Ariel's needs.

> "Mr. Payne, these are all fine properties, but we would like a property with two very similar, ideally identical, houses. It would be helpful to have a third building, such as a guest house, to address our security needs. Finally, we are interested in buying a property in the Fairacres Historic District. Is there anything like that available?"

> "Yes, there is a property that comes to mind that I think you'll love. Let me make a quick call to the listing agent to see if she's available, and then we can see the house, hopefully right away. It's a special place."

Mr. Payne went to work on the phone outside, where he could speak freely, and after a few minutes returned to the sitting room.

> "Ok, I spoke with the listing agent. There is a house on Davenport St. which has a house behind that borders it, and there's a small house next to it—all of them are available. You would be assembling your own compound. Do you want to see all of them today?"

> "Ariel?" Katie questioned with her eyes and Ariel nodded approvingly. "Yes, of course, thank you Mr. Payne."

The tour lasted almost three hours. Robbie attended too, and after seeing the first house, he asked the security team to immediately visit the home to assess whether the future compound was fully defensible. Neither Katie nor Ariel knew that they had twenty-four-hour professional protection—discreet, layered, and constant—beyond their live-in child carers. No matter how much Katie didn't want the children to know about the family's financial situation, it was becoming increasingly visible.

After visiting all three houses, Katie and Ariel had a long discussion about whether the compound would be a good place to raise their four children. They both concluded that it suited their needs perfectly and that they would consult with their husbands about the facilities.

While they were consulting with their husbands—the new generals—Robbie was negotiating the purchase on the assumption that it would proceed. It was more complicated than usual—they were negotiating with three separate sellers. As Robbie often said, cash does not argue—it accelerates. Mr. Payne was shocked when Katie and Ariel returned and confirmed the deal.

"Robbie, how quickly can we finalize the closing and when can the interior designers get started? We also need to discuss Catholic schools, synagogues, and the Catholic diocese."

"Well, this is known as a Catholic city because of Creighton University, which means there are plenty of Catholic schools. Ariel, it's going to be more difficult for your family. I haven't found a Jewish school yet or seen how the community reacts to your faith. I did find a wonderful organization in Omaha called the Jewish Federation of Omaha. They seem to be a very stable organization. They were formed in 1925, so they are over 25 years old."

Ariel was suitably satisfied.

"Robbie, you never cease to impress me. You're now beginning to understand the Jewish faith and the measures we take to make sure our children can maintain our culture and beliefs."

"Working with you is such a pleasure, Mrs. Green. Now, I have some news to share with both of you. The sellers, after talking to the officers at JP Morgan, decided to move out immediately. We will take possession of the properties in seven days. The decorators and security services will arrive tomorrow. We expect you to be able to move in within three weeks."

CHAPTER NINETEEN—FAMILY COMPANY MEETING

"Paul and I would like to welcome all of you to our new home. We would also like to thank you for your outstanding performance since the inception of The Family Company. Besides coming up with a better company name than 'Family Company', I don't think there's anything we could improve. Over the past few years, Robbie and I have met regularly to review the results, and I am thrilled beyond my own expectations. One of my best decisions ever—aside from marrying my epically talented and brilliant husband—was asking Robbie to manage the organization. I want to thank each of you for your accomplishments. Upon your return home, you will find a small gift to express our appreciation. Robbie, thank you for your help, and congratulations on your achievements on our behalf; you have the floor."

"Thank you, Katie, Paul, Mother Murphy, and our relatively new friend Wes, whom we have come to know as both an exceptional rancher and businessman. We also recognize and welcome General and Mrs. Green, whose family has been very successful in the diamond industry in New York City for over 100 years. Today, we will review last year's income statement, balance sheet, and projections for the upcoming year. I know that each of you has had a week to review the financial statements and balance sheet, so feel free to ask questions at any time. The one thing I believe you will come to understand is that, assuming no major setbacks, The Family Company will generate approximately $190 million in excess cash that we haven't yet found a suitable investment vehicle for. Furthermore, the company retired its last long-term debt in 1949. This is another reason why, in 1950, the company will generate such an extraordinary cash return. In 1949, the company increased its assets by approximately $180 million. Net assets rose by approximately $250 million after settling all long-term debt. Part of this growth came from selling a division that underperformed. We finished 1949 with a total net worth of $2.0 billion. We expect the company to generate excess cash at or around $190. Last year, we ended with roughly $500 million in cash and U.S. Treasury Bonds. The bonds are arranged on a 5-year ladder, meaning the longest maturity of any bond is five years. As each of you know, we have consistently achieved a 10.5% compounded increase in The Family Company's net worth throughout our relationship, while maintaining a very conservative balance sheet. One of the reasons we are meeting today is a problem we face. We are finding it increasingly difficult to find investments that meet our management quality criteria and are priced so that the company and the management team can earn a strong return. One of the new businesses we have explored, based on Katie's strong suggestion, is to offer our services to other high-net-worth families. When we first met with Wes, he expressed some dissatisfaction with how the ranches' cash was reported, used, and available on a consolidated basis. We undertook a cash management project, and I believe that we have helped the ranches to pay off their $1.0 million working capital line of credit and develop a minimum cash balance of approximately $1.4 million. Wes, thank you for letting us undertake that project."

"Robbie, thank you for your help. I am truly impressed by what your team has accomplished. All of the individual ranches have become very fond of their team. I expected many people to complain about losing control of cash, but that did not happen. The ranchers all embraced the idea of having centralized group review invoices, sales results, and ensure we were paid correctly and not overcharged. Robbie's team worked with both our lawyers and accountants. His team was able to improve their quality of work and reduce their fees. Robbie, thank you so much for everything your team has done."

"It was a pleasure working with you, Wes. It shows what we can accomplish when we collaborate and what we can offer to others. However, I'm concerned that those third parties we assist may start competing with the family business, and that would be like cutting off your nose to spite your face. Paul, what are your thoughts on this?"

"That's an interesting point, Robbie. Who are you using for your accountants and lawyers?"

"Well, it depends on the situation. For operational matters, we have an internal team of about 10 lawyers. When a major issue arises, we turn to Sullivan & Cromwell in New York. Allen Dulles's brother is the managing partner."

"Wes, who are you using?"

"We usually use a local lawyer in each ranch's hometown. When something big comes up…we shop around for a lawyer."

"Robbie, could your team handle the significant matters or oversee Sullivan & Cromwell for Wes's ranches?"

"Sure, we might need to add a lawyer or two. Wes, how many ranches, pairs of Black Angus cattle, and acres are you managing now?"

"I usually wouldn't answer that question. Out west, that's like asking a man how long his equipment is. But I'm among friends. We have 20 ranches, 8,000 pairs of Black Angus, and about 800,000 acres or 1,250 sections."

"Are all of these properties located in Idaho?"

"Yes, Robbie, they are."

"Who do you use for accountants?"

"I work with about 15 local accounting firms, Paul. They generally aren't that good. After seeing what Robbie's accounting firm, Arthur Andersen, did for us, I am considering switching our work to them."

"Mom, I am starting to wonder whether we should have Robbie's firm handle the legal and accounting work or if we should combine our operations with Katie's. It seems that, technically, I own 50% of her business and she owns 50% of mine. We are all managing it for the benefit of our children, your two grandchildren. The Family Company is having trouble finding businesses to invest in; they love you and Wes and have over $100 million to invest each year. If the combined company invests, say, $20 million next year, the ranches could see significant growth. That was a bit disjointed, Mom, but what do you think?"

"I'd like to hear what Wes thinks first. Wes, you've been managing the ranches for over 20 years. This is a pretty major move. What do you think?

"Well, okay. I do think it's a great idea. That said, everything depends on how it's managed. People might think that the business is run by a group of 'financial animals' who don't understand ranching or the Mountain West. If we proceed carefully with the existing ranches and acquisitions it should work great. The 'home office' folks need to show genuine care and respect for the ranchers. If they ask questions and review the proposals with the ranch managers before making changes, we could just hit a home run. Building relationships will be the key. Robbie's team has been fantastic on these kinds of issues so far right Mrs. M?

"I couldn't agree more with your assessment, Wes. I also want to see written due diligence procedures in place before we make any purchases. Some of the ranches will be operated by untrustworthy or financially incompetent individuals. I don't want to bite into what we think is a beautiful beef steak and find out it's dog meat. Additionally, I would like Wes to be responsible for making decisions, unless you two disagree on any issue. If that happens, I'd like you to bring the decision to Paul, Katie, and me. Robbie, does that work?"

"That's just good corporate governance, Mom. I agree. I believe the next step should be to create a term sheet that outlines the equity participation for the new company. Robbie can take care of that. We also need a name for the new company. I have two proposals. We have ensured that the brands are clear in Idaho, Wyoming, Montana, and all neighboring states. If you don't like these names or brands, just let us know. The first is Lone Wolf.

LONE WOLF RANCH

The Lone Wolf cattle brand features an "L" with a stylized wolf head symbol (A) that represents both the wolf and the mountain wilderness.

LA

The second option is Thunder Basin Ranches."

"Whoa. Wait a second." Wes took to his feet with a smile on his face. I worked in Australia for over 10 years. 'Thunder Basin,' although fabulous, is reminiscent of an Australian outhouse. They call it a "thunder box," but Thunder Basin is close enough."

The room exploded with laughter and brought levity to a very serious meeting. Once they regained composure, Paul continued with his third branding option.

"Well, thank you, Wes. You might have saved us from an embarrassing branding mistake there. We do have a third option that—considering option two is pretty much down the toilet, so to speak—may I suggest Sky Rider?"

Once again, the room erupted in laughter.

Katie's eyes lit up. "I like the third option very much, but what do you all think of Sky Rider Ranches? Allen took the floor.

"Oh, I like that. Especially with the family's history of flying and the big sky nature of the land that houses the ranches, it sits well."

"Yes, I like it too." Ben started to scribble in pencil on his notepad. "The brand could be wings with the initials; here is a rough idea."

Ben finished sketching out the brand concept and passed it around.

Paul and Katie immediately loved both rough logos and the one brand. Paul wanted to make sure it was equally accepted by all.

"Mom, what do you think? After all, it's a continuation of what Dad and you created."

"Paul. It's a mix of what Dad and I built, plus what Katie's parents started. The sky favors the bold. I like it a lot."

"I kind of liked the name Lone Wolf." Katie was deep in thought. "It reminds me of Paul somehow, but this is about doing things together, not alone. I think Sky Rider is perfect. Let's fly!"

"Ok. Sky Rider it is. We need a clean corporate structure and a light board. The politics will matter—we must remain tight and agile.

Robbie stayed in the room with Wes and all the owners for discussion on the finer details. Katie began proceedings to get the political strategy clear.

"Folks, the first thing I want to confirm is that there will be no notes from this or any other meetings on this subject. I know that none of you ever records any meeting due to the sensitive nature of some of the topics, but I wanted it tabled so it's official. With that understanding, assuming we succeed in acquiring considerable property in both Montana and Wyoming, our political influence on a national level will become significant. We already have strong relationships with the Senators from New York and California, as well as with those from Idaho thanks to the Murphy cattle empire, now Sky Rider. With the new acquisitions, I believe that we will develop strong relationships with both Senators from Montana and Wyoming. That would give us meaningful representation in ten Senate seats. It would ensure we are heard—clearly—on matters that affect the land, capital, and industry of this country."

"Yes, Katie, our New York lawyers—or is it animals?—have an extensive (and expensive) political compliance division. I will find us a point person and provide each of you with their contact information. Finally, I will prepare an equity term sheet and a valuation of each of the businesses. Once the documentation is ready, each of you should have your own lawyers' review. Wes, if you'd like some help finding a lawyer for this, I have some suggestions for some guys in Salt Lake City and Denver you could interview."

"Thanks, Robbie, but that won't be necessary. I already have someone who has helped me with these issues. He's pretty good."

"Alright then. Well, that brings us to the end of the first joint meeting of Sky Rider Ranches and The Family Company. As a final item, do we think we can do better than the name Family Company? On one hand, I feel like the entire empire could be named Sky Rider, but on the other hand, a degree of anonymity is called for. Katie, any thoughts?"

"Thank you, Robbie. As I mentioned, a name is a name, but I think it should be humble and reverent. Something that denotes that great wealth comes with gratitude and responsibility. Maybe we could explore something in Latin, Paul?"

"Well, my Latin is somewhat limited to begin with, and certainly rusty, but one phrase comes to mind that always stuck with me. Deo Adjuvante. It means, 'with the help of God' or 'God Aided.'"

"Wow. That's powerful, Paul. Deo Adjuvante. What does everyone think?"

A quiet, reverent applause welled through the room, and everyone added their agreement. Robbie took to his feet to officially close the meeting.

"Well, it would seem we have a new name for The Family Company. Deo Adjuvante Corporation. I'll get the legalities started immediately. And with that, I declare the first meeting of Deo Adjuvante Corporation adjourned. Thank you all."

CHAPTER TWENTY—OFFUTT AIR FORCE BASE

Paul and Ben's first months at Offutt Air Force Base were anything but quiet. General Curtis LeMay had inherited a Strategic Air Command that he believed had grown complacent, and he intended to change that immediately.

At the time, SAC's bomber force was a strange mixture of old and new. The aging B-29 Superfortress still formed the backbone of the command, even though it had carried the United States through the final years of the Second World War. Alongside it were the enormous B-36 Peacemakers—piston-driven giants designed for intercontinental missions—and the new B-47 Stratojets, sleek and promising but still plagued by developmental problems.

Neither Paul nor Ben believed that this patchwork fleet represented the future.

LeMay wanted something different: a bomber that could strike anywhere in the world without relying on foreign bases. Something fast, high-flying, and capable of delivering the nuclear weapons that now defined American strategy.

That challenge landed squarely on the desks of officers like Green and Murphy.

A large part of their assignment at Offutt was to help develop the operational requirements for the next generation of strategic bomber. Working with Air Force Materiel Command, subordinate SAC units, and Boeing engineers, they began constructing what was essentially a blueprint for the aircraft the United States would need in the nuclear age.

The early requirements were ambitious.

The new bomber would have to operate independently of overseas bases, flying intercontinental missions directly from the United States. It would require a large crew capable of sustaining extremely long flights, including relief personnel for missions that could last more than a day. The aircraft would need to cruise at high altitude—above thirty-four thousand feet—and maintain a range measured not in hundreds but in thousands of miles.

Speed was equally important. Strategic planners wanted an aircraft capable of cruising at roughly four hundred miles per hour, faster than any piston-driven bomber then in service. It also needed to carry a heavy payload of nuclear weapons while remaining capable of operating in all weather conditions.

Over time those early ideas evolved into a more concrete design.

Boeing's proposal eventually became known as the Model 464-49. The aircraft would feature swept wings—similar to the revolutionary B-47 design—and eight jet engines mounted in four pods beneath the wings. Engineers proposed an unusual bicycle landing gear system, supported by small outrigger wheels near the wingtips, which allowed the thin swept wings to remain structurally efficient. The main landing gear could even pivot slightly off center to allow the aircraft to land safely in strong crosswinds.

There were still problems. Early jet engines consumed enormous amounts of fuel, which threatened the range the Air Force demanded. LeMay was unwilling to compromise.

Between 1949 and 1951, he personally pushed Boeing to enlarge the design into a bigger aircraft—what became the Model 464-67—to ensure the bomber could reach intercontinental targets. He also insisted on a practical cockpit layout, replacing the tandem seating arrangement used in the B-47 with a side-by-side configuration. LeMay believed that two pilots working shoulder to shoulder would operate more effectively during the exhausting missions SAC envisioned.

For officers like Green and Murphy, translating these strategic ideas into operational requirements was exhausting work. They often spent more than sixteen hours a day in meetings, drafting documents, comparing performance estimates, and negotiating with engineers who had to turn theory into metal.

Their mandate was clear: define the aircraft that Strategic Air Command would rely on for decades.

The requirements they finalized described a bomber capable of flying thousands of miles without refueling, carrying nuclear weapons at high altitude and high speed, and operating in any weather conditions. It would use jet propulsion, swept wings, advanced navigation and bombing systems, and eventually aerial refueling to extend its already formidable range.

If the design succeeded, the aircraft would become the backbone of

America's strategic deterrent.

And in time, the world would come to know it as the B-52.

CHAPTER TWENTY-ONE—THE KOREAN WAR

The demands of Ben's and Paul's positions increased dramatically on June 25, 1950, when North Korean forces crossed the 38th Parallel and the Korean War began.

Most of Washington immediately focused on the tactical disaster unfolding on the peninsula—retreating armies, collapsing defenses, and the desperate struggle to hold the Pusan perimeter. Strategic Air Command, however, had to think differently.

Generals Curtis LeMay and Hoyt Vandenberg were not merely concerned with Korea. Their responsibility was ensuring that the United States possessed the strategic air power necessary to deter a much larger war.

Ben and Paul had become deeply involved in that effort. The primary mission requirements and strategic specifications for the B-52 had already been drafted, but publishing the requirements was only the beginning. The real work lay in turning those requirements into an aircraft capable of meeting them.

Early in their assignment at SAC, Ben and Paul had decided to share an office to speed communication. Each technically had his own office suite, complete with aides and secretaries, but they rarely used them. Instead, they worked side by side at a large partner's desk in a joint workspace.

The arrangement puzzled many officers at Offutt. Two young generals sharing a workspace like junior staff officers seemed unusual. But no one questioned the pair who had the confidence of General LeMay

They were debating the selection of a subcontractor when the scrambler phone on Paul's desk rang

It was an AN/GSQ-3 "Junior X" secure line, one of only ten such phones in all of Strategic Air Command.

Paul lifted the receiver.

"Headquarters Strategic Air Command, Directorate of Plans and Operations. Brigadier General Paul Murphy speaking. This line is currently unsecured. How may I assist you, sir?"

"Paul, this is General Hoyt Vandenberg."

Paul straightened.

"Sir."

"I believe you're sitting next to a phone that can go secure."

"Yes, sir."

"Let's engage it."

Paul flipped the switch.

"Sir, my line indicates secure."

"Mine as well."

There was a brief pause.

"Paul," Vandenberg said, "have you ever received a direct call from the Chief of Staff before?"

Paul allowed himself a small smile.

"Yes, sir. Usually after speaking with a secretary, then a deputy, and waiting about twenty minutes."

Vandenberg chuckled.

"Well, today we're skipping the bureaucracy."

His tone hardened.

"I have a complete mess in Korea. The Air Force is on trial there, and leadership is going to decide whether we succeed or fail."

Paul said nothing.

"I need someone who understands both tactics and strategy," Vandenberg continued. "Someone who isn't afraid to ignore peacetime procedures when the mission demands it."

Another pause.

"I once heard about a young lieutenant colonel who told a major general: 'Sir, I know my mission, I know my authority, I understand the classification of this operation—and you are not cleared for any of it.'"

Paul winced.

"And then," Vandenberg said, "that lieutenant colonel had the general arrested."

Paul sighed.

"Yes, sir. I remember the incident."

"Well Paul," Vandenberg replied, "that lieutenant colonel was you."

Ben leaned back in his chair.

"I need you in Korea," Vandenberg continued. "You'll technically report to Fifth Air Force, but I want a direct report from you every week. If anyone interferes with your mission, inform them you are operating under my authority."

"Yes, sir."

"You leave today."

Paul blinked once.

"Yes, sir."

"I want you in the Pusan area tomorrow."

Another pause.

"You're a triple ace in the P-51. Are you current in the F-86?"

"Yes, sir."

"Good. Requisition one immediately and fly it to Korea."

"Yes, sir."

"Who are you taking with you?"

"Sir, if he's available, I'd like Major Paul Payton."

"Why Payton?"

"He solves problems."

Vandenberg laughed.

"That's the right answer."

"Anyone else?"

"Yes, sir. Chief Master Sergeant Jones."

"Done."

Paul hesitated.

"Sir… I'd also like General Green assigned if possible."

"Not this time," Vandenberg replied. "I need him exactly where he is. You may take him as an observer for one week from Japan."

"Yes, sir."

The line went silent.

"Paul," Vandenberg added, "pack your B-4 bag and helmet bag. If anything gets in your way, call me."

Click. The line went dead. Ben stared at him.

"Was that the Chief of Staff?"

"Yes."

"You're going to Korea today?"

"Yes."

"Does LeMay know?"

"Not yet."

"Does Katie know?"

"Not yet."

Ben stood slowly.

"Where are you going to get an F-86?"

Paul shrugged.

"I'm going to borrow one."

Offutt Flight Line

Ben walked to the tower while Paul packed. At that moment four F-86 Sabres taxied in from a training sortie. A lieutenant colonel climbed out of the lead aircraft. Paul approached him.

"How are the aircraft?"

"Brand new," the officer spouted proudly. "Perfect condition."

Paul nodded.

"Excellent."

Minutes later he walked into Base Operations, displayed his general officer identification, and impounded two of the aircraft.

The master sergeant behind the desk blinked.

"Sir… impounded?"

"Vandenberg Operational Command Order," Paul announced calmly. "You can verify with the Chief of Staff if necessary."

Within the hour the base commander arrived.

"General Murphy," the master sergeant boomed angrily. "You cannot simply take my aircraft."

"There's a war in Korea," Paul replied calmly. "The Chief of Staff has ordered me to Korea immediately. I'm taking them."

The Provost Marshal arrived moments later with several MPs. After a tense exchange the truth became clear. Murphy had direct authority from the Chief of Staff of the United States Air Force. The base commander stepped aside.

Flight Planning

Lieutenant Colonel William Philbrick, commander of the 336th Fighter Interceptor Squadron, joined them.

"General," he said, "my squadron already prepared a ferry plan for deployment."

He spread the chart across the table.

"Offutt to Eielson Air Force Base in Alaska. Then Misawa Air Base in Japan. From there to Taegu in Korea."

"The total distance," Philbrick continued, "is approximately 6,390 miles."

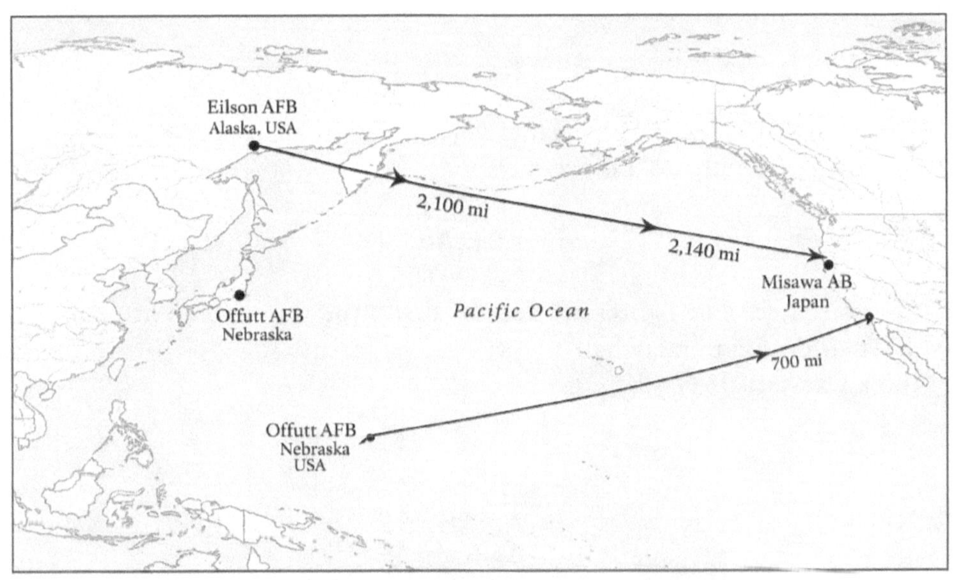

Ferry route flown by Generals Murphy and Green from Offutt Air Force Base to the Korean theater, June 1950.

Murphy studied the route.

"That's a long way in a fighter."

"Yes, sir."

Murphy nodded.

"Boots," he said, reading the call sign on Philbrick's jacket. "Get us a weather briefing."

"Severe clear for seventy-two hours, sir."

Murphy grinned.

"Ben," he said, "are you ready?"

Ben pulled on his helmet.

"Ready."

Departure

The two Sabres rolled onto the runway.

"Offutt Tower," Murphy called. "Flight of two F-86s ready for departure. Direct Eielson."

"Flight of two cleared for takeoff."

The engines roared. The Sabres accelerated down the runway and lifted into the sky. Their destination lay half a world away.
And a war had already begun.

CHAPTER TWENTY-TWO—THE MERGER

"Katie, we've completed the appraisals and the relative valuation model. They were shipped to you overnight. Would you like to discuss them, and if so, should anyone else join us?"

"Thanks, Robbie. Paul isn't available. He's flown to Korea and has taken command of all U.S. fighter and fighter-bomber operations there. We should probably include Mrs. Murphy and Wes in the discussion. Do you have any idea when we could arrange that?"

"I think we could meet later this week in Driggs, Idaho," Robbie replied. "I can pick you up in the Connie and fly there nonstop. Let me call Mrs. Murphy and see if she and Wes are available. We kept the model fairly simple. I'll also send them the Deo Adjuvante Corporation audit. Are you comfortable with that?"

"Of course, Robbie. Send them everything you would want to see if the positions were reversed."

Robbie hesitated.

"Oh, and Katie... when the accounting team was auditing the ranch business, they noticed a few minor discrepancies."

"What sort of discrepancies?"

"Just a few invoices that appear to have funneled payments to an unfamiliar corporation. It may be nothing, but the auditors flagged it for further review."

Katie paused.

"Alright. I'll leave that to you."

Robbie gathered the reports and attached a short note.

Katie, Wes, and Mrs. Murphy,
Enclosed are several documents summarizing the activities of Deo Adjuvante Corporation, including a detailed income statement and balance sheet. I have also included a proposed equity allocation table for discussion.

These materials are intended only as a starting point for our meeting.

I look forward to seeing you on Friday.

Sincerely,
Robert A. Johnson
CEO
The Management Company, Inc.

Wes wandered into the ranch house and sat down heavily at the kitchen table. Mrs. Murphy entered a moment later and found him staring at the documents spread across the table.

"Good evening, Wes. Are you alright? You look like you're carrying the weight of the world."

"Hey, Mrs. M. I'm fine. I've just been reading through these reports. It's a lot to take in."

She sat across from him.

"Tell me something," Wes continued. "Do you think Paul had any idea about Katie's wealth when they got married? What was he—eighteen? Nineteen?"

Mrs. Murphy shook her head.

"No, I don't believe he had the slightest idea. They were young and in love. If anything, I suspect the wealth might have frightened him away."

She gestured toward the papers.

"It really is remarkable what Robbie has accomplished. Last year alone they cleared more than two hundred million dollars. And they're sitting on over a billion dollars in cash."

Wes let out a low whistle.

"That's an unbelievable amount of money."

He leaned back in his chair.

"So much so that I think Katie may be being overly generous. Their operation earns fifty times what we do. We run a fine ranch business—but we're not even in the same league."

Mrs. Murphy smiled.

"Katie and Paul already own half of everything the other has. So in many ways, this is a fait accompli."

"A what?" Wes asked.

"A French legal phrase. It simply means the outcome is already decided."

She tapped the documents.

"This new structure simply formalizes everything—and gives us room to grow."

She paused thoughtfully.

"I do have one concern, however. I believe we should also take care of you. I've been thinking about issuing you shares so that a percentage of the ranch income is distributed to you."

Wes shook his head.

"Mrs. M, you've always been generous. You pay me well, and that's more than enough."

"We'll see about that," a faint smile creeping slowly across her face.

"I also think Katie is being overly generous to me," she continued. "But in the end her children will inherit everything—both her family's holdings and mine. When you look at it that way, the precise terms of this agreement hardly matter."

"What do you think?" she asked.

Wes shrugged.

"To be honest, I think we could simply agree and skip the meeting. There's a mountain of paperwork ahead, and we want everything finished before the end of the year."

He leaned forward, his eyes lighting slightly.

"I'd rather get back to buying ranches in Montana and Wyoming."

"Quietly, of course."

Mrs. Murphy shook her head.

"No. We should still have the meeting."

"Why?"

"Integration."

Wes looked confused.

"Integration? What does this have to do with Black folks or Indians?"

Mrs. Murphy stared at him for a moment.

"Business integration, you nitwit," she quipped dryly. "Lawyers. Accountants. Financial systems. You can't imagine the work involved in merging operations of this size—especially if we want to keep everything quiet."

Wes grinned.

"Mrs. M, I was joking."

She sighed.

"You know me, Wes. Humor has never been my strong suit."

CHAPTER TWENTY-THREE—DAEGU AIR BASE

Korea—August 15, 1950

Paul and Ben reached Misawa Air Base, Japan, after a grueling ferry flight spread over two days and more than fourteen hours of stick time. The weather had not been "severe clear." They skirted thunderstorms whose tops climbed past fifty thousand feet, riding the edges of violent air that wanted to throw the Sabres off their wings. By the time they reached Misawa, conditions had deteriorated into solid instrument weather. They broke out low—one hundred percent overcast, a ceiling barely a hundred feet, and visibility reduced to three-quarters of a mile. It was the kind of arrival that took more out of a pilot than a dogfight, because there was no adrenaline to borrow against the fatigue.

They slept a few hours at Misawa, then launched at first light for Korea.

> "Taegu Tower, this is a flight of two F-86s. We're two brigadier generals, call sign Minsch, requesting landing instructions."

> "Minsch, Taegu Tower. Runway three-one left available, two thousand five hundred meters. Altimeter two-niner-

niner-two. Ceiling one thousand five hundred, runway visual range two thousand meters. You are cleared to land."

Paul glanced at Ben through the canopy. "You wanted to observe. Well—you got it. Look at the damage."

Ben's voice came tight. "Are they expecting us?"

"No. But there's the follow-me truck. Let's get the aircraft secured. And tonight it's non-alcoholic beer—this field was evacuated on August fifth. The engineers only just finished the runway we landed on. We're wheels-up at oh-four-hundred back to Japan."

"Fair enough."

They rolled to a stop amid the harsh geometry of a war zone: cratered earth, sandbagged revetments, scorched patches where fuel had burned, and the blunt improvisation of men building an air base in the path of an advancing army. A young captain jogged up, breathless.

"General—sir—we weren't expecting you. Where did you fly in from?"

Paul smiled without warmth. "Shangri-La."

The captain blinked, unsure whether he'd missed a memo. "Sir… we're scrambling to find housing. Also—are these your personal aircraft? We don't have trained crew chiefs for F-86s on station."

"No problem. Secure them for now. My crew chief is meeting us in Japan. But first—where's the COMMCEN?"

"The—sir?"

"The communications center. I have a message to send. And I need a message pad."

The captain produced one. Paul wrote fast, tore the page clean, and handed it back.

Z:151600K AUG 50. CDR, FIGHTER FORCES, KOREA AOR. GENERAL HOYT S. VANDENBERG, CHIEF OF STAFF. ARRIVED TAEGU (K-2), KOREA. END.

The captain read it, then looked up as if he'd just realized what he was holding.

"Sir… we can't send FLASH traffic without the COMMCEN commander's approval. He isn't here."

Paul's gaze sharpened. "Then find whoever is acting for him."

"Sir—the order was approved by the air base chief of staff, Colonel Johnson."

Paul nodded once, the kind of nod that meant the conversation had ended. "Captain, go get that REMF out of wherever he is and have him report to me within fifteen minutes. That is a direct order."

"Yes, sir."

Two minutes later a colonel appeared as if he'd been launched out of a cannon.

"Sir—Colonel John Duffy, Chief of Staff, forward detachment, reporting as ordered."

Paul did not invite him to sit. "Colonel Duffy, when I sign a message marked FLASH, does it require your signature to be treated as FLASH?"

"Sir, it's not quite that simple—"

Paul cut him off. "Yes or no. And don't make me call the Chief of Staff over this."

Duffy's jaw worked. "Yes, sir."

"Good! Then have the COMMCEN send it FLASH now."

Duffy hesitated. "General… one more thing."

Paul looked at him.

"We have a unit about five miles from here—Marines. They're in extremis. They're close to being overrun. We can provide fuel and ordnance, but we have no aircraft on strip alert. Your two Sabres are the only aviation assets we have right now. Would you and General Green consider flying close air support before you return to Japan? Sir, I know what I'm asking."

Paul's expression went flat. "You don't have a single aircraft on ramp alert at Taegu?"

"No, sir."

Paul exhaled once. "Then someone made a decision that may get this airfield taken. Load and arm my aircraft."

He turned to Ben. "You probably should not fly this mission."

Ben's reply was immediate. "Bullshit. I'm flying. I need the airtime on this equipment."

Paul held his gaze for half a second, then nodded. "Fine. Load both aircraft. Button one—controller frequency. Button two—Johnson for recovery. Nav two—approach setup for Johnson."

"Sir," an NCO said, stepping in, "correction—no FAC airborne. We have a Tactical Air Control Party with the Marines."

Paul's eyes narrowed. "Call sign?"

"Bulldog Control," the NCO replied officiously. "Frequency is loaded on button one. Ordnance—two five-hundred-pound general-purpose bombs and full .50-caliber ammunition per aircraft."

Paul looked at Ben. "Pack your gear, grab the map, and let's plan the runs."

They were airborne again within minutes.

USAF—5th AF MISSION REPORT (SUMMARY)

DATE: 15 AUG 1950
TIME: 1110–1245 KST
AIRCRAFT: F-86A
CALL SIGN: VICTOR FLIGHT
CREW:
>Victor 6 (Flight Lead): BG Paul Murphy
>Victor A: BG Benjamin Green

MISSION:
>Close Air Support (CAS)

LOCATION:
>Vicinity of Hill 303 / Taegu approaches

CONTROLLER: TACP
>"Bulldog Control"

SITUATION:
>Marine elements under heavy attack; position threatened; airfield risk elevated due to proximity of enemy forces and lack of local air assets.

EXECUTION:
>Victor Flight established contact with Bulldog Control, received target description (bunkers/trench line and troops on reverse slope), conducted two low-level attack runs with 500-pound bombs and sustained .50-caliber strafing to suppress enemy movement and neutralize key positions.

RESULTS:
>Enemy positions suppressed; mortar fire ceased; Marine elements reported ability to counterattack and stabilize the line.

EXPENDITURE:
> 4x 500-lb bombs total; approximately 1,500 rounds .50 cal total.

DAMAGE:
> None reported to friendly aircraft in-flight; post-flight inspection revealed extensive AAA impacts.

REMARKS:
> Controller coordination effective; mission executed under heavy ground fire; contributed directly to stabilization of threatened position.

The letter arrived like a grenade in a plain envelope. Ben was the one who saw it first.

> "Paul," he said, voice rising. "Oh hell—look what came in the mail."

Paul read the header, then the first paragraph, and his face tightened into something that looked almost like pain.

> "The Marines recommended both of us, Paul."

> Paul exhaled. "We were doing what any aviator should do."

> Ben's mouth twisted. "The problem is—someone is going to treat it like we were trying to be heroes."

Paul's thoughts snapped briefly into focus, sharp and cold. I might still be an LTC, he thought. Did I ever even finalize discharge paperwork? How many recalled officers have I met who didn't know they still held a reserve commission?

> Ben glanced up. "Did any generals get the Medal of Honor in World War II? Because that may be the only argument that keeps this from turning into a political circus."

> Paul stared at the letter again. "We have two defenses."

> "Go on."

"First—what else should we have done? Ignore the request and let Marines die? Let Taegu fall? Potentially lose the last viable lodgment on the peninsula?"

Ben nodded slowly.

"Second," Paul continued, "what example would that have set for my command? If we refused, everyone would have known. Every pilot. Every squadron. That would poison the culture before it even formed."

Ben's expression hardened. "And the third defense?"

Paul's mouth tightened. "Ariel and Katie."

Ben almost smiled. "You're forgetting one thing."

"What?"

"Even if the Pentagon doesn't kill us, Ariel and Katie just might."

Paul snorted. "Not wrong."

At that moment Command Chief Master Sergeant Jones entered the office.

"General, VIP call. Headquarters."

Paul took the receiver. The voice on the other end was furious.

"General Murphy—what in the goddamn hell were you thinking? I sent you there to organize fighters and fighter-bombers. I did not send you there to get yourself—and a visiting flag officer—killed. Every staff officer in the Pentagon is reading a Marine general's recommendation letter and deciding you're a loose cannon."

Paul let him finish. Then he spoke, calm and controlled.

"Sir, what else should we have done? We were the only air assets available. Marines were close to being overrun. The airfield was at risk. Declining that request would have been an indefensible command decision. I did not ask for any recommendation. I do not want the medal. I will not accept it."

"You put your command at risk by flying a mission that wasn't yours to fly."

"Sir, you selected me because I don't confuse peacetime procedure with wartime necessity. That was a battlefield decision. A simple one."

The voice snapped back, hotter. "You're playing a game where you don't know the rules."

Paul's tone sharpened. "Then we should continue this conversation on a secure line, sir."

A pause.

"You little prick."

Click. Ben watched Paul lower the receiver.

"I see that went well."

Paul didn't look up. "About as well as I expected."

He turned to Jones. "Get me Katherine on my encrypted personal line. She'll be at Victor."

"Yes, sir."

A beat later: "Sir—Mrs. Murphy is on the red phone."

Paul took the call.

"Darling," he said, voice instantly softer, "I'm sorry to bother you, but I need you to start making calls. A Marine commander has recommended Ben and me for the Medal of Honor. Headquarters is furious."

Katie's voice came back sharp and steady. "What did you do?"

"What any officer should do. Nothing more."

"And you didn't ask for this?"

"No. I don't want it. I won't accept it."

"Then we handle it. Try to stay out of trouble for five minutes, darling."

Paul exhaled. "Doing my best."

"I love you."

"I love you too."

The Next Morning's News

August 20, 1950—AP, Pusan, Korea

COMMANDER OF U.S. MARINE FORCES RECOMMENDS YOUNG AIR FORCE GENERAL FOR MEDAL OF HONOR

According to the recommendation, Brigadier General Paul Murphy was cited for conspicuous gallantry and intrepidity at the risk of life above and beyond the call of duty while engaged in combat against enemy forces near Hill 303, in the vicinity of Taegu (K-2) Air Base, Korea.

When questioned, President Truman remarked, "Where do we find men like this?"

Ben read the clipping twice, then looked at Paul.

"You can breathe now. Katie and Ariel are amazing."

Paul's mouth twitched. "Yes."

Ben folded the paper neatly. "And now that they've covered your ass—there will be hell to pay."

Paul looked up at him. "I know."

Outside, the airfield was already coming alive again, and the war did not care what the newspapers said.

CHAPTER TWENTY-FOUR—A CRACK IN THE ARMOUR

Gerald Forsyth, CPA
Business Office
Driggs, Idaho

Robbie, Katie, Mrs. Murphy, and a small group from both organizations gathered in Driggs ahead of the formal merger meeting. They convened in the business office of the ranch accounting firm—soon to be replaced—owned by its chief CPA, Gerald Forsyth. The conference room smelled faintly of coffee, paper, and old ledgers, the kind of place built to make numbers feel permanent. Mrs. Murphy stood at the head of the table as people settled into their seats.

"Robbie, welcome to Driggs. I don't believe I've formally introduced you to the ranch management team. Folks, this is Robert A. Johnson—Robbie—CPA and CEO of Katie's company since its founding. He has a personality unlike most accountants."

"Robbie, would you please introduce your senior officers and their roles?"

Robbie nodded, as if he were taking the floor in a boardroom instead of a ranch valley.

"Yes, certainly, Mrs. Murphy. This is Robert Varn, CFA—Chief Financial Officer and Chief Investment Officer."

"And this is Charles R. Pickering, Esq.—General Counsel and Chief Operating Officer."

He paused, then smiled politely. "That's enough for now."

Mrs. Murphy turned slightly, her tone becoming more procedural.

"Before we begin the general meeting, we need thirty minutes for a smaller group to review one matter. Robbie, Katie, Mr. Forsyth, Mr. Varn, and Mr. Pickering—please join me. I expect it will take thirty to forty-five minutes. I appreciate everyone's patience."

The larger group remained outside. Inside, the smaller group closed the door. Robbie placed a thin folder on the table and opened it with deliberate calm.

"Mr. Forsyth, I have a few questions before the official hand-off to the New York office."

"Yes, of course, Mr. Johnson. I'm all ears."

"During our audit, we noticed payments made against invoices from a consulting firm called Nymbol Consulting. What can you tell me about those invoices?"

Forsyth cleared his throat. "Nymbol has offered services since Wes joined the ranch operation. Wes trusted them. They provided consulting to ranch managers."

Robbie's expression didn't change. "That's what I expected you would say. We investigated ownership and the nature of the services."

He slid a page forward. "Nymbol Consulting is owned through an offshore corporation registered in Saint Lucia.

Locals there jokingly refer to the entity as a vehicle for 'bogus outstanding liabilities.' Internally, we call it BOL."

Forsyth blinked. "I—I didn't know that."

Robbie continued, not raising his voice. "We did more digging. The beneficial owner is Wes Bowen."

Mrs. Murphy's face drained of color so subtly that, for a moment, it looked like the light in the room had changed. Robbie's tone remained careful, as if he were reading facts in court.

"There's one more piece. Murphy Ranch Company has been billing Nymbol for consulting services. The amounts billed back to Nymbol are approaching half of what the ranch paid out to Nymbol in earlier years. Also, the external billing from BOL to the ranch stopped nearly eight years ago."

He looked directly at Forsyth. "If this repayment pattern continues, the ranch will effectively be reimbursed for the full amount within roughly two years."

Robbie let the numbers sit. "Mr. Forsyth—do you understand these transactions?"

Forsyth slumped back in his chair. For the first time, his voice sounded less like a professional and more like a man defending twenty years of work.

"The way I see it, Wes is a good man. When he came here, he came from a rough background. He didn't trust people. Over time he matured. He learned how honest you are—how honest Mrs. Murphy and Paul are. I think guilt got to him."

He swallowed. "I think this is a crisis of conscience. He tried to fix what he did without embarrassing anyone—repaying it quietly. If your firm hadn't audited this, he might have repaid it entirely without anyone knowing."

Mrs. Murphy stared at the table, hearing the words but trying to make them fit the Wes she had known—Wes who worked before dawn, who could calm a frightened horse, who knew every man on every ranch by name. She also knew one other thing, equally true: Forsyth should have questioned the invoices years ago. The fact pattern didn't add up—fake consulting fees going out, "repayment consulting fees" coming back. That was not clean accounting. That was improvisation.

She lifted her eyes.

"So, Robbie—what does this mean? In plain terms."

Robbie answered gently, but without any softening of substance.

"It means Wes controlled the consulting entities that billed the ranch for services that do not appear to be real."

He held up a hand, anticipating the obvious objection. "Yes—Wes has provided tremendous value. But the billing structure itself was concealed."

He nodded once. "Then, later, he appears to have initiated a quiet repayment through invoices flowing the other way, likely to undo what he did without confessing it."

He met her gaze. "Whatever his motivation, the original activity is hard to explain—especially now, when the merger will put everything under a brighter light."

Mrs. Murphy's mouth tightened. "He has repaid most of it."

"Yes," Robbie agreed. "And that does reflect something. But we have to make decisions as if a third party will discover everything—because eventually, someone always does."

Mrs. Murphy sat very still for a moment, then spoke with honest conflict.

"This is disappointing. And yet—he built our operations into something extraordinary. I'm not sure the ranch would be what it is without him."

She exhaled. "If he stopped years ago, and he's repaid what he took… I don't know how to balance justice and gratitude."

Robbie nodded. "Here's the balance I recommend."

He spoke clearly, as if laying down a policy that would survive the next decade. "Wes should not receive equity in Deo Adjuvante Corporation or any subsidiary, including the ranches. That creates reputational risk we cannot defend."

He continued, carefully. "However, I agree we should retain him. He is essential operationally, and we do not have a replacement ready."

Robbie looked to Katie. "Katie—how do you feel, hearing these facts?"

Katie leaned forward, eyes steady. "I hear what you're saying. He's worth the money—so forgiveness may be the price of keeping him and protecting the business."

She glanced toward Mrs. Murphy. "If we can handle this cleanly, I'm comfortable doing so."

Robbie nodded once. "I can present an offer non-confrontationally. We keep this contained. We protect Wes's dignity, and we protect the company."

He closed the folder. "Let's handle it now. Mr. Forsyth—please ask Wes to join us."

Forsyth called his receptionist. Robbie rose, and when the door opened a few minutes later, Wes stepped into the room with the easy confidence of a man who believed he belonged there.

"Come in, Wes," Robbie welcomed Wes warmly, as if nothing unusual had happened. "Good to see you. Please take a seat."

He looked to Mrs. Murphy. "Would you like to start?"

Mrs. Murphy's voice softened, the way it did when she was trying to preserve a relationship without surrendering truth.

"Yes. Wes, as I've told you, I wanted you to become a shareholder of Deo Adjuvante Corporation—so you're officially and appropriately rewarded for all you've done."

She turned slightly to Robbie. "Robbie—would you take it from here?"

Robbie kept his tone respectful.

"Yes. Wes—Mrs. Murphy's desire to grant equity speaks to how much you've meant to this operation. But during due diligence we discovered that you own Nymbol Consulting, that Murphy Ranches paid a substantial amount to that firm without disclosure of your ownership, and that those amounts appear to have been quietly repaid over time."

He paused. "If that history became public, it could create the appearance of a scandal even if your intent later was to make it right."

Robbie held Wes's eyes. "So—no equity. But we do want you to earn significant money through compensation. We want you to stay. We want your incentives aligned with performance. And we want a structure that is simple to explain."

Wes sat frozen. The room went quiet in a way that made even paper feel loud. When he finally spoke, his voice came out smaller than expected.

"Mrs. Murphy… you knew about my shell company?"

Mrs. Murphy did not flinch.

"I knew there were consulting invoices, Wes. I did not know you owned the company that sent them."

She leaned forward, her tone controlled. "But I do know your value. And I do know you've tried to repair the harm without making a spectacle."

She let that settle. "Your salary will remain. And you will have a path to earn far more—properly."

Wes lowered his head. Tears gathered, not dramatic—just real. He held his hat in his hands like a man in church.

"I am overwhelmed. I tried to fix it completely. I just… didn't have enough time."

He swallowed. "Your grace is more than I deserve. Mrs. Murphy—I will owe you forever."

"That's alright, dear. We all need help, sooner or later."

Robbie stood and addressed Forsyth with polite finality.

"Mr. Forsyth, thank you. We won't need you for the remainder of this discussion. Would you give us the room?"

Forsyth rose quickly, grateful to leave. He had lost a client, but not his reputation—at least not today.

The door closed. Robbie returned to the table and shifted the conversation into numbers—the place he could make clean what life had made messy.

"Wes, as you know, The Management Company does not own the underlying businesses. We are compensated for oversight and performance."

He kept it simple. "The management fee structure is twenty percent of returns above an eight percent hurdle. For 1949, we've already collected fifty million dollars in addition to salaries, bonuses, and expenses. We're awaiting the final audit for the remainder."

Wes blinked, genuinely stunned.

"Jesus," he muttered under his breath.

Robbie allowed the smallest smile. "That's a reasonable reaction."

He then returned to the point. "Because of the historic consulting arrangement, we need a compensation plan for you that no outside party could misinterpret."

He held up one finger. "Option one: we stop all Nymbol billing permanently, execute releases covering past matters, and we compensate you through a transparent performance arrangement."

He held up a second finger. "Option two: a larger catch-up payment plus a continuing share of ranch earnings."

Robbie slid two pages forward.

"Option one is this: your salary, bonus, vehicles, and expenses as usual, plus three percent of the Management Company's twenty-percent profit split above the eight-percent hurdle."

He tapped the paper. "Based on last year, that would have produced roughly three million dollars—plus your normal compensation and benefits."

He nodded once. "Option two: a ten-million-dollar catch-up payment plus five percent of ranch earnings each year."

Wes stared at the pages as if they might burn through the table.

"I'm sorry," he said, voice thick. "Jesus save me. They're both more than fair."

Robbie nodded. "There is one catch."

He didn't smile now. "You must stay with us. If you choose the catch-up alternative, we pay it in installments—one million per year for five years—and we gross-up the payments so taxes don't erode the intent."

He pointed to the last paragraph. "But there will be a claw-back if you leave early."

Wes sat back, eyes wet, and for the first time in the room, his voice sounded like relief rather than fear.

"Mother Murphy… Katie… Robbie… it's simple."

He looked at each of them. "I love the ranches. I want to be part of the team. I want the first deal—aligned interests."

He paused. "And Robbie—I want to learn. I don't want to be alone anymore."

Robbie nodded, satisfied. "Good."

He looked around the table. "Then we have documents to finish. Is it acceptable if my team returns to New York today so we can complete everything quickly?"

Katie's face broke into something like celebration, restrained by the seriousness of the moment.

"Absolutely."

Mrs. Murphy nodded. "Absolutely."

Wes cleared his throat, still emotional. "Absolutely."

Robbie closed the folder, the sound crisp and final.

"Then let's get this done."

PART IV—THE PATH TO LEGACY

CHAPTER TWENTY-FIVE—KIMPO

December 11, 1950
General Douglas MacArthur visits Kimpo Air Base.

MacArthur's arrival had the effect it always did—everyone stood a little straighter, and every flaw in the operation suddenly felt like an accusation. He walked the line with a small knot of officers trailing him, coat collar up against the cold, eyes moving over the field with the impatience of a man who believed war should bend to willpower.

"Paul, why in the hell don't you have any F-86s here? The Reds are twenty miles away, and things are tight."

"Sir, we've been holding the Sabres back for a reason. We have a major operation planned—possibly a war-changing one."

MacArthur's gaze didn't soften. "Go on."

Paul continued. "We're launching a deception operation in MiG Alley. The F-86s will fly F-80 profiles—F-80 speeds, F-80 altitudes—and they'll use F-80 call signs. We want the MiGs and their controllers to think they're seeing Shooting Stars. Once they commit, we kill them with Sabres."

> MacArthur's mouth tightened. "And why aren't they flying today?"

> "They're being ferried in now, sir," Paul confirmed. "They'll be here on the fifteenth. Upon arrival they'll be armed, fueled, and preflighted. Then we'll move them to Kimpo on the afternoon of the sixteenth, refuel and preflight again, and launch the operation on schedule."

MacArthur stared at him for a long moment, weighing the plan against the risk.

> "It had better work."

> "Yes, sir."

F-86A Sabre jets began arriving shortly thereafter, their presence changing the mood on the field. Even the ground crews moved differently around them—more careful, more possessive. The aircraft looked fast sitting still. They looked like they belonged to a different war.

Lieutenant Ward Hitt, writing home, tried to make it sound ordinary in the way young men often do when they are trying to keep fear from becoming real.

> "Our planes arrived today," he wrote, "so I guess I'll be in business tomorrow. Don't worry about me—we're flying top cover here, and no one is getting shot down in jets anyway. The Reds are twelve miles away."

December 17, 1950
Northwestern North Korea—"MiG Alley"

Mission Briefing

Lt. Col. Bruce Hinton, Commander
336th Fighter Interceptor Squadron

Lieutenant Colonel Bruce Hinton kept the briefing simple because the plan itself was simple. They would bait the MiGs. The Sabres would mimic F-80 flight profiles—same speed, same altitudes, even the same call signs—so that the Communist pilots and their ground controllers would commit to the fight under false assumptions.

The route would carry them northwest from Kimpo toward the Yalu River, into the narrow stretch of sky already being called MiG Alley. The objective was direct: draw the enemy into the air, engage decisively, and reassert control of the skies.

There was only one rule, delivered without flourish.

Do not cross into China.

On December 17, 1950, the deception worked. What followed became the first jet-against-jet engagement of the war—an F-86 Sabre victory over a MiG-15—and with it came the unmistakable sense that a new era in aerial combat had begun.

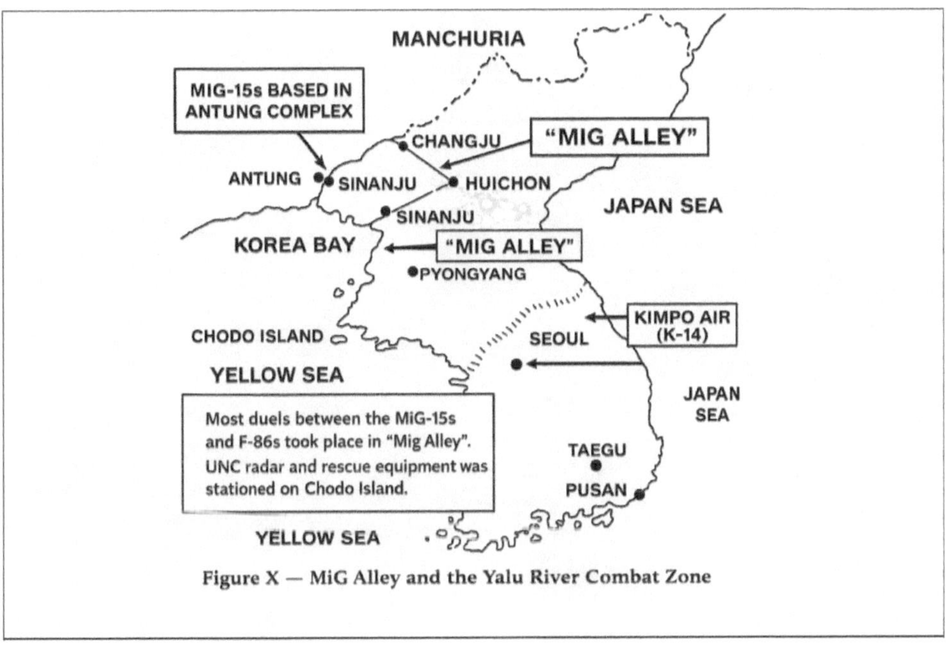

Figure X — MiG Alley and the Yalu River Combat Zone

CHAPTER TWENTY-SIX—YES MR. PRESIDENT

"Sir, you have another VIP call on your red phone, and no, sir, I don't know how they found this phone number."

"James, please figure that out. Who is calling?"

"Sir, it's Colonel Sidney L. Huff. I believe he is General MacArthur's aide."

"Yes, Colonel Huff. What can I do for you?"

"General MacArthur would like to speak with you, if you have a few minutes, General Murphy."

"Certainly. Colonel, I was just wondering how you obtained this phone number—and the encryption methodology."

"General, I apologize for using your personal number and encryption, but I believed it would be the fastest way to find you. If you weren't there, I assumed Command Chief Master Sergeant Jones would be able to reach you immediately. My source was AT&T. They have always been helpful to General MacArthur. Sir, here is the General."

"Paul, you are everything the President said you were. You are an officer who gets things done immediately. I find it amazing that we ever let you out of the Army. I also know the losers who went to West Point—while making up a very small part of the Association of Graduates—make up a very large part of the WPPA. Some of them even get four stars. I will let the President know I have personal knowledge of your skills, tact, diplomacy, and effectiveness. You should be in the Pentagon running operations for either the Air Force or the Chairman's organization. The MiG Alley raid was just what you said it would be. What a morale boost. We are going to kick those red bastards in the butt and win this war quickly. Congratulations. I don't like losing you, but the Air Force needs you back home to fix some problems. By the way—how old are you?"

"I was born in 1923. Twenty-seven, sir."

"Goodness. Paul, are you the youngest flag officer on active duty? Maybe I should promote the youngest battalion commanders to flag rank. If they're as effective as you, it could change this war quickly. I need to consider this." Click.

"Jones."

"Yes, sir."

"Jones, have you heard anything about me being reassigned back to the States? General MacArthur suggested I may be assigned to the Deputy Chief of Staff for Operations position. Have you heard anything like that?"

"No, sir. That said, I was asked yesterday if I would be willing to take a position to provide dedicated support to the Chief Master Sergeant of the Air Force. I told them I was very happy in my position with you."

"This just gets curiouser and curiouser. Well, what will happen will happen. Let's get to work planning the next big mission."

"Sir, you have another VIP call on your red phone, and no, sir, I don't know how they found this number either."

"Please figure that out. Now who is calling?"

"Sir, it's John R. Steelman. I believe he is, effectively, President Truman's chief of staff."

"Yes, Mr. Steelman. What can I do for you?"

"President Truman would like to speak with you, if you have a few minutes, General Murphy."

"Of course."

"Paul."

"Mr. President."

"I was briefed about the mission you put together. It was a whopping success. Once again, you have exceeded everyone's expectations. Paul, can you spare the time to come to Washington to see me? I would consider it a great favor. I don't know how good your XO is, but could he handle it for a few weeks?"

"Sir, just tell me when to be there, and I will be there. My XO can handle almost anything. I am recommending him for flag rank."

"My Chief of Staff will call you back within the day, Paul. We want to make sure you have efficient transportation both ways. I look forward to seeing you." Click.

"Command Chief Master Sergeant Jones, that was the President, summoning me to Washington. He didn't say why. Two requests. First, can you come with me to see the President? Second, can you see if you can find out why I'm being summoned?"

"Yes, sir. To both requests, of course."

Jones took another call.

"Headquarters 8th Air Force Fighter and Fighter-Bomber Command, Command Chief Master Sergeant Jones speaking. This line is not secure. How may I help you, sir?"

"Boy, that's a long title, Command Chief Master Sergeant Jones. This is John Steelman, the President's Chief of Staff. Would you be handling the General's schedule?"

"Sir, that is correct. I understand he is heading to Washington soon. He has asked that I also accompany him."

"There will be a Lockheed VC-121A Constellation ready for departure at your facility—Kimpo airfield—tomorrow morning at 0700. One requirement: only you and the General are authorized to be on board."

"Sir, sometimes we have injured soldiers and Marines who need transport. Would it be acceptable to take them? If yes, where should the first stop be?"

"The first stop would be Pearl Harbor, but it would take between ten and fifteen hours to get there. I will let the Colonel who is flying both of you know you asked. You two are always thinking about the combat-injured. Thank you for not letting rank interfere with taking care of the wounded. You are a class act."

Thirty minutes later, a retired Army Air Forces Colonel called Command Chief Master Sergeant Jones on the encrypted phone and identified himself as Steve Payton. He said he needed to find out who was in charge of transporting patients at the evacuation hospital. He informed Jones that it might add a few hours to their trip to Washington.

"Jones, what is your first name?"

"John, sir."

"John—or do your friends call you JJ? No matter what, if you are willing to call me Steve, or by my call sign, Bandit, would you think it disrespectful for me to call you JJ or by your call sign?"

"Sir, we're going to get along great. And I will absolutely end up asking for an explanation of your call sign."

"Understood. I will call the hospital. I think we can transport forty litter wounded if they can supply the necessary equipment and nurses. Would you please let the General know I am his pilot in command, after being recalled to active duty?"

"Yes, sir."

"And let the General know we're waiving the regulations and taking as many wounded as we can fit on the aircraft."

"Bandit, that will not be a problem."

A few minutes later that evening, General Murphy arrived on the flight line.

"Paul. Good to see you. How old is the General now? Have you achieved the age of twenty-eight yet?"

"Almost."

"You may want to know I only fly specific Constellation missions for specific people who happen to know either the President or Katie. And I have not missed a flight for Katie yet."

"Steve, thank you for taking care of my family. I really appreciate your help."

"No problem, sir. When will I be flying you back from Washington? I understand I'll have enough rest time to make that flight. They must think a lot of you if you're getting the VIP Connie."

"Steve, I have absolutely no idea why I'm going to see the President. Neither I nor JJ can find out. And thank you for finding out JJ's call sign. I love it."

"General, you need to get some rest. You're in for a long flight."

"No way. Much to Katie's displeasure, I will be helping the nurses take care of the wounded all the way to Hawaii. They're understaffed. It will also boost morale. I need to start my work."

"Ma'am, I am Paul Murphy. Do you know where the chief nurse is? I want to offer my assistance."

"Oh, General, you have found the chief medical officer. My name is Lieutenant Colonel Beverly Warren. I took this mission to meet you. When I accepted the flight, I thought it would only be you and the Command Chief Master Sergeant.

I was shocked to hear you were taking all our critical wounded. You could be saving thirty-eight to forty lives. Thank you, sir."

"Do they always ask the hospital to provide a doctor for these flights?"

"I believe so."

"That's absurd if they don't take all the critical wounded. I will bring this up when I speak with the President. I know Steve—or should I call him by his call sign, Bandit—arranged everything once I asked for the aircraft to carry as many wounded as we could. I know him well. In civilian life he's the chief pilot for my company."

"Sir, did you say the chief pilot for your company? You own a business that owns a Connie?"

"Well, yes and yes. We have a finance company, like a bank, and an operating business. Additionally, we own ranches that, as of the last time I checked, covered over one million acres and housed fifteen thousand pairs of Black Angus cattle. It's quite an operation, and we need reliable transportation to get around. But enough about me. Where are you from? Where did you go to college and medical school? And how did you get into the Army?"

"The Army has a program through which I attended medical school at a U.S. government facility. It covered all my medical school costs, and I was paid as a commissioned officer during medical school and residency. In exchange, I committed to serve as an active-duty MD for seven years, in addition to the years I spent in training. That makes me a lifer."

"And where are you from?"

"A small town in Montana near the Canadian border, not far from an Indian reservation called Cut Bank. Few folks ever escape it."

"So, doctor—why did you accept this flight? You said you thought it would only be me and the Command Chief Master Sergeant. Did you have something you wanted to say?"

"Well, sir, you have a reputation for looking out for soldiers and Marines. I think you need to know they are not getting the right quantity or quality of supplies. My hospital runs continuously low—antibiotics, anesthesia medicines, even simple wound-closure supplies. We have money for equipment, but not the basics for the wounded. That makes no sense."

"Lieutenant Colonel Warren, are you willing to put your name and reputation on the line with these issues? If you say yes, I will give you a direct order to accompany me and JJ to meet the individual who has summoned us. He will fix the problem, but it may affect both our careers."

"The answer is yes, General. I acknowledge the order and will follow it. I also understand the ramifications."

"Steve, how long do you expect the flight to last?"

"The weather looks like we'll get a tailwind—about one hundred ten knots once we reach altitude—if we can get clearance to climb directly to Flight Level 230. If we get that, we'll make it in under ten hours."

"Use our Presidential VIP status and critical-casualty status to get us up there now, Steve."

"Yes, sir."

Approximately one hour before landing, Colonel Steve Payton called Tripler

Army Medical Center in Hawaii to notify them of their imminent arrival. He provided the names, IDs, and injury details for all the wounded. The Connie landed eleven hours after it took off from Seoul due to favorable winds that negated the need for a fuel stop. Because of Lieutenant Colonel Warren and the nurses, thirty-nine of the forty critical patients survived the flight. Upon landing at Honolulu International Airport, the wounded were loaded into ambulances and transported to Tripler. The nurses were released to return to Seoul. Steve arranged to have the Connie cleaned and serviced. The medical equipment was removed from the cabin and secured in the aircraft's cargo hold. Steve, JJ, Lieutenant Colonel Warren, and Paul ate dinner at the Moana Surfrider, where each of them ordered lamb chops.

"Lieutenant Colonel Warren, you can still avoid a career disaster if you choose to. You could file an anonymous IG complaint and send a copy to JJ and me. That way no one in authority would know it was you."

"General, Command Chief, I will not back down. I believe I have a chance to raise an issue that can be resolved. If I don't, young men will die. It's as simple as that. I hope I'm not putting you in a tough spot."

"Colonel, take time to organize your thoughts and then get some sleep. JJ and I are heading to bed right now. JJ, did we have time to load my dress uniform—with all awards and badges?"

"Sir, we have both complete uniforms ready to go."

"Thank you, JJ. Good night."

"General, we will be landing in San Francisco in a while. We will pick up a supplemental air crew for the flight to Washington. That leg will take about five and a half hours. Please get a few more hours of rest. We will wake you and JJ about an hour out so you can dress. With the time changes, we expect to land at 2000. I'm not sure whether the President will see you tonight or in the morning. Good night, sir."

"Good night."

Washington National Airport, 2000, December 22, 1951.

"Steve, that was a wonderful flight. Do we have any updates about meeting the President? Second question—can we stay at my home here? It would be nice to see it sometime this decade."

"Well, Paul, I think we should inform President Truman's scheduling secretary that we are available whenever it's convenient. Then we'll let them know we'll be staying at the Murphy home, Embassy Row. Is that okay with you, Paul—and with you, Lieutenant Colonel Warren?"

"Paul, you have a home named after you on Embassy Row? Are you joking?"

"No, Colonel Warren, we aren't joking. We purchased that home a few years ago. Steve, that's good with me. I should call the house and let them know you, JJ, and Colonel Warren will be staying there. JJ—did I miss anything?"

"No, sir. Colonel Steve has taken care of the White House. I notified the house and arranged transportation. All we need to do is get into the car and go."

December 23, 1951—The Murphy Home.

"Paul, we are scheduled to meet President Truman at 1330 today. We should arrive at the security office no later than 1300."

"That means we leave by 1200. Traffic is unpredictable. Does anyone know if Payton is in town? I want my 'aide' to attend if possible. Steve, I don't know if you will be invited. Colonel Warren, I want you to participate in the meeting.

You will probably be asked to join after the President finishes giving me an assignment. JJ, you will be with me. Does everyone agree with that plan?"

"Sir, Lieutenant Colonel Payton—or, rather, Minister-Counselor Payton—is on a plane to Korea right now. He doesn't know we've been ordered here."

"JJ, when did he make lieutenant colonel? I thought he was a captain."

"Sir, Mr. Dulles operates in mysterious ways. Colonel Payton will be on a plane to Washington as soon as he lands anywhere."

The White House.
Yellow Oval Room.
The President's Office.
1600 Pennsylvania Avenue NW, Washington, D.C.

"Sir, I don't think you're in any trouble. The meeting is in the Yellow Oval Room—second floor, in the residence. I have never been there."

"Command Chief Master Sergeant Jones, how many times have you been in the White House?"

"I didn't keep track, General. When I was a junior sergeant, I worked in the White House communications section."

"General Murphy, welcome to the White House and my favorite working location—the Yellow Oval Room."

"Thank you, Mr. President. It's a pleasure to meet you in person and to see this remarkable place. Sir, I would like to introduce several people with me, if you don't mind."

"Paul, go ahead."

"The first is Command Chief Master Sergeant Jones. He's my right hand. I met him in 1946 when I returned from World War II. I understand he served here in the communications section."

To everyone's shock, the President extended his hand to JJ.

"It's been too long since I've seen you."

"Mr. President, JJ always surprises me—and your friendship is another surprise. The next guest is Lieutenant Colonel Beverly Warren. Colonel Warren is a medical doctor and chief medical officer at the 121st Evacuation Hospital. She was the medical officer on our flight, where she tended forty critical wounded. She raised issues I believe you will want to hear."

"Paul, how would you like to proceed?"

"Sir, our two guests can step out to give us private time when it's convenient for you."

"Paul, let's talk about a new job for you. To start, it should be just you and me. JJ, please escort the doctor to the waiting room. We'll bring both of you in shortly."

"Paul, the first thing I need to tell you is that you will be awarded the Medal of Honor, and so will Colonel Benjamin Green. Ben is probably unaware, but he has not fully transitioned to civilian life. Once we pin his medal, we will correct that administrative oversight. And I don't want to hear one word about you objecting. Understood? The White House Military Office will coordinate with both families to set an appropriate date."

"Your new position will be: Special Assistant to the President, Pentagon Liaison Officer."

"Your responsibilities will be to ensure clear communication between me and the Department of Defense, including the Joint Chiefs. This is a critical position. I want to understand what is going on each day. As you know, MacArthur is not the easiest man to work with. I am not beyond relieving him if it comes to that, but I hope to avoid it. Do you have questions?"

"Yes, sir. Two. Can I pick my staff? And when do I start?"

"Yes. Except JJ will be announced as Chief Master Sergeant of the Air Force. In that role, he can assist you with communications. As for when you start—you started a few minutes ago."

"Sir, I would also like Lieutenant Colonel Payton—Minister-Counselor Payton—with the State Department. I need him to retain his role and title with State. His position entitles him to compensation at the rank of a major general. He has done excellent work. He should be promoted to major general as soon as possible."

"We'll figure that out, Paul—but it will happen. Now tell me what the doctor is going to brief me on."

"It's simple, sir. She will tell you soldiers and Marines are not getting the correct quantity or quality of supplies—food, ammunition, clothing. Her hospital frequently runs low on critical antibiotics, anesthesia medications, and basic wound-closure supplies. Men are dying as a result. That makes no sense."

"Bring them in."

"Mr. President, this is Lieutenant Colonel Beverly Warren, Chief Medical Officer of the 121st Evacuation Hospital."

"Mr. President, we have a problem. In June 1950, the medical departments were short of everything. The most acute shortage was doctors—especially specialists. As you know, a doctor draft was instituted in August 1950, and the first medical draftees will arrive in Korea in January 1951. We appreciate your support. But we are chronically short on anesthesia, critical antibiotics, and basic wound-closure supplies. This is unacceptable. The food provided is unacceptable. Cold-weather gear is insufficient. These failures will cause needless casualties—casualties that will become deaths. This requires investigation at the highest level and should be reported to you immediately. Thank you for your time, Mr. President."

"Paul, your first assignment as Special Assistant is to investigate these matters without attributing any information to Colonel Warren. I want an update within two weeks. If her position is correct, I want a corrective plan executed within days, not weeks—specifically within sixteen days from today. Colonel, is that sufficient?"

"Yes, Mr. President."

"That concludes our meeting. Paul, your office will be directly outside mine in the West Wing. And Mr.—or should I say Colonel—Payton's office will be within fifty feet of yours. I expect both of you on the job within forty-eight hours. Would you like to look at offices once you receive your award?"

Paul was given a map of the West Wing of the White House, and President Truman had ordered him to select an office that was very close to his own. The one thing Paul did not want to do was to bump someone from their office. He also needed to be aware of the locations of each of the Armed Forces Congressional Liaison Offices.

Paul stared at the hastily-printed West Wing layout Rose Conway had handed him-close enough to the Oval Office that he could feel the building's pulse through the paper.

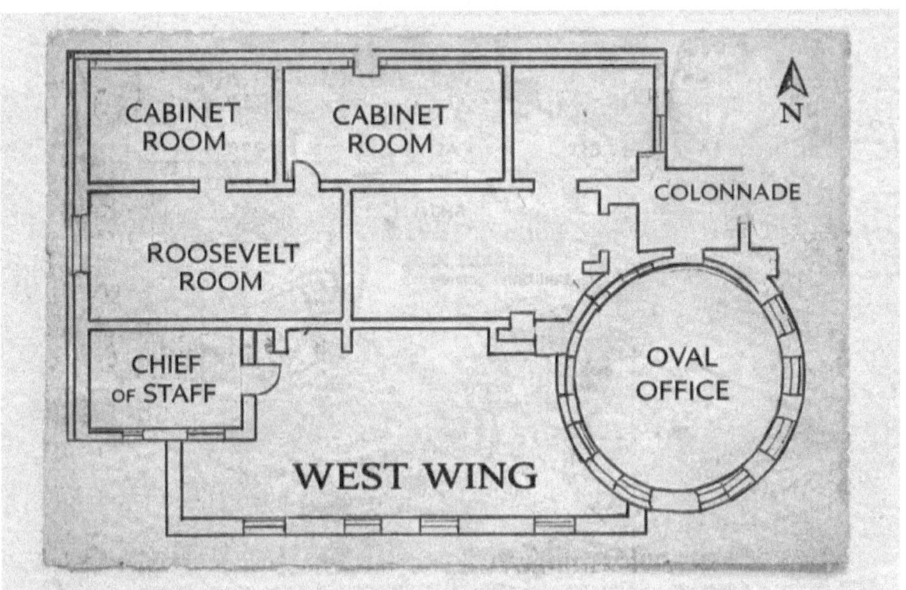

Medal of Honor Ceremony.
Brigadier General Paul Murphy.
January 15, 1952.

"Commander, I believe Mrs. Murphy, Mrs. Katherine Murphy, Tommy Murphy, and Nathan Murphy will want to be on the stage for the ceremony."

"Yes, sir, Mr. President."

The Commander began placing each family member in their designated spot. It felt less like ceremony and more like herding cattle. He could not understand why there were so many dignitaries present: the Joint Chiefs, Cabinet officers, senior intelligence officials, undersecretaries, generals—and two U.S. Senators from New York, California, Idaho, Montana, and Wyoming. Herding cats, he thought, except the cats had ribbons and stars on their shoulders. Just when he felt he had the group under control, the President took over.

"Commander. Post the orders."

"Attention to orders."

"The President of the United States of America, authorized by Act of Congress, March 3, 1863, has awarded, in the name of Congress, the Medal of Honor to Brigadier General Paul Murphy, United States Air Force…"

(Orders continue as read.)

Remarks by President Harry S. Truman.

"Well, once again, I have had a great privilege…"

(Remarks continue.)

"Ladies and gentlemen," the Navy Commander announced, "there will be a small reception in the adjoining room where we will honor General Paul Murphy."

Paul turned to Ben. "Ben, it will be your turn next week. The President has promised to ensure the Army's records accurately reflect the correct day your service ended in 1947. That way you won't be subject to recall."

"Please tell the President thank you."

"Dad," Tommy asked, "what does this mean? Are you a hero?"

"No, Tommy. I'm an officer doing my duty. The biggest beneficiaries of these awards are you and Yosef."

The President, overhearing, added, "Because both of your fathers have been awarded the Medal, both of you will receive automatic Presidential appointments to West Point or any of the other service academies."

"That's cool, Dad. Maybe Yosef and I can go to the same university."

"You still need to work hard in school and extracurriculars, Tommy. The academies evaluate the whole person—not just the awards your parents earned."

After the ceremony, President Truman handed Paul a map of the West Wing and ordered him to select an office near the Oval Office. Paul's one rule was simple: he would not bump a working staffer out of an office if there was any other way. The only options that satisfied the President's requirements involved reshaping the dining space adjacent to the Oval Office—or temporarily putting Paul into the Chief of Staff's closet until construction was complete. Paul needed five minutes with "Zipper Lip," the President's secretary, Rose Conway.

"Mrs. Conway, would it be possible to get five to ten minutes of the President's time tomorrow?"

"General Murphy, as you may know, that is a big request. I will have to ask him. Is there anything he needs to see in advance?"

"No, ma'am. Nothing in advance."

"Where can I find you today? I know you don't have an office yet."

"I will be in either the Navy Mess or the White House Military Office in the EOB, ma'am."

Paul went down to the basement of the West Wing, where the Navy facility was located. He needed coffee, the Washington Post, and the Navy Times.

He wanted to see whether the press had caught wind of the allegations about the government's failure to care for its troops. He immediately found an article about General MacArthur's emergency requests for supplies, including desperately needed medical equipment. Blood shortages were worsening, and the young Air Force Medical Service was struggling to expand by nearly three hundred percent. Paul's mind drifted back to the opening months of the war—the rapid advance, the counter-advance, the Chinese intervention, the renewed collapse of lines. The pace had strained logistics everywhere, but nowhere more brutally than medical support. Postwar budget cuts had hollowed the force. That erosion had to be corrected—and corrected publicly—before adversaries concluded America could not respond at scale.

"General Murphy, this is Rose. The President has a few minutes now, if you can get here promptly."

"Ma'am, I'm in the Navy facility downstairs. I'll be there directly."

"He said for you to come right into the Oval Office."

"Paul, there you are. I didn't expect to see you for a few more days."

"Sir, I have always thought time is the enemy. I wanted to identify office alternatives and seek your advice."

"That's the correct approach. What do you propose?"

"Sir, if my understanding is correct, the Oval Office dining space will be downsized. If so, there will be a new private office for you, a more intimate dining room, and room for an additional office. I also understand there may be a new office for Mr. Steelman, and his current office—his closet—may be made available. Either of those would meet your requirement that I be close at hand."

"Rose, get me Mr. Steelman."

"John," the President appealed with authority when Steelman came on, "I require that General Murphy have an office very close to me. He has brought two alternatives. I don't want this drawn out. Get with him, choose one, and begin construction today. I want it finished by close of business Thursday."

"Mr. President, where is he now—and what is his title?"

"He will be in your office in five minutes, and his title is Special Assistant to the President. Any other questions?"

"No, sir."

"Paul, let me know immediately if there are any hang-ups. Approve the plan and move in Thursday night. I want you fully functional Friday morning. Rose will find you an administrative assistant."

"Yes, Mr. President."

Everything moved faster than Paul thought possible. Steelman made it happen. The new office—adjacent to the President's private office—would be completed by Thursday evening. Payton would be given the closet office until a better space could be arranged. Going home that night, Paul considered calling a Deo Adjuvante meeting. With the principals in town, it was the right moment to take the temperature of the new structure.

"Katie, I'm home. Do you have a minute to discuss a few things?"

"I'm in the library with your mom having a drink. Please join us."

Paul loosened his tie, took off his jacket, and stepped into the library.

"Mom, I'm glad to see you. How was your day? I have something I want to discuss with you and Katie."

"My day has been wonderful. My son received the Medal of Honor, the President thinks my son and daughter-in-law are two of the smartest people in the United States, and our family business is making more money each month than I can count. This day—and every day—is wonderful."

"Mom and Katie, since you, Robbie, and Wes are in town, do you think we could have a quick meeting on how the company—and our relationships—are developing?"

"Let me call Robbie," Katie walked to the phone. "He planned to stay a few more days. Wes is staying with him. Paul, as Special Assistant to the President, when will you have time?"

"Anytime Saturday or Sunday works. Sunday is probably better."

Katie coordinated the meeting for Sunday and arranged a reception for their congressional friends for Saturday night. What began as a casual question became two significant gatherings—one political, one financial. While Paul worked the West Wing, Katie handled catering, valet, and invitations like a general officer organizing a campaign.

Over the following days, Paul continued his work on Colonel Warren's complaint. It turned out her concerns were valid—and if anything understated. Shortages of antibiotics, anesthesia, and basic medical supplies were chronic. The items were readily available in CONUS. The solution was obvious, and his findings concluded:

We must establish a prime vendor responsible for stocking required medical items, including med-surg supplies, medications, and surgical anesthesia.

All medical units—including medical components of line units—must be able to order directly from the prime vendor.

Supplies must be delivered directly to unit medical components.

Shortages of critical items must be reported immediately to the respective DCSLOGs and Chiefs of Staff.

Prime vendors will be judged on anticipation of demand and cost control.

When Paul moved into his office, a new assistant was waiting: Beverly Finkle. On his first night, he handed her his report on the medical supply issue and his proposed fix. She typed it in the format Truman preferred:

To: President Truman
From: Brigadier General Paul Murphy
Subject: Solving the Reported Shortage of Critical Medical Supplies

1. Issue
2. Short Answer
3. Discussion
4. Recommendations
5. Implementation Plan
6. Cost

Attached as a separate memorandum was Paul's recommendation that Colonel Beverly Warren be appointed OIC of the new agency supervising medical supply—and that she be promoted to flag rank. Whoever's ox she had gored, a star would make it harder to bury her work and easier to finish the mission.

The best surprise of his first assignment was Beverly Finkle. She was well-read, curious, and relentless, and the staff respected her. The one complication was her wardrobe—too glamorous for a war-footing West Wing. After a few days, Paul asked her, politely and directly, to dress more conservatively, especially when presenting documents over his desk. She was embarrassed, apologized, and corrected it immediately.

By the end of the week, Paul looked forward to dinner and cocktails with the senators they had cultivated for years. The family's political influence had to remain subtle, but the relationships were real. Mother Murphy and Katie prepared the house. The food would be excellent, and because the company owned one of California's best vineyards, the wine would be spectacular.

> "Katie, the house, the food, and the wine look like the
> best I've ever seen at any reception in Washington."

"Thank you," Katie said, "but I need to review something important. We have to discuss it with each of the senators tonight."

"Okay."

"There is a fundamental tax issue for Robbie and his team. It is called carried interest. Robbie and his team's interests in our portfolio companies are taxed as capital gains when we sell businesses. If Congress changes the law, their gains could be taxed as ordinary income—up to ninety-two percent—instead of the current capital gains rate. We must get our congressional friends to stop this."

"Are you kidding me? We get capital gains treatment, and they get ordinary income? That is insane."

The Political Reception.

Attendees.

U.S. Senate
California: William F. Knowland; Richard Nixon
Idaho: Henry Dworshak; Herman Welker
Montana: James E. Murray; Zales N. Ecton
New York: Herbert H. Lehman; Irving M. Ives
Wyoming: Joseph C. O'Mahoney; Lester C. Hunt
Deo Adjuvante Corporation
Robert "Robbie" Johnson, CPA, CEO
Katherine Murphy, Chairman
Betty Murphy, Vice Chairman
Paul Murphy
Wesley "Wes" Bowen, GM
Robert Varn, CFA, CFO

The party began at 7:30 p.m. The first to arrive was always the senior senator from New York. He was early, as usual, and wanted time with Katie—wanted the agenda before the room filled. Tonight, he found Robbie, Katie, and Paul, who was the least tactful of the three.

"Senator James, I just heard about a proposal to drive a wedge between Robbie and the family. That is unacceptable. Frankly, it makes me want to find the best candidate to run against you and write him a million-dollar check."

"What in the world are you talking about, Paul? I don't have a clue."

"Senator, this is the only time I will accept that answer. There is a fundamental tax issue for Robbie and his team—carried interest. If Congress changes the law, their gains could be taxed as ordinary income—up to ninety-two percent—instead of capital gains. That is total bullshit. I want it fixed, and fixed tonight. Any of you can threaten leadership and make it disappear. If ten senators take that position, the problem no longer exists. Do I make myself clear?"

"General, I now understand why you became the youngest general officer in the last hundred years. Your orders are clear. We will obey. May I quietly meet with the other senators as they arrive so we can remove this from the night and enjoy ourselves?"

"Certainly. We have the library set up for exactly that."

"Will you direct them there when they arrive?"

"Certainly."

Robbie whistled the moment the senator was out of earshot. Katie stood speechless.

"Paul, I have never heard you speak like that at one of these gatherings," Robbie quipped respectfully. "But I am grateful. My team will be beyond themselves when they hear what you just did."

"It pissed me off. Punishing your people for working hard—those political hacks aren't worth a pimple on a goat's ass. I can't do that often. But if you only speak on substance every ten years, people tend to listen. And politicians listen when you mention a million-dollar donation to their opponent."

Katie, Paul, and Robbie laughed until the senators emerged from the library with a promise: the issue would disappear by ten a.m. the next morning. The rest of the evening went beautifully.

Sunday morning, Deo Adjuvante's management meeting convened. Robbie and five senior officers from the Management Company attended. Robbie opened by thanking the family for resolving the tax threat and then began his report.

"Mrs. Murphy, Katie, and Paul, we'd like to provide a summarized report on the traditional business and the ranch operations. Over the past twenty-four months, the historic business has maintained its level of profitability. We have seen a compounded ten-point-four percent increase in asset value, net of management fees. The financial statements have been audited by Arthur Andersen & Co. We are proud that Andersen suggested no audit adjustments. Due to the confiscatory tax rates in the United States, we have moved a reasonable level of assets overseas. Andersen will continue to audit all operating businesses wherever located. We continue to carry no debt. Revised total assets grew to $13.5 billion at the end of 1950 and increased to $14.8 billion by year-end 1951. We have retained a sixty-five percent cash and cash-equivalent ratio during this growth period."

"Now the ranch operation. Upon completing the merger, the company had approximately one million acres under management. Since closing, we acquired an additional three hundred thousand acres, substantially in Montana and

Wyoming. We've acted as a rescue agent for community banks with troubled ranch loans—special situations, estate tax crises, distressed sales. Liquidity lets us buy when there are no other buyers. We now have approximately sixteen thousand pairs of Angus cattle. Cash has been expertly managed and has more than doubled since before closing. The audits bear out these numbers. The question we must ponder is how much concentration in real estate we want in this geographic area."

Being the President's Special Assistant made Paul a hybrid—chief of staff without the title, aide-de-camp, and director of research. One major initiative was ensuring SAC received the intellectual and financial resources it needed. LeMay was pleased.

Paul also met regularly with the Air Force Chief of Staff, and the relationship repaired itself. Two weeks after Paul's appointment, he met with General Vandenberg.

"Paul, it's good to see you again. While your office isn't as grand as mine, you have immediate access to the President. Truman has spoken highly of your work."

"Thank you, General Vandenberg. That was kind. I want to apologize for our last interaction."

"That is water under the bridge. You were not—and will not be—the last combat commander with whom I disagreed. You did magnificent work running fighter operations in Korea. LeMay wrote in your efficiency report that you are the only officer in his career he felt he should be working for, not the other way around. Paul, I may reuse his words, but that's not why I'm here."

"You now occupy one of the most powerful positions in the Air Force. As the President's right hand, people will try to get you to use your influence for matters that are not in the best interest of the country—or the President. I want to hear about it whenever it happens. You will have an open line to me. If you need me, call. If you don't get me, ask for my aide and you'll have me within ten minutes."

"You understand the Air Force's real needs as well as anyone alive. Do not let anyone—including me—influence you to contradict those needs. That's all I had. Do you have anything for me?"

"Sir, I occasionally meet with the gentlemen I disclosed to you on that contentious call in Korea. Would you like to be invited? I am cautious about invitations. However, if you—or a single individual you appoint who understands confidentiality—would like to attend, I will make that happen."

"You are every bit as smart and effective as LeMay said you are. I would personally like to join you on one of those occasions. Thank you."

CHAPTER TWENTY-SEVEN—THE TRUMAN–EISENHOWER TRANSITION

After two years serving President Truman, Paul expected the usual turnover that followed an election. Instead, when Dwight D. Eisenhower won the presidency, he asked Paul to stay on as Special Assistant—indefinitely.

For Paul, the request carried a kind of quiet gravity. Eisenhower was a war hero with his own orbit, his own rhythms, and his own way of deciding who belonged in the room. Paul understood what it meant to be retained. It meant the new President had looked at the machinery of the West Wing and decided that one of its moving parts should remain unchanged.

Six months later, the flag officer promotion board announced Paul's selection for promotion to Major General.

He had been a Brigadier longer than most of his peers thought prudent. The promotion, like so many of the turns in his career, arrived without warning and without theatrics. One day he was a senior one-star; the next he was told he'd be adding a second star. The only thing that changed immediately was the way people looked at him—less like a gifted subordinate and more like a future problem to be managed.

Paul called Katie from his office.

"They picked me up."

Katie did not ask what that meant. She understood promotion boards the way some spouses understood weather. She also understood Washington, which meant she understood how quickly a private moment became a public event.

"When?" she asked.

"My anticipated date is August fifteenth."

There was a brief pause on the line. Paul could hear her doing the calculation, not just of dates, but of consequences—who would attend, who needed to be seen attending, and what this meant for the next move.

"Good," she said, already moving. "We'll do it properly."

One of the jokes that spread through Paul's circle was that he was moving from being one of the senior Brigadier Generals to being one of the junior Major Generals. Paul smiled when he heard it. In Washington, rank was truth and comedy at the same time.

Katie set the party for October 15, 1956. She drafted the invitations and, after a brief skirmish with preference and protocol, settled on using the Air Force protocol office's formal invitation. She wanted the invitation to speak in the language the city respected—clean, official, unmistakable.

The party surpassed even her expectations.

General Curtis LeMay, newly installed as Vice Chief of Staff, attended. There were senators and congressmen—enough to make the event feel less like a celebration and more like a marker placed on a map. The Secretary of Defense was present. Vice President Nixon came as well, which in Washington meant someone had decided this was not merely a social obligation. It was a signal.

Katie moved through the rooms like she owned the air.

Paul watched her work and felt the familiar mixture of gratitude and astonishment. The D.C. house had been her insistence, her argument, her wager. Once again, she was correct. A home in the right neighborhood was not a luxury. It was leverage.

Late in the evening, LeMay drew Paul aside. The General had a way of speaking that made everything sound like an order, even when it was advice.

"You've commanded joint units, Paul, but you've never served a Joint Staff tour."

Paul waited. With LeMay, impatience was a kind of kindness. It meant the man respected your time.

"If it's offered," LeMay continued, "take it."

Paul understood the logic immediately. A Joint Staff assignment wasn't glamour. It was wiring. It showed you how Washington actually moved—how decisions were shaped before they ever reached a President's desk, how the services negotiated with one another, how the Pentagon turned disagreement into direction. It was also a credential that could not be substituted for with heroism or flying hours.

The party continued around them, loud with laughter and clinking glasses, but Paul felt the evening narrowing toward a single reality—the promotion was not an end. It was a hinge.

After the guests left and the house finally quieted, Katie poured them each a drink. Paul loosened his collar. The formal uniform, the medals, the endless handshakes—Washington demanded that a man perform his life as if it were someone else's story.

Katie sat across from him and studied his face.

"You're thinking about what comes next."

"I am."

Katie's delight in Washington was not simple vanity. She loved the city because it offered a kind of power that could be shaped with discipline. She believed in being seen, in building relationships that didn't feel like transactions. She also believed that the appearance of comfort could be as useful as comfort itself.

Paul, privately, hoped his next assignment would keep them in the Washington area. If Katie continued to expand her social and political presence, it would help him—but it would also fulfill something in her that he could not deny was real.

A week after the promotion was announced, Paul received a call from General Balkcom, who ran the MMO2 office. The General wanted to discuss Paul's next assignment.

There was no theatrics in Balkcom's voice. It was the tone of a man laying out a plan.

Balkcom believed the best next step for Paul was a Joint Staff assignment—Vice Director for Operations (J-3) at the Directorate of the Joint Chiefs of Staff, in the Pentagon.

It was, in every way that mattered, a high-visibility position disguised as staff work. The assignment would place Paul inside the nerve center of

American military planning and give him exposure to nearly every major operation, initiative, and inter-service negotiation moving through Washington.

Paul listened carefully as Balkcom outlined the role and its reach. He understood what the General was really saying: this was not merely a job. It was a set of doors.

When Balkcom finished, Paul let a beat of silence pass.

"Sir," Paul said, "I would like to take some time to think about this. Would it be acceptable for me to get back to you tomorrow afternoon?"

"Of course," Balkcom replied. "Take your time."

That evening, Paul talked it over with Katie.

She did not need persuading. She understood LeMay's counsel without being told. A Joint Staff assignment kept them close to Washington, close to the center, close to the people who mattered. It also positioned Paul for whatever came next—because in the military, advancement was never only about merit. It was about being prepared when history presented an opening.

The next day, Paul called General Balkcom.

"Sir," he said, "I will accept the Joint Staff assignment."

Balkcom's satisfaction was audible even through his restraint.

"Good! We'll proceed."

Paul hung up the phone and stood for a moment in the quiet of his office, looking out at the city that had taken so much from him and, in its own cold way, rewarded him for it. He thought of LeMay's warning—how quickly a man became a figure others wanted to control or cut down. He thought of Katie—how she could turn a home into a platform, a party into a signal, a life into strategy.

Then he sat back down at his desk, pulled a clean sheet of paper toward him, and began outlining the next chapter of his career.

CHAPTER TWENTY-EIGHT—SHADOWS OVER THE CANAL

September 1954
Israel

When Aluf (General) Benjamin Green returned to Israel from the United States, he was met at Lod Airport by Aluf Dan Tolkovsky, the commander of the Israeli Air Force. The two senior officers passed quickly through immigration and stepped into the waiting staff car.

"We're not going to headquarters," Tolkovsky informed Ben. "I'm taking you to Ramat David Air Base."

Ben nodded. When the commander of the Air Force personally met you at the airport and immediately drove you to a secure facility, it meant something important was waiting.

At Ramat David they entered a small briefing room where several senior officers were already assembled. Tolkovsky closed the door behind them.

"Ben," he said, "welcome home."

The tone in the room shifted. Tolkovsky spoke slowly, carefully choosing his words.

"You were sent to the United States for two reasons. First, to develop long-term relationships with the American military establishment. That mission alone may prove to be the most strategically important assignment any Israeli officer has ever carried out."

He paused.

"Second, you ensured that Israel obtained the resources it needed to win its War of Independence. That mission secured the survival of this country."

Tolkovsky looked directly at him.

"Because of that, you are one of the most valuable officers in the history of the Israeli Air Force."

Ben shifted slightly in his chair. Praise from a superior officer was rare in the Israeli military and usually brief. This sounded more like the preface to something else.

Tolkovsky continued.

"Effective immediately, you will command all fighter and bomber units in the Israeli Air Force. You will also supervise the development of all operational plans."

Ben absorbed the assignment quietly. After years of strategic work abroad, he was returning to operational command.

It took several weeks for him to reorient himself. The Israeli Air Force had begun transitioning into the jet age. Ben spent long hours relearning operational procedures and training in the Gloster Meteor, Israel's first jet fighter.

The Meteor was not the most advanced aircraft in the world, but it represented something far more important—Israel had entered the modern era of air combat.

The aircraft could reach speeds of nearly six hundred miles per hour and climb above forty thousand feet. Armed with four twenty-millimeter cannons, it was a formidable platform in the hands of skilled pilots.

But aircraft alone would never determine Israel's survival.
Strategy would.

Operation Kadesh

Early in September 1954, Ben received a call from the Chief of Staff of the Israel Defense Forces.

Rav Aluf Moshe Dayan wanted to see him immediately.

Dayan's office carried the quiet tension of a place where decisions about war were made daily. The famous eye patch gave Dayan a severe appearance, but the man's real intensity came from his mind. Dayan thought several moves ahead of almost everyone around him.

> "Ben," Dayan gestured toward a chair, "I have a project for you."

Ben listened carefully.

Dayan outlined the broad concept of what would later become known as Operation Kadesh—a military plan to seize the Sinai Peninsula and capture the Suez Canal.

Egypt had grown increasingly hostile toward Israel. President Gamal Abdel Nasser had positioned himself as the dominant power in the Arab world, and his rhetoric made clear that Israel's destruction remained a central goal.

Dayan explained that Britain and France were quietly considering cooperating with Israel. Both nations had deep strategic interests in the canal and were increasingly alarmed by Nasser's policies.

Ben listened without interruption. When Dayan finished, Ben spoke cautiously.

> "Sir, I have concerns."

Dayan leaned back slightly.

> "Go on."

> "If Israel attacks Egypt to seize the canal, the United States and the Soviet Union will strongly object. I believe the global reaction will be severe."

Dayan did not interrupt.

> "Furthermore," Ben continued, "the British public is no longer in the mood to fight colonial wars. If this operation

becomes public knowledge, there may be political consequences inside Britain itself."

Dayan's expression remained neutral.

"You may be right, but that does not change the strategic situation."

Ben understood what that meant. His job was not to debate the policy decision. His job was to ensure that if the war occurred, Israel would win it.

Over the next months he developed the operational plan.=

The invasion of the Sinai Peninsula would begin with a rapid airborne and armored assault. The entire campaign was designed to conclude quickly.

Ben estimated the operation could be completed in less than one hundred hours.

Speed would be the key to success.

A Visit to the Holy Land

During the winter holiday season of 1954–1955, the Murphy family made their first trip to Israel.

Paul, Katie, and their children arrived in Tel Aviv on December 15. Ben and his wife Ariel welcomed them at their home in the Ramat Aviv Gimmel community.

Because of Ben's senior military position, Israeli security services treated the visit with exceptional caution.

Shin Bet, Israel's internal security service, had increased protection for senior military officials in response to rising regional tensions. Hosting the family of a senior American officer raised the security level even further.

When the two families traveled to Jerusalem, nearly two hundred security personnel were quietly assigned to their protection.

After witnessing the extraordinary precautions, Ariel and Katie decided the remainder of the visit should be spent somewhere quieter. They moved their gatherings to the Elram Center, a private country club that allowed both families to relax away from the constant attention.

The highlight of the trip was watching the growing friendship between the two boys—Tommy Murphy and Yosef Green. The boys were inseparable. It soon became obvious that the friendship between the sons mirrored the relationship between their fathers.

Both boys had already begun discussing their futures.

They wanted to attend the same American service academy.

West Point seemed the most likely destination. Because both Paul and Ben had received the Medal of Honor for their wartime service, their sons were eligible for presidential appointments to U.S. service academies.

To the adults watching them laugh and argue over basketball games, the future seemed very far away.

The Suez Crisis

By early 1956 tensions across the Middle East had escalated dramatically.

Ben had continued refining the plans for Operation Kadesh for nearly two years. By then the invasion concept had become well known among Israel's senior military leadership.

In July 1956 the situation exploded when Egyptian President Nasser nationalized the Suez Canal.

Britain and France saw the move as a direct threat to their strategic interests.

The possibility of war moved from theory to probability.

Despite his role in developing the original operational plan, Ben was excluded from several of the political negotiations that took place during the summer and fall of 1956. Adjustments to the plan were made without his direct involvement.

The invasion began on October 29, 1956.

The Israeli assault moved rapidly through the Sinai Peninsula. Air superiority was quickly established, and Israeli ground forces advanced with remarkable speed.

Ben's original estimate proved accurate.

Within roughly one hundred hours, Israel had achieved all of its military objectives. But the political consequences unfolded exactly as Ben had predicted.

The United States and the Soviet Union both condemned the operation. International pressure mounted almost immediately. Only hours after the campaign concluded, Paul Murphy arrived in Israel unannounced. Ben met him privately.

> "Ben, we've been friends our entire adult lives. What I'm
> about to tell you isn't pleasant."

Ben waited.

> "Tomorrow President Eisenhower and Secretary of State John Foster Dulles will demand that Israel withdraw from the Sinai."

Paul's voice remained calm.

> "If Israel refuses, the United States will consider economic sanctions. The Soviets are already threatening far worse."

Ben exhaled slowly. None of this surprised him.

> "So," Paul thinking carefully, "my advice is simple. Withdraw."

Within hours of their meeting, Israel began pulling its forces back from the Sinai Peninsula.

The military victory remained intact, but the political reality was unavoidable. Israel could not fight the entire world.

A New Mission

Ben's performance during the campaign did not go unnoticed.

His operational leadership, his strategic planning, and his accurate predictions about the international response earned him widespread respect inside the Israeli defense establishment. Soon afterward he was promoted again.

His new responsibilities placed him in charge of overseeing the development of Israel's air force and coordinating many of its future operational strategies.

For the next two years Ben traveled extensively across Europe and the United States seeking new technologies, aircraft, and intelligence relationships that could strengthen Israel's military.

During that period he developed a close relationship with one of the most powerful figures in Israeli intelligence.

Isser Harel.

Harel was the architect of Israel's intelligence empire. As director of both Mossad and Shin Bet, he oversaw nearly every intelligence operation conducted by the young nation. Few men inside Israel's government were more feared—or more respected.

In late 1958, Harel summoned Ben to a private meeting. He did not waste time.

"Ben," Harel said, "I want you to become my deputy."

Ben was silent for a moment.

Deputy head of Israel's intelligence services was not simply a promotion. It was entry into a world where strategy, politics, and covert operations were inseparable. Harel studied his reaction.

"We have a mission," Harel continued quietly.

Ben waited.

"We have located Adolf Eichmann."

The room seemed to grow very still. Eichmann had been one of the principal architects of the Holocaust. Since the end of the Second World War, he had disappeared.

Now Mossad believed they knew where he was hiding.
Harel leaned forward slightly.

"Your job," he said, "is to bring him home."

CHAPTER TWENTY-NINE—THE JOINT STAFF

Washington, D.C.
Pentagon

Paul Murphy arrived at the Pentagon as Vice Director for Operations (J-3) at the Directorate of the Joint Chiefs of Staff during a period when the Cold War was shifting into a far more dangerous phase.

The assignment placed him at the center of American military planning. From his office he could watch how the Army, Navy, Marine Corps, and Air Force negotiated strategy before any decision ever reached the President's desk.

For a relatively young Major General, it was an extraordinary education. One of his primary responsibilities was working with the Operations Deputies, known throughout the Pentagon simply as the OPSDEPS. The group served as a preparatory body for the Joint Chiefs of Staff, examining operational issues before they were formally presented to the Chiefs themselves.

Below the OPSDEPS sat another working group known as the Deputy Operations Deputies, or DEPOPSDEPS. These officers were typically the senior planners from each service. They handled the first rounds of analysis and coordination, forwarding issues upward only after the major disagreements had been ironed out.

It was complex, often tedious work. But it revealed something Paul had long suspected: military power was not created solely on battlefields. It was created in rooms filled with maps, intelligence reports, and arguments between professionals who understood the cost of being wrong.

Paul thrived in the environment. Within months he had developed a reputation for being able to cut through arguments quickly and push discussions toward decisions. The ability served him well as Washington increasingly turned its attention toward a new strategic concern—the Soviet Union's rapidly expanding missile and nuclear capabilities.

By the time Paul had completed his third year on the Joint Staff, he began thinking about what his next assignment might be.

The call came unexpectedly.

One afternoon his secretary informed him that the office of Allen W. Dulles, Director of the Central Intelligence Agency, had requested a meeting.

Dinner in Georgetown

September 15, 1957

The meeting took place at Martin's Tavern, a quiet Georgetown restaurant that had long been a discreet gathering place for Washington's political and intelligence communities.

When Paul arrived, Allen Dulles was already seated. With him was a younger man Paul had not yet met.

> "Paul," Dulles chirped warmly as he stood up, "good to
> see you again."

Dulles made the introductions.

> "Richard Bissell. He manages one of our more sensitive
> programs."

Bissell nodded politely.

After the waiter took their drink orders, Dulles began the conversation with a question that seemed casual but was anything but.

> "Paul, when you served as Assistant to the President
> during Eisenhower's first term, were you ever involved in
> reviewing proposals for…special aircraft?"

Paul smiled slightly.

> "That depends on what you mean by special."

Dulles leaned forward.

"Let's be direct. High-altitude reconnaissance aircraft."

Paul took a moment before answering.

"Allen, you know I cannot discuss classified matters unless the appropriate authority authorizes the conversation."

Dulles nodded.

"You have that authority now."

Paul looked briefly at Bissell.

"Then yes. I'm familiar with the concept."

Dulles seemed satisfied.

"Good! Because the program is now operational."

He gestured toward Bissell.

"Richard is the program manager. The project is called Aquatone."

Bissell took over the briefing.

"The program is a partnership between the CIA and the United States Air Force. While the CIA maintains operational control, the Air Force provides pilots, engines, and technical support."

Paul listened carefully.

The aircraft being discussed was the U-2, a high-altitude reconnaissance platform designed by Lockheed's legendary Skunk Works division. Its mission was simple in concept and extraordinarily dangerous in practice. The aircraft would fly above seventy thousand feet—far higher than most fighters could reach—and photograph Soviet military installations.

For the first time since the beginning of the Cold War, the United States would be able to see what was actually happening inside the Soviet Union. Bissell outlined the program's progress.

The U-2 had completed its first test flights in 1955. By April 1956 it was fully operational. Within months it had already conducted reconnaissance missions over the Soviet Union, capturing detailed photographs of critical military facilities.

The intelligence gathered had already begun reshaping Western strategic planning. Dulles waited until Bissell finished. Then he asked the question that had clearly been the purpose of the dinner.

"Paul," he said, "how would you feel about joining us?"

Paul leaned back slightly.

"In what capacity?"

Dulles spoke carefully.

"I've been discussing this with Admiral Radford, Chairman of the Joint Chiefs. We believe the CIA needs a senior military officer who can coordinate directly with the armed services."

He paused.

"The position will initially carry two stars, but it will almost certainly become a three-star billet."

Paul understood what that meant.

"You would like me to serve as Associate Director for Military Support."

Dulles nodded.

"Yes."

Paul was silent for a moment.

"You know how Katie and I make decisions. If it's acceptable, I'd like to talk with her tonight."

"Of course," Dulles replied. "Take the time you need."

Katie's Advice

That evening Paul drove home thinking carefully about what had just happened. Dulles never offered opportunities without several layers of intention behind them. If the CIA director wanted a military officer in that role, it meant something larger was unfolding.

When he walked into the house Katie immediately noticed the expression on his face.

"You've had an interesting evening, my darling."

Paul poured himself a drink.

"That's one way to describe it."

He told her about the dinner, the U-2 program, and Dulles's proposal. Katie listened quietly.

"What happens to the current occupant of the position?" she asked.

"He's being reassigned as Commander in Chief of Pacific Command," Paul replied. "A four-star job."

Katie nodded slowly.

"So the position is a stepping stone."

"That's what it looks like."

Katie leaned back in her chair.

"Then the question isn't whether you should take the job. The question is where it leads."

Paul smiled slightly.

"That was exactly my thought."

They discussed the possible career path that might follow. Senior military leaders who aspired to the very top positions often needed experience beyond traditional command assignments.

A senior intelligence role could provide that.

Katie finally looked at him directly.

"Before you decide," she said, "there's one person you should talk to."

"Who?"

"General LeMay."

Paul nodded. She was right.

The Monocle

The following evening Paul met General Curtis LeMay for dinner at The Monocle, a restaurant favored by senior military officers and members of Congress. LeMay wasted no time.

"So" LeMay began as the drinks arrived. "Allen Dulles offered you the CIA job."

Paul smiled.

"News travels quickly."

LeMay shrugged.

"This town has no secrets."

Paul explained the position and what Dulles hoped to accomplish.

LeMay listened carefully. Finally he spoke.

"You should take it."

Paul had expected that answer.
LeMay continued.

"It's the right time for your third star. After that you'll need a major command if you want to stay on track for the very top positions."

Paul nodded.

"Sir, I'd love Tactical Air Command someday."

LeMay allowed himself a small smile.

"One step at a time."

Then he leaned forward.

"Tell Dulles you'll accept the job."

Paul understood what the conversation meant. LeMay had just quietly endorsed his next move.

A New Direction

The following morning Paul called Allen Dulles.

"I've discussed the matter with my wife, Allen. And with General LeMay."

Dulles waited.

"I will accept the position."

Dulles sounded pleased.

"Excellent. Welcome to the Agency."

Paul hung up the phone and sat quietly for a moment.
His career had already taken him through combat, diplomacy, and the

highest levels of military planning.

Now it was about to take him into the secret war that defined the Cold War.

And he suspected the most dangerous part of the journey had only just begun.

CHAPTER THIRTY—PROJECT AQUATONE

October 15, 1957
Central Intelligence Agency Headquarters
McLean, Virginia

Paul Murphy drove slowly through the gates of the Central Intelligence Agency headquarters on Colonial Farm Road.

The campus, set quietly among the wooded hills of northern Virginia, looked almost ordinary from the outside. There were no outward signs that some of the most secret operations of the Cold War were planned inside those buildings. At the security checkpoint Paul presented his credentials. Waiting for him on the other side was a young man in a dark suit.

"Good morning, General Murphy. My name is Eddie Francis. I'll be your executive assistant."

Eddie handed him a folder.

Inside were his new identification badge, parking authorization, office credentials, and the all-area access card that granted him entry to most of the Agency's restricted sections.

Eddie then climbed into the passenger seat and directed Paul to his assigned parking space.

From there he escorted the General through the building to his new office. On the way Eddie offered a brief introduction to the staff.

"You'll also be working closely with Patty Byrd," he explained. "She's your private assistant. Frankly, sir, she's the best one in the building."

Paul smiled.

"I'm glad to hear it."

When they reached the office, Patty greeted him warmly. She was efficient, calm, and immediately organized the rhythm of the office.

"We have a simple protocol, General," she explained. "Anyone who arrives to see you will be announced first."

Paul had been in the chair less than five minutes when his phone rang. It was Allen Dulles.

"Paul," Dulles said, "welcome to the Agency."

"Thank you, sir."

"I believe you've met Richard Bissell."

"Yes, we had dinner together in Georgetown."

"Good. Dick will brief you today. The program he manages is one of the most important intelligence efforts we have underway."

Paul understood immediately what that meant. The U-2 program.

The Dragon Lady

Richard Bissell arrived shortly after the call. Paul greeted him warmly.

"Dick, it's good to see you again."

"Likewise, General."

They sat down and began reviewing the program. Bissell summarized the history of Project Aquatone.

In 1954 the United States approved development of a high-altitude reconnaissance aircraft capable of flying above seventy thousand feet. Lockheed's Skunk Works division had designed the aircraft with one goal: to fly so high that Soviet fighters and missiles could not reach it.

The aircraft was called the U-2. The Air Force referred to it by another name. —Dragon Lady. The first test flights took place in 1955 from a remote dry lakebed in Nevada. Within a year the aircraft had entered operational service. By mid-1956 the U-2 was flying reconnaissance missions over the Soviet Union.

The photographs the aircraft captured were astonishing. For the first time Western intelligence could see Soviet airfields, missile test ranges, and industrial complexes in remarkable detail. Analysts could count aircraft, measure runways, and track the construction of new military installations. The intelligence was already reshaping American strategy.

Paul listened carefully.

"Where do we stand today?"

Bissell nodded.

> "We're continuing reconnaissance missions over the
> Soviet Union. The objective is to determine the true strength
> of their missile program."

The fear dominating Washington at the time was the so-called missile gap— the belief that the Soviet Union might be developing far more intercontinental ballistic missiles than the United States.

The U-2 offered the only reliable way to know the truth.

Bissell continued.

> "In June of last year one of our aircraft reached seventy-
> four thousand feet during testing. That altitude gives us a
> comfortable margin above Soviet fighter capabilities."

Paul nodded.

> "But not necessarily above their missiles."

Bissell smiled slightly.

"You're exactly right."

The briefing continued for most of the afternoon. By the time they finished, Paul had a clear understanding of the scope of the program. The U-2 was no longer simply an experimental aircraft. It had become one of the most important intelligence tools in the Cold War.

Sputnik

Three weeks before Paul arrived at the CIA, the Soviet Union had stunned the world. On October 4, 1957, the Soviets launched Sputnik, the first artificial satellite. The event shook Washington.

If the Soviets could launch a satellite into orbit, they could almost certainly launch nuclear warheads across continents. The U-2 program suddenly became even more important. American intelligence needed to determine the true status of Soviet missile development. The reconnaissance missions would expand accordingly.

Paul's responsibilities at the CIA grew quickly. He coordinated military support for the program, oversaw operational planning, and ensured cooperation between the Agency and the armed services. The work required careful balance. The missions were incredibly valuable. They were also incredibly risky. If a U-2 aircraft were ever shot down inside Soviet territory, the political consequences could be severe.

Still, the intelligence gathered was proving invaluable. The photographs demonstrated something surprising. The Soviet missile program was far smaller than American intelligence analysts had feared. The so-called missile gap appeared to be largely an illusion.

Promotion

March 30, 1958

Paul had been at the CIA for several months when Patty Byrd entered his office carrying a sealed envelope. Behind her stood Allen Dulles, Richard Bissell, and General Curtis LeMay.

A photographer waited in the hallway.

"Open it," LeMay ordered.

Paul broke the seal and unfolded the document. It was a formal memorandum from the Chief of Staff of the United States Air Force. The President of the United States had nominated him for promotion to Lieutenant General. The Senate had unanimously approved the appointment. The promotion was effective immediately.

Paul looked up from the document.

LeMay grinned.

"Well," he said, "where's the extra star?"

An aide produced the insignia.

"Since Katie isn't here," LeMay continued, "who do you want to pin it on?"

Paul turned toward Allen Dulles.

"Director Dulles. If you don't mind."

Dulles smiled.

"Not at all."

LeMay attached the star to one shoulder while Dulles attached the other. The photographer captured the moment as the two men stepped back. Paul Murphy was now a three-star general.

Patty Byrd entered with glasses and a bottle of Scotch.

"To General Murphy," someone raised a glass.

The room echoed the toast. Paul raised his glass.

"To our comrades in arms—living and dead—and to those we left behind."

The room fell silent for a moment before the glasses touched. As the celebration wound down, LeMay pulled Paul aside.

"You're now the youngest Lieutenant General in the Air Force."

Paul nodded.

"That means people will be watching you very carefully. Some will be hoping you make a mistake."

LeMay placed a hand on his shoulder.

"Don't give them one."

Paul smiled slightly.

"Yes, sir."

As LeMay left the office, Paul looked down at the new stars on his uniform. The Cold War was entering its most dangerous phase. And somehow, he had just moved one step closer to the center of it.

CHAPTER THIRTY-ONE—TACTICAL AIR COMMAND

December 1959
Langley Air Force Base

By the end of his second year at the Central Intelligence Agency, Paul Murphy understood that his time there was nearing its end.

The U-2 reconnaissance program had matured into one of the most effective intelligence tools of the Cold War. The missions had provided photographic evidence that dramatically reshaped Western understanding of Soviet military capabilities. The feared "missile gap" had proven largely mythical.

The intelligence gathered during those missions had given the United States and its allies something priceless—clarity.

Shortly before Christmas, Allen Dulles sent a formal letter of commendation to the Chief of Staff of the Air Force praising Paul's leadership of the military liaison and operational elements of the program.

Dulles wrote that Murphy had created a climate of cooperation between the intelligence community and the armed services that allowed the program to succeed. He also noted something Paul had been saying privately for months.

The risks of continuing reconnaissance flights over the Soviet Union were growing. Sooner or later, he warned, one of the aircraft would be shot down. It was not a question of if. Only when.

The letter circulated quietly through the highest levels of the Air Force. A few days later, the phone rang in Paul's office. It was General Curtis LeMay.

"Murphy," LeMay said, his voice unmistakable even over the line, "you need a new assignment."

Paul waited.

"Tactical Air Command just opened up."

TAC was one of the Air Force's most important operational commands. Responsible for fighter aircraft and tactical air operations, it was the spearhead of American airpower outside the strategic nuclear mission.

"You're a fighter pilot," LeMay continued. "You're a triple ace. You've been running intelligence operations for two years."

LeMay paused.

"It's time you got back to command."

Paul did not hesitate.

"Yes, sir."

The decision was made within minutes. Paul Murphy would become the new commander of Tactical Air Command. The Monocle—Again Before the announcement became public, LeMay invited Paul to dinner.

The meeting took place once again at The Monocle, the familiar restaurant near Capitol Hill where many of Washington's quiet decisions were made. When Paul arrived, the owner personally escorted him into a private dining room. LeMay arrived shortly afterward. Paul had already ordered martinis and the first course.

"Bomber," Paul boomed as LeMay sat down.

LeMay nodded.

"Murphy."

The waiter appeared briefly to confirm the dinner order.

Paul took charge. "Crab meat imperial to start. Then rib-eye steaks, medium rare, onion rings, and creamed spinach."

LeMay nodded approvingly.

"Sounds good."

The wine—a bottle of 1945 Petrus—had already been opened and was breathing quietly on the table.
LeMay leaned forward.

"The Chief and I agreed. You'll take command of Tactical Air Command effective January first."

Paul exhaled slowly.

"Thank you, sir."

LeMay studied him.

"TAC is a four-star billet. But you're still a relatively junior lieutenant general."

Paul understood immediately what LeMay was saying.

"There will be competition."

LeMay smiled thinly.

"You could say that."

The Air Force at the time had only a handful of four-star generals. Dozens of three-star officers were waiting for an opportunity to move up.

"Keep your head down. Do the job well."

Paul nodded.

"Yes, sir."

The rest of the dinner moved more comfortably. They spoke about aircraft modernization, tactical doctrine, and the evolving balance between nuclear strategy and conventional airpower.

When they finally finished dessert and coffee, LeMay stood.

"You'll do well there."

Paul hoped he was right.

Langley

Langley Air Force Base sat near the Virginia coast, just outside Norfolk. It had been the headquarters of Tactical Air Command since the end of the Second World War. Paul arrived a few days before Christmas.

Instead of traveling by transport aircraft, he flew down himself in an F-105F Thunderchief, with an instructor pilot occupying the rear seat. The flight from Andrews Air Force Base took less than twenty minutes.

As they approached the Langley training area, Paul asked the instructor pilot if they had enough fuel for a few maneuvers.

"Plenty, sir."

Paul smiled.

"Let's stretch her legs."

For the next several minutes the aircraft rolled and climbed through a series of high-performance maneuvers before finally descending toward Langley. The landing felt like coming home.

After the post-flight debriefing Paul drove to the visiting officers' quarters where his staff had arranged temporary accommodations. Later that afternoon his senior aide met him for a briefing.

Paul's instructions were simple.

"Schedule a staff meeting for January fifth. I want updates on three things."

The aide waited.

"First, our support for counterinsurgency operations. Second, our commitments to reinforcing NATO air forces in Europe. Third, the state of our training programs."

The aide nodded.

"Yes, sir."

Paul paused for a moment.

"And we'll need to discuss the staff organization. I may make some changes."

The aide smiled slightly.

"We expected that, sir."

Deo Adjuvante
December 28, 1959

A few days after Christmas, Paul and Katie held the annual meeting of their family company, Deo Adjuvante Corporation.

Robbie Johnson presented the financial results.

"Our net worth will be approximately $33.2 billion once the audit is completed"

Paul raised an eyebrow.

"Another good year."

Robbie nodded.

"Twenty-one billion of that is in cash or cash equivalents. The ranch operations continue to expand. We now operate more than 2.5 million acres."

Katie smiled.

"That's remarkable."

Robbie continued.

"After taxes and management fees, our projected earnings for 1959 are approximately $2.1 billion."

Paul leaned back in his chair.

"Robbie," he said, "you've done an extraordinary job."

But the conversation soon turned toward another subject. Katie's Senate campaign.

She had already begun receiving endorsements from agricultural groups, law enforcement associations, and several regional newspapers.

"I haven't officially announced yet. But I will soon."

Robbie nodded thoughtfully.

"You'll need a campaign manager immediately. And a chief of staff."

Katie agreed.

"The real question," she said, "is whether I should run as a Democrat, a Republican, or an independent."

Robbie thought for a moment.

"If Kennedy wins the presidency," he said, "running as a Democrat might be advantageous."

Katie shook her head slightly.

"I'm leaning toward running as an independent."

Paul looked at her curiously.

"Why?"

"So I can vote my conscience. And so no one can claim they own my vote."

Robbie smiled.

"That approach will require a very strong ground organization."

Katie nodded.

"I know."

She outlined her idea. Campaign offices in nearly every community in the state. Constant travel. Personal meetings with as many voters as possible. Paul listened quietly. He knew something the others in the room were beginning to realize. Katie Murphy was not simply running for office. She was building something. Preparing for the Next Step

Later that evening Paul and Katie sat together in their Washington home. Paul mixed martinis.

"To TAC," Katie said, raising her glass.

"To TAC."

They talked about logistics. Paul would spend most of his time at Langley, but the family would remain in Washington so the children could stay in their schools and Katie could continue her campaign preparations.

Langley was only a few hours away by car or a short flight by military aircraft. It would work.

As Paul finished his drink, the phone rang. It was General LeMay.

"Murphy," he said, "I have some news for you."

Paul listened.

"The President has submitted your name to the Senate for promotion to General—four stars."

Paul was silent for a moment.

"That soon?"

"Yes."

LeMay continued.

"If I become Chief of Staff next year, there will be an opening for Vice Chief. To be eligible, you need to hold four stars for at least a year."

Paul understood immediately. LeMay was planning ahead.

"Congratulations," LeMay boomed.

Paul thanked him and hung up the phone.
Katie was watching him carefully.

"Well?" she asked.

Paul smiled.

"They're giving me my fourth star."

Katie laughed softly.

"Paul Murphy," she said, "you are becoming very difficult to keep up with."

Paul leaned back in his chair. The next year would bring new commands, new responsibilities, and new risks.
But for the moment, the future seemed wide open.

CHAPTER THIRTY-TWO—OPERATION FINALE

May 1960
Buenos Aires, Argentina

For nearly fifteen years after the end of the Second World War, Adolf Eichmann had lived quietly under a false name.

He worked a series of ordinary jobs—mechanic, factory laborer, clerk. To the neighbors in the modest suburb of San Fernando, he was simply Ricardo Klement, a quiet middle-aged man who rode the bus home from work each evening.

Few people suspected that the thin, balding man was once one of the principal architects of the Nazi regime's Final Solution.

Fewer still knew that Israeli intelligence had been searching for him since the founding of the State of Israel.

The man who had organized the deportation of millions of Jews to extermination camps had disappeared at the end of the war. Like many Nazi officials, he had slipped through the chaos of post-war Europe and escaped through clandestine networks that moved fugitives to South America.

For years the trail had gone cold. But in 1957 a German-Jewish refugee living in Argentina sent a letter to the Israeli authorities suggesting that a man living nearby might actually be Adolf Eichmann. At first the claim seemed unlikely. But the Mossad began to investigate.

By early 1960 the evidence had become difficult to ignore. The man calling himself Ricardo Klement looked remarkably like the photographs of Eichmann taken during the war.

The Israeli government faced a difficult decision. Argentina had not requested Eichmann's arrest. There was no guarantee the country would extradite him if formally asked. Yet the crimes he had committed were among the most horrific in human history. Prime Minister David Ben-Gurion made the decision. Eichmann would be captured and brought to Israel to stand trial.

Surveillance

For weeks Mossad agents quietly observed the small house on Garibaldi Street.

Each evening at precisely the same time a bus stopped near the intersection. The same man stepped off. He walked the short distance down the dirt road toward the modest house where his family lived.

The routine never varied. The agents confirmed the man's identity through photographs and careful observation. There was no longer any doubt. Ricardo Klement was Adolf Eichmann.

The Capture

May 11, 1960

The Mossad team positioned themselves along the road shortly before dusk. A car with its hood raised sat at the side of the street as if it had broken down. Two agents pretended to examine the engine. Another waited in the shadows nearby.

At 7:40 p.m. the bus arrived. The man stepped off. He began walking down the dimly lit road toward his home.

When he approached the car, one of the agents spoke.

"Un momentito, señor."

Eichmann turned slightly. In that instant the agents seized him. He struggled briefly before being forced into the back seat of the waiting car. Within seconds the vehicle disappeared into the darkness.

The operation had taken less than a minute. For the first time in fifteen years, Adolf Eichmann was in custody.

The Safe House

Eichmann was taken to a secure safe house where Mossad agents interrogated him and confirmed his identity. At first he refused to cooperate.

But the evidence was overwhelming.

Eventually he acknowledged who he was. The next challenge was far more complicated. The agents needed to remove Eichmann from Argentina without alerting the authorities. If Argentina discovered the kidnapping before Eichmann was gone, the operation could turn into a diplomatic crisis.

The solution required careful planning. Israel was preparing to celebrate the anniversary of its independence. An official Israeli delegation would soon arrive in Buenos Aires.

The Mossad decided to move Eichmann out of the country aboard the same aircraft that would return the delegation to Israel. On the evening of May 20 the agents disguised Eichmann as an airline crew member who had been injured in an accident.

Sedated and dressed in a flight uniform, he was quietly escorted onto the aircraft.

The plane departed Argentina without incident. Only after it was safely in international airspace did the world begin to learn what had happened.

The Announcement
May 23, 1960
Jerusalem

Prime Minister Ben-Gurion addressed the Israeli Knesset.

> "I have to inform the Knesset," speaking solemnly, "that Adolf Eichmann—one of the greatest Nazi criminals responsible for what they called the Final Solution—has been found."

A ripple of shock moved through the chamber.

> "He is already under arrest in Israel."

The announcement reverberated across the world within minutes. For survivors of the Holocaust and for families of those who had been murdered, the news carried profound meaning.

One of the principal architects of their suffering would finally face justice.

Washington

The story reached Washington quickly. Paul Murphy read the first reports early the next morning.

Katie joined him at the breakfast table as he folded the newspaper.

"Eichmann. They caught him."

Katie nodded slowly.

"Good."

For a moment neither of them spoke. The horrors of the war still lived vividly in their memories.

They had both seen too much to ever forget.

"Where was he hiding?" Katie asked.

"Argentina."

She shook her head.

"All these years."

Paul leaned back in his chair.

"It was only a matter of time."

The Trial

The trial began in Jerusalem in April 1961. For the first time the world heard detailed testimony about the machinery of the Holocaust. Survivors described the deportations.

The ghettos. The trains. The camps.

Eichmann sat inside a glass enclosure in the courtroom as witnesses recounted the systematic destruction of millions of lives. The proceedings lasted months. When the verdict was finally announced, Eichmann was found guilty on multiple counts of crimes against humanity and war crimes.

He was sentenced to death. On June 1, 1962, Adolf Eichmann was executed in Israel. His ashes were scattered at sea beyond Israeli territorial waters.

No grave would ever mark the place.

Reflection

Late one evening Paul sat alone in his study. The news coverage of the trial had stirred memories he rarely allowed himself to revisit.

The war had ended fifteen years earlier. But its shadows still stretched across the world.

Katie entered the room quietly.

"You're thinking about it again."

Paul nodded.

"The things we saw. The things people did."

Katie sat beside him.

"And the things people stopped."

Paul looked at her.

"That's true."

For a moment they sat together in silence. Justice, even delayed, had finally reached one of the men responsible for the darkest chapter of the war.

But both of them understood something deeper. The world had not become safer.

The Cold War was intensifying. New dangers were already emerging. And the next chapters of their lives would unfold in that uncertain world

CHAPTER THIRTY-THREE—THE U-2 INCIDENT

May 1, 1960
Peshawar Air Station
Pakistan

At dawn the weather briefing room was quiet. The pilot sat alone reviewing the flight plan spread across the table.

The mission would take him across thousands of miles of Soviet territory. The aircraft would climb to more than seventy thousand feet and photograph missile installations, airfields, and industrial sites before exiting the Soviet Union over Norway.

The aircraft waiting outside the hangar was a Lockheed U-2 reconnaissance plane. The pilot was Francis Gary Powers. He had flown similar missions before, but every flight carried the same understanding.

If something went wrong, there would be no rescue.

The aircraft would be alone.

The Mission

Shortly after sunrise the U-2 lifted from the runway at Peshawar and began its slow climb toward the upper atmosphere.

At those altitudes the aircraft flew near the edge of aerodynamic capability. The margin between stall speed and structural limits was dangerously narrow.

Pilots called it "coffin corner." For the first several hours the flight proceeded exactly as planned. Powers crossed deep into Soviet territory. The aircraft's cameras photographed air bases, missile sites, and industrial complexes as it followed its route across the heart of the Soviet Union.

But Soviet radar operators had already detected the aircraft. Air defense forces began tracking the flight almost immediately. Fighter aircraft attempted to intercept but could not climb high enough to reach the U-2.

Missile batteries were another matter. Near Sverdlovsk, Soviet air defense commanders made the decision to fire. A volley of SA-2 surface-to-air missiles streaked upward toward the high-flying aircraft.

One exploded close enough to shatter the fragile wings of the U-2.

The aircraft broke apart. Powers was forced to eject. He parachuted to the ground and was immediately captured by Soviet authorities.

Washington

The news did not reach Washington immediately. At first American officials assumed the aircraft had simply disappeared. But two days later Soviet Premier Nikita Khrushchev made a dramatic announcement.

A United States spy plane had been shot down over the Soviet Union. At first the American government attempted to deflect the accusation. NASA issued a statement suggesting that a weather research aircraft had gone missing after the pilot experienced oxygen problems.

The explanation might have worked. Except for one problem. The Soviets had the pilot. And they had the aircraft. When Khrushchev revealed that Gary Powers was alive and in custody, the American cover story collapsed instantly.

Langley Air Force Base

Paul Murphy was in his office at Tactical Air Command when the first confirmed reports arrived. His aide stepped into the room carrying a message.

"Sir, Washington just confirmed it."

Paul looked up.

"The U-2?"

"Yes, sir."

Paul leaned back in his chair. He had warned about this possibility two years earlier. The reconnaissance missions had been extraordinarily valuable, but every flight carried enormous risk.

Eventually the Soviet defenses would improve. Eventually one of the aircraft would be lost. Now it had happened. The political consequences were immediate.

A summit meeting between President Dwight Eisenhower and Soviet Premier Khrushchev had been scheduled in Paris. The incident destroyed any hope that the meeting might ease Cold War tensions.

Khrushchev demanded a public apology. Eisenhower refused. The summit collapsed before it even began.

Moscow

Gary Powers was taken to Moscow and interrogated by Soviet intelligence officers. The Soviets treated him carefully. They wanted him alive. They wanted a trial.

The captured pilot—and the wreckage of the aircraft—provided undeniable evidence that the United States had been conducting espionage flights over Soviet territory.

The trial began in August 1960. Powers admitted flying the mission but explained that he had simply followed orders. He was convicted of espionage and sentenced to ten years imprisonment.

The Aftermath

The incident sent shockwaves through Washington. Reconnaissance policy had to change. Within months the United States accelerated development of a different form of intelligence gathering.

Satellites.

If cameras could be placed in orbit above the Earth, photographs could be taken without violating national airspace. The concept had already been under development. The U-2 incident pushed the effort into overdrive.

For Paul Murphy the event carried a more personal significance. He had helped build the operational framework for the U-2 program. He knew the risks better than most.

And he knew something else. The Cold War was entering a new phase— one in which technology, intelligence, and nuclear weapons would intersect in increasingly dangerous ways.

A Conversation

Late that evening Paul sat with Katie in their Washington home. The television news replayed the story again. The captured aircraft. The pilot. The collapse of the summit.
Katie switched off the television.

"You expected this, didn't you?"

Paul nodded slowly.

"Yes."

"Could it have been avoided?"

Paul thought about the question.

"Maybe delayed. But not avoided."

Katie studied him.

"Does this change anything?"

Paul looked out the window toward the darkening city.

"It reminds everyone how fragile the peace really is."

He paused.

"And how close we are to something much worse."

Katie reached for his hand.

"Then let's make sure we stay ahead of it."

Paul smiled faintly.

"That's the plan."

CHAPTER THIRTY-FOUR—A NEW ADMINISTRATION

November 8, 1960
Washington, D.C.

The election results came in slowly that evening. Paul Murphy sat in the living room with Katie, the television quietly reporting the vote tallies from across the country. The race between Senator John F. Kennedy and Vice President Richard Nixon had been close from the start.

By midnight the outcome was becoming clear. John F. Kennedy would become the next President of the United States.

Katie watched the screen for a moment before turning it off.

"Well," she said, "that changes things."

Paul nodded.

"It always does."

The change of administrations in Washington rarely altered the daily work of the military overnight, but it always shifted the strategic landscape. New advisors, new priorities, and new political realities would soon ripple through every branch of government.

For Paul, the transition meant that his position at Tactical Air Command would soon come under the scrutiny of a new Secretary of Defense and a new civilian leadership team.

For Katie, the political implications were more direct.

If she decided to run for the Senate, she would now be doing so during the rise of a new generation of national leadership.

The New Team

When Kennedy began assembling his cabinet, the appointments reflected his determination to modernize the nation's defense posture.

Robert McNamara, the dynamic president of Ford Motor Company, was selected as Secretary of Defense.

McNamara brought with him a radically different approach to military planning. Numbers. Systems analysis. Efficiency.

He and the group of analysts he assembled—soon nicknamed the "Whiz Kids"—believed that military strategy could be improved through rigorous quantitative analysis. The approach impressed many in Washington. It also made many senior officers uneasy. The armed services had always relied on experience, judgment, and battlefield knowledge.

The idea that war could be reduced to spreadsheets and statistical models did not sit comfortably with many commanders.

Langley

At Tactical Air Command headquarters, Paul watched the changes unfold carefully. The strategic emphasis of the Kennedy administration was shifting.

Instead of relying almost entirely on nuclear retaliation—as had been the doctrine during the Eisenhower years—the new administration wanted the military to develop a broader range of options.

The concept was called Flexible Response. It meant preparing forces that could respond to conflicts at many different levels—conventional wars, limited conflicts, and counterinsurgency operations.

For TAC, the implications were enormous. Fighter aircraft would no longer be viewed primarily as nuclear delivery platforms. They would once again be expected to fight conventional wars.

Paul welcomed the change. Fighter pilots had always believed that airpower's greatest strength lay in flexibility and speed. Tactical air forces could respond quickly to developing crises anywhere in the world. Now the new doctrine seemed to recognize that fact. Still, the transition would not be easy. Training programs needed revision. Aircraft modernization had to accelerate. And budgets would inevitably become battlegrounds between competing priorities inside the Pentagon.

A Call from LeMay

One evening the phone rang in Paul's office.

It was Curtis LeMay.

"Murphy."

"Bomber," Paul replied.

LeMay did not waste time.

"Looks like Kennedy's people are serious about this flexible response idea."

Paul leaned back in his chair.

"That's what it sounds like."

LeMay snorted.

"Well, somebody still has to make sure we don't lose the nuclear deterrent while they're experimenting."

Paul understood exactly what he meant.

LeMay had built Strategic Air Command into the most powerful nuclear force in the world. He was determined to keep it that way.

"You're going to see more attention on tactical forces now," LeMay continued.

"Good."

LeMay laughed.

"Don't get too comfortable. When budgets tighten, everyone starts fighting."

Paul smiled.

"That's Washington."

Katie's Decision

While Paul navigated the changing military environment, Katie's political future moved closer to a decision point. The Senate seat from Idaho would soon be contested.

Several political figures had already begun positioning themselves as potential candidates. Katie spent weeks speaking with advisors, community leaders, and longtime friends.

One evening she sat across from Paul at the kitchen table.

"I've decided."

Paul looked up.

"You're going to run."

Katie nodded.

"Yes."

Paul studied her for a moment.

"Independent?"

"Yes."

He smiled.

"That's the hardest path."

"I know."

Katie leaned forward.

"But it's the honest one."

She explained her reasoning. Running as a Democrat or Republican would give her an established political organization and access to party resources. But it would also mean aligning herself with positions she might not always support.

Running as an independent would allow her to vote her conscience.

Paul nodded slowly.

"That's exactly why people might vote for you."

Katie smiled.

"I hope so."

Campaign Beginnings

The campaign began quietly. Small gatherings. Community meetings. Visits to farms and small towns across Idaho.

Katie spoke about issues that mattered deeply to the state—agriculture, water rights, education, and rural development. She also spoke about something broader.

Responsibility.

"Government," she often told voters, "should exist to serve people—not to control them."

Her message resonated. Word spread quickly. Newspapers began covering the campaign. Political analysts in Washington began taking notice of the unusual independent candidate building support in a traditionally partisan race.

Gathering Storms

As winter turned to spring, the international situation continued to grow more tense. The Cold War showed no signs of easing. Berlin remained divided.

The Soviet Union continued expanding its missile programs. And in a small Caribbean island ninety miles from Florida, a revolution led by Fidel Castro was rapidly transforming Cuba into a Soviet-aligned state.

Paul followed the developments carefully. Events were beginning to move faster. Much faster. One evening he looked up from a stack of intelligence summaries.

Katie noticed the expression on his face.

"What is it?" she asked.

Paul closed the folder slowly.

"The world... is getting ready to test us again."

Katie studied him.

"Then we'll be ready."

Paul hoped she was right.

Because somewhere beyond the horizon, the Cold War was approaching one of its most dangerous moments. And when it arrived, both of them would be drawn directly into its center.

CHAPTER THIRTY-FIVE—SUMMER VACATION

By the summer of 1961, the Murphy and Green families had earned a rare stretch of quiet.

The Korean War was long behind them, and the tensions of Washington had not yet fully intruded into their lives. For the first time in years, both families were able to spend time together without the constant pressure of military operations or political battles.

They gathered on the beaches of Martha's Vineyard.

Paul and Katie had purchased the property several years earlier, a wide stretch of land overlooking the Atlantic. The house was large enough to hold both families comfortably, with room for guests and the occasional political visitor. But for this week, the house belonged only to family.

The children were no longer really children.

Tommy Murphy and Joseph Green had grown into young men. Both had been accepted to the United States Military Academy at West Point, and their departure for the academy was only weeks away.

The two had spent most of the morning walking along the beach, talking about what lay ahead.

> "You realize," Joseph said, skipping a stone across the water, "this is probably the last summer we'll ever have like this."

Tommy nodded. West Point was not simply college. It was a commitment—one that would shape the rest of their lives.

The academy demanded discipline, endurance, and sacrifice. And both young men knew that graduation almost certainly meant war. The Cold War had made that reality unavoidable.

Back at the house, the adults watched them from the porch. Katie sat beside Paul, a glass of iced tea in her hand. Betty Murphy and Ben Green sat nearby, quietly observing the boys.

"They look older every day," Betty began.

"They are," Ben replied. "West Point will finish the job."

Katie turned toward Paul.

"Are you worried?"

Paul considered the question carefully.

"Of course, I am. But I'm also proud of them."

He had spent most of his life in uniform. War had shaped nearly every important decision he had ever made. Now the next generation was stepping onto the same path. Neither he nor Ben had pushed the boys toward military service. If anything, they had tried to explain how difficult that life could be.

But the decision had been the boys' alone. Later that afternoon the two families gathered for dinner outside, overlooking the ocean.

Katie had arranged a simple meal—fresh seafood, vegetables from the garden, and several bottles of wine from the family's California vineyard. The conversation moved easily between laughter and reflection.

Ben raised his glass.

"To the next generation."

Everyone lifted their glasses. Tommy and Joseph exchanged a glance. They both understood the weight behind the toast.

Paul looked at the two young men and felt a mixture of pride and concern. He had seen too much of war to pretend that military service was glamorous. But he also knew that leadership required sacrifice. And the country would soon need leaders again.

As the sun set over the Atlantic, the families remained at the table, talking late into the evening. For now, the world felt peaceful. But Paul Murphy knew better than most that peace rarely lasted. In only a few weeks, the boys would leave for West Point. And once they stepped through those gates, their lives—and perhaps the course of history—would begin to change.

CHAPTER THIRTY-SIX—THE SENATOR

Washington had changed dramatically by the early 1960s, but one thing remained constant: power in the capital still depended on relationships.

Katie Murphy understood that better than most. Her campaign for the United States Senate had begun quietly, almost cautiously. At first many in the political establishment had dismissed the idea entirely. Washington was still a place where women were rarely seen as serious contenders for major office.

But Katie had never been intimidated by expectations. She approached the campaign the same way she approached every major undertaking—with careful planning, disciplined execution, and a deep understanding of the people involved.

Her network was already formidable.

Over the years, she and Paul had built relationships with senators, military leaders, intelligence officials, and influential figures across both political parties. Their home had quietly become one of Washington's most important informal meeting places.

Katie knew how to bring people together—and just as importantly, she knew how to listen. The campaign itself moved quickly once it began.

Her reputation for intelligence and discretion attracted strong support from both political moderates and members of the national security community. Many respected her judgment, and others simply trusted her ability to navigate complex problems without unnecessary drama.

When election night arrived, the result was decisive. Katie Murphy was elected to the United States Senate by a comfortable margin.

At home that evening, Paul poured two glasses of champagne and handed one to her.

"Well, Senator," Paul smiled warmly.

Katie laughed softly.

"I suppose I should start getting used to hearing that."

The victory placed her in the middle of a rapidly evolving political environment.

A new generation of leadership was emerging in Washington, and the election of John F. Kennedy had accelerated that transformation. Younger politicians, many of them veterans of the Second World War, were beginning to replace the older generation that had dominated American politics since the New Deal.

Katie entered the Senate at exactly the right moment.

Her colleagues quickly discovered that she was neither timid nor easily influenced. She asked direct questions, studied issues carefully, and avoided the theatrical speeches that many senators seemed to enjoy.

Within months, she had become a respected voice in several critical areas, particularly those involving national security and international affairs.

Her ability to bridge relationships between the Senate and the military establishment also made her unusually valuable. One evening not long after taking office, Katie and Paul attended a small dinner at the White House.

President Kennedy had invited a handful of political leaders and advisors to discuss several emerging foreign policy concerns. The gathering was informal, but the discussion was serious.

Kennedy greeted them warmly as they entered.

"Paul, Katie—it's good to see you both."

"Mr. President," Paul replied.

Katie shook his hand.

"Congratulations again on the election, Katie. Washington needs more people who actually understand how the world works."

They took their seats at the table as the conversation turned to the growing tensions between the United States and the Soviet Union.

The Cold War was entering a new and uncertain phase.

Berlin remained a flashpoint. Cuba had suddenly become a strategic concern. And across Southeast Asia, the situation in Vietnam was becoming increasingly unstable.

Kennedy listened carefully as several advisors presented their assessments.

At one point he turned toward Katie.

> "Senator Murphy, what's your view?"

Katie paused for a moment before answering.

> "Mr. President, the most important thing is clarity. Our allies need to understand our commitments, and our adversaries need to understand our resolve."

Kennedy nodded.

> "That's a rare quality in Washington."

The discussion continued late into the evening. As the guests eventually left the White House, Paul and Katie walked together down Pennsylvania Avenue toward their car.

> "You handled that well," Paul smiled warmly.

Katie smiled slightly.

> "I've been listening to strategic conversations in our living room for years. Eventually you start to recognize the patterns."

Paul laughed quietly.

> "You may end up becoming one of the most influential people in Washington."

Katie looked ahead at the Capitol building rising in the distance.

> "I'm not interested in influence for its own sake. I'm interested in making sure the right decisions get made."

Neither of them said it aloud, but both understood that the coming years would test the country in ways few people yet fully understood.

And now they were closer to the center of those decisions than ever before.

CHAPTER THIRTY-SEVEN—VICE CHIEF OF STAFF

By the early 1960s, Paul Murphy had spent most of his adult life in war or preparing for it.

World War II had forged him as a combat leader. Korea had tested his ability to command under pressure. Now, in Washington, the battlefield had changed.

Strategy had replaced tactics.

When the call came from General Curtis LeMay, Paul already knew the conversation would not be casual.

LeMay did not waste time.

"Paul, I need you in the Pentagon this afternoon."

"Yes, sir."

When Paul arrived at LeMay's office later that day, the Air Force Chief of Staff was standing near the window overlooking the Potomac.

LeMay turned.

"I'm recommending you for Vice Chief of Staff of the Air Force."

Paul absorbed the statement quietly.

"That's a significant responsibility, sir."

LeMay nodded.

"It is. And you're the right man for it."

The Vice Chief position placed Paul at the center of the Air Force's operational planning and strategic development. It meant overseeing everything from force readiness to long-term planning in a world that was becoming increasingly unstable.

LeMay sat down and motioned for Paul to take a chair.

"The Cold War isn't cooling off. If anything, it's heating up."

Berlin remained a flashpoint between East and West. The Soviet Union was expanding its nuclear arsenal. And in Southeast Asia, the situation in Vietnam was becoming steadily more dangerous.
LeMay leaned forward.

"The President needs clear military advice. Not politics. Not guesswork."

Paul nodded.

"That's exactly what he'll get."

Within weeks of his confirmation, Paul moved into his new office at the Pentagon.
The Vice Chief's office was less ceremonial than powerful. From this room flowed much of the planning that shaped the Air Force's global posture.
Maps covered several walls—Europe, the Pacific, Southeast Asia. Paul spent long hours reviewing reports and meeting with commanders responsible for different operational regions. Increasingly, those discussions returned to the same troubling topic.

Vietnam.

The United States had begun expanding its advisory presence in South Vietnam, sending military advisors to assist the South Vietnamese government in its fight against the communist Viet Cong insurgency.

On paper, the mission seemed limited. But Paul had seen enough wars to recognize the warning signs. Advisors became trainers. Trainers became combat leaders. Combat leaders eventually required full military support.

The pattern was familiar. One afternoon, Paul met with several senior planners reviewing intelligence updates from Southeast Asia.

The briefing officer pointed to a map.

"Viet Cong activity has increased significantly across multiple provinces," he explained. "Their ability to operate in rural areas continues to expand."

Paul studied the map carefully.

"What about infiltration from the north?"

"We believe North Vietnam is providing logistical support, though the scale remains unclear."

Paul leaned back slightly in his chair.

"That will change."

After the meeting ended, Paul remained in the conference room reviewing the situation alone. The conflict in Vietnam was still considered a secondary issue by many policymakers in Washington. Europe and the Soviet Union remained the primary strategic concern.

But Paul's instincts told him something different. Insurgencies had a way of growing slowly—and then suddenly.

Later that week he met again with General LeMay.

"Paul. You've been reviewing the Vietnam briefings."

"Yes, sir."

"And?"

Paul answered without hesitation.

"If the situation continues to escalate, we're going to face a difficult choice."

LeMay waited.

"Either we commit the resources necessary to win the conflict quickly," Paul continued, "or we risk becoming trapped in a long war that drains both our military and our political capital."

LeMay nodded slowly.

"That's exactly what I've been worried about."

For the moment, however, Washington had not yet made that choice. Policy discussions continued. Advisors were deployed. Reports were written. But the strategic direction of the conflict remained uncertain.

Paul returned to his office and stood for a moment looking at the large map of Southeast Asia on the wall. Vietnam appeared small compared to the vast geography of the Pacific.

Yet something about the region drew his attention again and again. He had learned long ago that the size of a battlefield rarely determined the scale of a war.

And increasingly, he suspected that the next major test of American strategy might begin in a place few Americans could even find on a map.

CHAPTER THIRTY-EIGHT—THE NEXT GENERATION

West Point had always been more than a military academy. It was a crucible.

For over a century, young men had arrived at the gray stone gates along the Hudson River as students and left four years later as officers responsible for the lives of others. The academy's traditions were demanding, its standards unforgiving, and its expectations absolute.

Tommy Murphy and Joseph Green quickly discovered that life at West Point was exactly as rigorous as their fathers had warned.

Their days began before sunrise and rarely ended before midnight. Between classes, military drills, physical training, and study periods, there was little time left for anything else.

Yet both young men thrived in the environment.

They had grown up listening to stories of leadership, sacrifice, and responsibility. For them, West Point was not simply a school—it was the next step in a family tradition that stretched back through the Second World War and Korea.

Still, the academy was changing.

The Cold War had reshaped the military's priorities. Officers were now expected to understand not only battlefield tactics but also the political and strategic realities of a world divided between competing ideologies.

During their third year at the academy, the two young cadets attended a guest lecture that would shape their future more than any classroom lesson.

The speaker was Captain Gray Johnson, a Special Forces officer recently returned from Southeast Asia.

Johnson did not look like the traditional West Point instructor. His uniform bore the distinctive green beret of the Special Forces, a unit that had gained growing attention within the military for its unconventional approach to warfare.

Instead of commanding large formations of troops, Special Forces teams operated in small units, often deep behind enemy lines. Johnson spoke calmly as he addressed the cadets.

"The nature of war is changing. In the future, many conflicts won't be fought by large armies meeting on open battlefields."

He paused, letting the room settle.

"They will be fought in villages, jungles, and mountains—often among civilian populations."

Several cadets exchanged curious glances.

Johnson continued.

"Success in those conflicts will depend on adaptability, intelligence, and the ability to work with local forces."

Tommy leaned slightly toward Joseph.

"That sounds like the kind of work we've heard about in Vietnam."

Joseph nodded.

When the lecture ended, several cadets approached Johnson with questions. Tommy and Joseph waited until the crowd thinned before stepping forward.

"Captain Johnson," Tommy said, "we were wondering if you had time for a few questions."

Johnson smiled.

"I always have time for future officers."

They spoke for nearly half an hour.

Johnson described the training required to join Special Forces: language instruction, survival training, unconventional tactics, and the ability to operate independently in difficult environments.

"The work isn't easy. But it's important."

Joseph asked the question both had been thinking about.

"Do you think Vietnam will become a major conflict?"

Johnson studied them for a moment before answering.

"It already is. Most Americans just don't realize it yet."

The conversation stayed with both young men long after the lecture ended.

Over the following months, Tommy and Joseph began discussing their own future assignments.

Traditional combat arms branches—infantry, armor, artillery— remained the most common career paths for West Point graduates. But Special Forces offered something different.

Smaller teams. Independent command. Direct involvement in emerging conflicts.

It also carried significant risk.

One evening during their final year, the two friends walked along the Hudson River overlooking the academy grounds.

"Are you thinking what I'm thinking?" Joseph asked.

Tommy nodded.

"Special Forces."

Joseph laughed softly.

"Our fathers are going to love that."

Tommy smiled.

"They taught us to serve where we're most needed."

Both men knew the decision would place them directly into the growing conflict in Southeast Asia.

But neither hesitated. Several weeks later they formally submitted their branch preferences.

At graduation, their orders confirmed the assignment.

Both Tommy Murphy and Joseph Green would begin their officer careers in the United States Army Special Forces.

When Paul Murphy received the news, he read the message twice.

Katie looked at him from across the room.

"Well?"

Paul folded the paper slowly.

"They're going Special Forces."

Katie exhaled quietly.

"I had a feeling."

Neither of them said what they were both thinking. Special Forces officers were often sent to the most dangerous assignments.

Paul walked to the window and looked out across Washington. He had spent years shaping military strategy at the highest levels of government.

Now his son was stepping into the very conflicts those strategies would create. History had a way of repeating itself.

And the next chapter of that history was already beginning to unfold in Southeast Asia.

CHAPTER THIRTY-NINE—SIGMA

The Pentagon
1963

War, Paul Murphy had learned long ago, rarely arrived the way planners expected.

By the early 1960s the United States possessed the most powerful military in the world. Its nuclear arsenal could deter any direct confrontation with the Soviet Union. Its conventional forces were stationed across Europe, Asia, and the Pacific.

Yet the greatest strategic challenge facing the United States was emerging far from those traditional battlefields.

Vietnam.

The conflict in Southeast Asia had begun quietly. At first it appeared to be little more than an insurgency—a local struggle between the South Vietnamese government and communist guerrillas supported by the North.

But by 1963 the situation had become impossible to ignore.

Reports arriving in Washington described an increasingly sophisticated enemy. The Viet Cong were expanding their operations across large sections of South Vietnam, supported by supplies and reinforcements moving south along hidden infiltration routes through Laos and Cambodia.

Within the Pentagon, senior military planners had begun studying the problem in detail.

The program was known as SIGMA.

SIGMA was a series of strategic war games designed to simulate how the Vietnam conflict might unfold under various policy decisions. Senior officers, intelligence analysts, and civilian strategists gathered in secure rooms to test different military and political strategies.

The goal was simple. Predict the future. Paul had been invited to observe several of the sessions.

The participants were divided into opposing teams. One group represented the United States and South Vietnam. Another played the role of North Vietnam and its communist allies. Each team attempted to anticipate the decisions of the other.

At first the exercises appeared manageable.

Initial American military assistance slowed the expansion of communist forces in several regions. Additional advisors improved the effectiveness of South Vietnamese units. Air power provided occasional advantages.

But as the simulations progressed, the patterns became increasingly troubling. Each time the United States introduced limited military pressure—small increases in troops, restricted bombing campaigns, incremental escalation—the opposing team responded by expanding their own commitment.

North Vietnam accepted heavy casualties. The communist leadership proved willing to endure enormous hardship in pursuit of long-term victory. Gradual escalation, the policy favored by many civilian leaders, failed repeatedly in the simulations. Instead of ending the conflict, it prolonged it. During one particularly intense session, a senior analyst presented the projected casualty estimates.

The room fell silent. If the war continued under a gradual escalation strategy, American combat forces could eventually exceed 500,000 troops in Vietnam. Casualties could reach tens of thousands. North Vietnamese and Viet Cong losses would be far higher—but the simulations suggested that those losses would not necessarily end the conflict.

Paul studied the charts carefully. He had seen war from the cockpit of a fighter aircraft. He had commanded operations in Korea. He understood how quickly optimistic plans could collapse under the pressure of combat.

The numbers on the screen were not abstractions. They represented young men who would be sent to fight. After the session ended, several participants remained in the room discussing the results.

Some believed the war could still be controlled through careful escalation. Others argued that a decisive strategy—either overwhelming force or complete disengagement—was the only realistic alternative.

Paul remained quiet.

He understood the political realities shaping the decisions being made in Washington. Presidents rarely had the luxury of choosing between perfect options.

Instead they faced choices between imperfect ones.

Later that evening Paul returned to his office. The Pentagon was unusually quiet. Most of the staff had already gone home, leaving only a handful of lights glowing across the vast building. He sat at his desk and opened the SIGMA briefing report once more. The casualty projections filled several pages.

As he read through the analysis, a thought returned that he had tried unsuccessfully to push aside all afternoon. Tommy. Yoseph.

Both young men had chosen careers in Special Forces. If the war expanded—as the simulations suggested it might—Special Forces units would almost certainly be among the first deployed.

Paul closed the report slowly. He had spent his life preparing for war, studying it, fighting it, and planning it.

Yet nothing in those years had prepared him for the possibility that the next great conflict might claim the sons of his own generation. Outside the Pentagon window, the lights of Washington stretched across the night.

The city appeared calm, even peaceful. But Paul knew how fragile that calm could be. On his desk the SIGMA report remained open to the final page.

The conclusions were stark. If current policies continued, the conflict in Vietnam would almost certainly expand. And once it did, it would be very difficult to end. Paul leaned back in his chair and looked again at the map of Southeast Asia hanging on the wall.

Vietnam was a small country. Yet the decisions being made about that small country could shape the lives of an entire generation.

He closed the report and placed it carefully in the classified folder. Somewhere far away, two young officers were beginning their military careers.

Paul Murphy knew he could not stop the forces already gathering in Southeast Asia. But he also knew that leadership meant trying.

He turned off the light in his office and walked out into the quiet corridor. The future of the war—and perhaps the future of the boys—had not yet been decided. But time was running short. And history rarely waited for anyone.

EPILOGUE

The paper smelled like carbon and fear.

Paul Murphy had read classified documents for two decades—loss reports, mission summaries, intelligence digests, the cold arithmetic of attrition dressed up in acronyms and careful prose. He had read casualty projections before. He had written them. He had signed off on them with the same mechanical certainty with which a man signs a mortgage when he believes the house is worth the risk.

This was different.

It wasn't the tone. The SIGMA summary was written the way all such documents were written—bloodless, tidy, pretending that language could disinfect what it carried. It wasn't even the scale, though the scale was grotesque.

It was the specificity.

A ninety-percent casualty rate for Special Forces personnel. Not a worst-case scenario. Not a "possible if." Not a hedge framed to protect the drafter's career. A projection. A forecast presented with the confidence of mathematics.

Paul sat in the small sitting area adjoining his office in the Pentagon, the door closed, the blinds half-drawn, the hum of ventilation the only sound. His aide had left the folder on the coffee table as if it were a menu. Paul had lifted it with two fingers, as if the paper might be contaminated. Now it lay open in his hands, the pages slightly bent where his thumb pressed too hard.

He read the line again. Then once more. Ninety percent. He felt the first wave of nausea and forced it down. That was the thing about command—if you allowed your body to revolt, your mind followed. He set the folder down carefully, aligning the edges, then stood and walked to the window.

From here, the Potomac was a gray ribbon, the sky a washed-out sheet. The city looked calm the way it always did from above, as if the Republic ran on schedule, as if men did not make decisions in quiet rooms that would ripple outward into jungles half a world away.

He could see the Washington Monument in the distance—white, stubborn, immaculate. He had once loved monuments. He had believed they were built to honor sacrifice.

Now he understood they were built to hide it. He turned back to the folder. The words did not change. They waited for him the way a verdict waits. Tommy. Yoseph.

His son and Ben's son—his godson.

Paul had watched the two boys grow like twin saplings, close enough to share sunlight, close enough that when one moved the other swayed. They were different in temperament—Tommy sharper around the edges, Joseph quieter, more analytical—but their loyalty to each other was a single, braided cord. They had entered West Point together, survived Beast together, and now talked about the future as if the future were a map with clear lines and predictable roads.

Infantry Officers Basic. Ranger School. Special Warfare. Green Berets. The boys said it with the calm certainty of youth, as if saying it made it safe.

Paul lowered himself into the chair again. He stared at the folder as if it might offer him a way out. It didn't. He had known this moment would come. Not this document, not this number. But the moment when the war— any war—reached into his home.

A father could accept risk for himself. A father could even accept risk for his country. A father could not accept risk for his son that was born of stupidity. And this was stupidity.

Gradualism. Incrementalism. The careful drip of commitment designed not to win, but to avoid embarrassment. A war conducted like a committee meeting, where no one wanted to be responsible for decisive action and everyone wanted the illusion of control.

Paul had heard Bomber's voice in his head—furious, profane, incandescent. I fucking hate gradualism. Paul hated it too. But hatred wasn't a plan. He needed a plan.

He flipped to the first page again, forcing himself to read the report not as a father but as the Vice Chief of Staff of the United States Air Force. He read the projected timeline. The assumptions. The likely escalation points. The political constraints embedded like land mines.

It wasn't only about Vietnam. It was about a pattern. Cuba, Laos, Berlin, the shadow wars that never appeared on the evening news until they were too large to hide.

The paper didn't say it outright, but Paul could hear it between the lines: the nation was walking into a long corridor with no exit sign.

He reached for the phone on the side table and stopped himself before he touched it. The instinct was to call Ben. Ben would understand the number the way an engineer understands the stress limit of a bridge. Ben would be quiet for a moment, then he would ask the question Ben always asked—the question that hurt because it was always the right one.

What do you want to do about it?

Paul wasn't ready to answer. He picked up his green notebook from his briefcase and opened it to a blank page. He wrote, slowly, deliberately, as if the act of writing might anchor the world.

SIGMA—What must happen now.

He underlined it twice. Then he wrote three names. Katie. Ben. Gray Johnson.

He sat back and stared at the page. Katie first.

His wife was a Senator now. An Independent, which was its own kind of weapon. She was not beholden to party machinery, not dependent on donors, not afraid of being uninvited from the right dinners. Katie had always played the long game, and she had always understood what men like Wagner never grasped—power was not granted; it was taken, held, and defended.

The question was clearance. SIGMA. TS-SCI protocols. Bomber had mentioned it at dinner with the air of a man tossing a match into dry grass.

Isn't Katie on the Senate Select Committee on Intelligence and the Defense subcommittee? So she may have a TS-SCI SIGMA clearance. You may want to check on that.

Paul had nodded at the time, filing the thought away like a contingency. Now it was not a contingency. It was the only moral road. He needed to speak with her. But he also needed to speak carefully.

They had built a marriage on discipline—two professionals who could love each other fiercely without turning their home into a leak. LeMay had once mocked them in Berlin with grudging admiration.

A couple who keep professional, political, and military secrets from each other.

It had been true. It had kept them alive. But what did you do when the secret threatened to kill your son?

Paul closed the notebook, stood, and walked down the hall to his private office. His aide looked up immediately, reading his face.

"Sir?"

"Get me my wife's office. Tell them I need to speak with Senator Murphy directly. Not her staff. Her."

"Yes, Sir."

Paul waited, hands clasped behind his back, staring at the framed photograph on the wall—a younger Paul and Katie on a tarmac, both laughing, both unaware of how much history would demand from them.
The phone rang.

"Paul?" Katie's voice was warm, amused. "Are you calling to tell me you've finally learned how to take a day off?"

Paul closed his eyes for a moment. The sound of her voice was a rope thrown across a canyon.

"No. I'm calling because I need to ask you a procedural question."

A pause—tiny, but enough.

"Go ahead."

"What is your current clearance level?" Paul asked. "And do you have access under SIGMA protocols?"

Silence, then the sound of a breath.

"I have TS," Katie considered carefully. "And I have SCI compartments tied to Intelligence and Defense work. SIGMA...depends on the subject matter. Why?"

"Because I have a SIGMA summary in my hands," Paul said, and hated how calm his voice sounded. "And it involves our son."

Another pause. This one longer. The amusement had vanished.

"Katie," Paul's voice became low and serious, "Tell me what you can tell me."

Paul looked at the door as if someone might be listening through it.

"I can't discuss content over this line. But I need to know if you can be read in. I need to know today."

"Paul," she said, and now there was steel in her tone. "If it involves our son, you will have an answer. I will call the Committee security officer right now. I will have Andrew arrange it. If I need to walk into a vault and sign a thousand papers, I will do it."

Paul exhaled slowly.

"Good. Because this cannot wait."

"Where are you?" she asked.

"My office."

"I'm coming. Don't argue."

He almost smiled at that—almost.

"Katie—"

"Paul," she cut in, and he could picture her face—the calm mask she wore on the Senate floor, the one that made men underestimate her until it was too late. "Don't argue. I'll be there within the hour. Tell your aide to clear your calendar."

"Yes, ma'am," Paul said, and heard the faintest softening in her breath. The line went dead.

He stared at the phone for a moment, then replaced it with a kind of reverence.

That was one piece. Now Ben.

Ben was in Israel most of the time now, a retired Colonel who was never truly retired, a man who carried two nations in his chest the way other men carried a wallet. Calling him to discuss a SIGMA projection would be perilous in every possible way. But Ben was not only a friend. He was the father of the other boy in Paul's mind. And he was the only person Paul knew who could stare at a terrible number and immediately begin building a solution.

Paul dialed Ben's secure contact through his aide, then waited, pacing the carpet. When Ben's voice came through—low, precise—Paul felt the world tilt.

"Rodeo! Is something wrong?"

"Yes… And no. Everyone is alive. For now."

Ben didn't fill the silence. He let Paul choose his words.

"I received the SIGMA summary. It projects—" He stopped, jaw tight. "It projects outcomes for Special Forces if we continue on this path."

Ben exhaled once, slow.

"Tommy and Joseph." It wasn't a question.

"Yes."

"Then we stop the path."

Paul felt a sharp, unexpected surge of gratitude.

"How?" Paul asked, and hated how small the word sounded.

Ben's answer was immediate.

"We do what we always do. We define the objective. Then we force everyone to confront reality. Politicians survive on ambiguity. Reality kills ambiguity."

Paul looked down at his green notebook and opened it again, writing as Ben spoke.

"We need two tracks," Ben continued. "One is operational—war games, honest scenarios, rigorous referees, no political theater. The other is political—Katie's world. Hearings, leverage, pressure points. And we need a messenger inside the White House who can speak truth without sounding like a threat."

Paul's pen hovered.

"A messenger," he repeated.

Ben didn't hesitate.

"Gray Johnson."

Paul felt the hairs rise on his arms. The name had been in his notebook before Ben said it, but hearing it from Ben made it real.

Gray Johnson—the Green Beret who had walked into the Oval Office and told the President the sky was blue. The young man Kennedy had elevated in a single morning, the kind of officer who frightened bureaucrats because he was competent and not impressed by them.

"Gray is close enough to the President to be heard, Paul. And he is young enough that he is not perceived as a rival. He is also not an Air Force general with a reputation for breaking furniture when frustrated."

Paul almost laughed, but the sound died.

"I'll handle Gray."

"Yes," Ben replied. "And Rodeo—tell me when Katie is read in. Ariel will want to be involved. She will pretend she doesn't, but she will."

Paul could picture Ariel's smile—the soft one that was never soft when her family was threatened.

"I will."

"Good," Ben answered. "Call me when you have dates."

The line clicked off. Paul remained still for several seconds, letting the plan coalesce.

Two tracks. Operational and political. War games and hearings. LeMay and Katie. And Gray Johnson inside the White House. It was audacious. It was also the only way.

Paul was still standing there when his aide appeared in the doorway.

"Sir, Senator Murphy is on her way. Her driver called ahead. She asked that your security detail be ready to escort her directly to your office."

Paul nodded.

"Clear the outer office. No interruptions unless the building is on fire."

"Yes, Sir."

When the aide disappeared, Paul returned to the window. The Potomac looked unchanged. The city looked unchanged. He wondered how many men had stood in this same building, looking out at the same river, thinking they could hold the world steady with their hands.

Katie arrived like weather—unavoidable, decisive.

She entered without ceremony, coat still on, hair immaculate, eyes already searching him.

"Close the door."

Paul did. The click sounded loud.

For a moment they stared at each other—husband and wife, General and Senator, two people who had built a life on strength and now faced the one thing strength could not prevent.

Katie stepped closer and lowered her voice.

"Tell me. Not the content. Tell me the shape of it."

Paul swallowed.

"It's a projection. And if it's even half right, it means one of the boys doesn't come home."

Katie's face hardened, not with anger but with clarity.

"Then we change the projection."

Paul felt something loosen in his chest.

"Can you be read in?" he asked.

"I already made the calls," Katie replied. "I can be read in this afternoon. If I have to sit in a vault until midnight, I will. Andrew is coordinating it now."

Paul nodded once. Katie took his green notebook from the table without asking and flipped to the page where he had written the names. She traced them with her finger.

"Good. You already know who matters."

She looked up.

"We are going to be very careful. And we are going to be very ruthless."

Paul met her gaze.

"Katie," he said, "I don't want ruthless."

Katie leaned in slightly, her voice barely above a whisper.

"Paul," she said, "ruthless is what you call it when the other side expects you to be polite."

She handed him the notebook back.

"Now," she continued, "tell me what you need from me."

Paul took a breath, and in that breath he felt the machinery of the next book begin to turn—the gears of Washington, the shadows behind the headlines, the dangerous intimacy between power and family.

"I need you," Paul said, "to look at the Senate the way you looked at Wagner."

Katie's smile flickered—cold, brief.

"Oh!. That won't be difficult."

"And I need Gray Johnson," Paul added, "inside the White House, telling the President the truth in a way the President will hear."

Katie's eyes narrowed thoughtfully.

"Then we invite him. Not as a soldier. As family."

Paul nodded.

Outside the window the river moved, indifferent.

Inside the room Paul Murphy—the Vice Chief of Staff of the United States Air Force—watched his wife set her mind like a blade.

For the first time since he had read the SIGMA summary, he did not feel sick.

He felt dangerous.

And somewhere far north, at West Point, two boys in gray uniforms marched in step, believing the world ahead of them was certain.

Paul Murphy stared at the green notebook in his hands and made himself a promise he did not write down.

Not this time. Not my son. Not Ben's son. Not if the Republic still belonged to men willing to fight for it. He picked up the phone again.

"Get me Major Gray Johnson," Paul told his aide. "And after that—get me General LeMay."

He paused, looking at Katie.

"This is going to get loud!"

Katie's answer was immediate.

"Loud it is."

THE END

www.ingramcontent.com/pod-product-compliance
Lightning Source LLC
Chambersburg PA
CBHW032143050726
47591CB00001B/65